PRINTHOUSE BOOKS PRESENTS

I0660869

Everlasting Romance

An American Love Story.

Fiction

ANTWAN 'ANT' BANK$

MELISHA ROSS

© ANTWAN 'ANT' BANK$; 2014

PRINTHOUSE BOOKS   Atlanta, GA.

Published 1-20-2014

www.PrintHousebooks.com

VIP INK Publishing Group; Incorporated

Cover art designed by SK7

ISBN – 978-0-9911719-9-6

Library of Congress Cataloging-in-Publication data

ANTWAN'ANT' BANK$

MELISHA ROSS

Everlasting Romance; *An American Love Story*

1.Romance 2.Urban Fiction 3.African American

4. Love 5.ANTWAN 'ANT' BANK$ 6.MELSIHA ROSS

From the backdrop of the ATL; the hottest city in the South, comes a compelling love story about several friends and their adventures in College at the A.U and their professional careers while in the city of Atlanta. Experience Love, Drama, infidelity and historic memories as you indulge yourself in this Romantic tale of fiction. Set in 2001-2002, you're sure to reminisce back when Jay-Z, Nelly, Luda, Missy, 112, Lil Jon, Alicia Keys and more were in heavy rotation on your favorite radio station. When T.I's album; I'm Serious had the city crazy, the clubs closed late and Ying Yang had those ATL Shake stages rocking and dollars raining.

Everlasting Romance, An American Love Story explores the essence of friendships, life, Love and how those bonds molded several individuals into a close knit family while in the hot city of Atlanta. Donnie, Quentin, Chantel, Cynthia and their friends; found themselves sharing love at every level; Brotherly, Sisterly and most of all intimately! But; at what cost!

Dedicated to Love and the institution of; that sacred vow.

ANTWAN'ANT' BANK$

MELISHA ROSS

Everlasting Romance

An American Love Story.

VIP INK Publishing Group; Incorporated

Atlanta; GA.

Table of Contents.

1. CAMPUS LIFE.

The fresh smell of clothes; drying, penetrate the atmosphere as the sound of spinning washing machines, knock against the dormitory, laundry room walls. Chantel is seated under the window closest to the dryers then turns the page of her romance novel as she waits on her clothes to finish drying. The sun light beams in the window, casting a shadow off the dull gray walls and cement floors. Bam! The steel double doors swung open, a gush of air brushes against her face and she looks up. "Girl you look good; want you back that ass up!" "Want you come over here and back that ass up!" "Damn you look sexy; come on and back that ass up!" Ummm-Ummm! Oh my bad baby! Yeah uh-huh! The tall, dark skin gentlemen walks over to the washer then removes one white dress shirt and heads over to the dryers. His long dread locks hung off his shoulders as he bent over to remove the load of clothes! Excuse me! What the hell; do you think you're doing?

Did you not just see my clothes in there? You must have fell and bumped your head. Maybe if you move those damn dreads out ya face, you probably would be able to see better! Girl I didn't know those were your clothes; there dry anyway! Why you tripping! I'm not tripping; you are the one tripping boy, I guess your manners are non- existent, I was sitting right here! If you would have asked then you would have known they were mine, but that would have sounded too much like right! Man look; are you gonna get these clothes or what? I have an interview to go to. I'm trying to get me a job; unlike your pretty ass! I'll move my clothes out of the way when you act like a man and ask nicely. Oh and my pretty ass has a job, so you catch up.

Hold up, you know what; let me regroup here; my parents taught me better than this. My name is Donnie; what may I ask is yours pretty lady? Mine is Chantel Sir! Nice to meet you Chantel! Umm-hmm; that's more like it! Ha-ha! You're a mess woman; can I dry my clothes now? Sure you can; on one condition! And what's that? Help me fold them and I'll think about it. Oh that's no problem I can do that but you have to go on a date with me. Man there you go! What you mean there I go?

How do you know that I don't have someone already? This is just a friendly date; you know; one where we can get to know each other. What do you think about that? Chantel; I said what do you think? I guess we could, friendly date right? I am not from here so where would we be going to on this date? Of course a friendly date; we can go shoot pool and grab some wings; I know a good spot. Are we going to be drinking there too Mister? Yes we can get a few beers. Pool huh? Well don't get mad when I wipe the table with your butt.

Shiiit; you must be crazy girl. You can't get none over this way; where are you from; you talk plenty junk! Michigan bruh! Wolverines; and do not say Detroit! That's what's up; I got a homeboy from Saginaw; is that where you from, Sag Nasty? Hell nah! Ok; Flint then? Last I heard there weren't any jobs in Michigan; I'm just saying.

Ha-ha! No I am not from neither of those cites as a matter of fact, a little too far to the west and not enough to the south. I am from Grand Rapids; Gun Ru; as they call it. As far as having any jobs, there is plenty; now you not having much since, is a different thing. Wow; ok, don't get all mean and evil, woman. I was only asking you a simple question. Come on over here and help me fold your clothes; damn you have a lot of thongs! Well the sentences that you were forming were statements not questions, assumptions so to speak. Never assume that you know things about someone, assuming makes an ass of you. Those thong's that you are holding sweetie, are from Victoria's secret; why I have so many is mine. Oh really; I like a woman that knows how to keep a secret. I'm feeling you; how come I never seen you around campus until now? Or is that a secret too? Don't worry boo; if it was that big of a secret, I sure wouldn't let you in on it. But since you find it such a mystery, the dorm that I was supposed to be living in was all filled up. I found out there was one vacancy here in co Ed, so here I am. Lucky for me huh! Yep!

Okay, enough about me, where do you come from? Are you from the big "A"? Nope; I'm from Sin City baby; home of the Players, Hustler's and Baller's. Have you ever been to Las Vegas? Sin city I can tell, player not trying to find out, and baller please! You don't even have a job yet. To answer your question though, no I have not been there before. Ha-ha! You are too much but I don't try to hide it; I claim Vegas all day Miss Chantel! You're that new breed of woman; yall just came out in 2000; my dad warned me about yall. New breed I am not, what I am is a thorough bread stallion, and my mother warned me against donkeys like you. Damn; you're brutal; you have to be one of those Law Students! I can tell; aren't you? Yes sir I am, this time your assumption paid off. Mind your testimony and confess nothing but the truth, because I can make your strongest defense weak. What is your major?

Well damn; since you put it that way. I'm a business major with a focus on Finance. My Uncle is in the Real Estate Investment Business and I'm planning on opening a branch here in Atl. On another note; I'm noticing that you don't have many bras in your laundry; what's that all about? It just seems kind of strange to me; I know it's not my business but it was on my mind. That is a wonderful field to go into especially with the economy. But Man, you are just too much. Switching the subject that quickly! While you will be this great business man, you are right; it is none of your business. The where about of my bra's, remain to you; simply a clue waiting to be found. I tell you what; when we go shoot pool later; we can bet on what secret you will tell me. I'm looking forward to this; you're a very interesting woman, not like most of these chicken heads around here.

See; why do you have to call woman chicken heads and you need to tell me where you plan on taking me before I say yes anyway, Donnie! Further-more; what makes you think that any amount of liquor will allow you to persuade me, to let you know the business! That is one bet I am willing to go in on; when you lose you can run tell that to your boys.

Yeah whatever; we'll see about that Chantel; I'm from Vegas remember; so don't get mad when you start losing; and don't quit either. But to answer your question; we're going to Club Strokers over on the East side. They have like; 6 pool tables, some good wings and cheap drinks too. I'll take it easy on you the first game though. Ha-ha! Take it easy on me, huh! What makes you think that I want it easy, I may be the type of girl that likes it rough, as well as hard; either way, don't be scared to bring it. Strokers never heard of it, sounds like fun.

Alright Chant; just don't write a check that your behind can't cash. If you want me to bring it; I will; since you're a big girl, a senior and all? I mean you are a senior right; that's the only time you can live here in co-ed anyway. Yeah I am a senior this year, but being a senior doesn't make me a big girl. I know my worth and what I have to look forward to, so don't try and bounce a quarter off of this brick house. But this living situation is okay, aside from having to smell the odors from you men lingering in the hallways.

Ha-ha! Girl I use Irish Spring; clean as a whistle; it aint me you smelling! But I'm looking at these clothes and my pile is bigger than yours; how is that and these are your clothes? What's up with that Chantel; you must be enjoying this huh? That, I am! You are too Donnie! As far as the actual folding, I think you should par take in some lessons. Whatever, are you going or not? Okay, so I guess I will say yes to going on this date with you. What time should I be ready? Wait, I thought that you had an interview to go to? We can meet up around 8 or so; I do have an interview but it's in an hour. I still need to let my shirt dry some more because I don't have an iron in the room, got to let the heat knock the wrinkles out; not unless you want to iron it for me. Come on, you can do this favor for your new friend; I did just fold your clothes.

Ha-ha! I'm just joking Chantel; you don't have to answer that.

I think that you must have mistaken me for the assistant janitor! Favor; this was supposed to be an even trade, as a matter of fact, folding these clothes is taking up less time than a date so, it really is not even. You are too funny for your own good, 8 will be better. Buzz!

Ok that's my Shirt; how will I contact you later? I don't even know what floor you're on. I don't know too much about you right now other than you are from Vegas, you think you are a baller, you can't fold, and you major in business, oh and maybe you are sexy. If I get more comfortable around you, then you will know but for now you will have to find me. Ok and thanks for that compliment but I'm sure I can find you. My team mate is the Dorm manager- Team mate? Oh I didn't tell you that I play on the Basketball team huh; I don't get much time though. That's neither here nor there but don't worry, I'll find your pretty ass.

Chantel looks at Donnie with a slight smirk; places her folded clothes in her purple basket and heads for the door. She stops at the door before going through, turns around, looks at Donnie then sings to him. "Don't ask my neighbor; come to me; don't be afraid of what you see." Donnie watches with a smile as she turns back towards the door and walks out.

Minutes later, Chantel enters her dorm room with her basket of clothes, and closes the door behind her. She sees her room-mate Cynthia; sitting on her bed with her earphones on, listening to Faith Evans. Cynthia a heavier set woman, light skin with light colored eyes, was always working but never had a problem finding time to start drama and mastered the art of being sneaky. She's the type of woman that always wants what she cannot have, and is very confident. If you looked at her you would think that she was a very kind woman, and she is but just miss understood. Cynthia grew up with her grandmother in a small country town and wanted more out of life. Ever since she was a little girl; Cynt always told herself that she would get more by any means necessary.

Their room was not a big one by far, two beds, a small kitchen and a closet. You could smell baby lotion and perfume all through the small area. Chantel walks over to Cynthia and taps her on her shoulder. You would never believe! What's that? I met this guy today. Pray tell; does he have a job? Girl damn; can you be more-straight forward with it? Sorry girl just making sure he ain't no buster. You are always thinking that someone is a buster. I don't know he seems different. And by different you mean? Chantel sits down on her bed that's on the other side of the room. Well, he seems as if he really has his head screwed on straight. Hmm, you sure it wasn't the other head guiding him Chant? He almost got on my damn nerves though, trying to take my dryer. Chantel leans back on her bed, arms folded under her head while looking up at the ceiling then crosses her legs. But them dreads and that build; I would swing off those vines anytime. Cynthia; raised up with intrigue. He got it like that girl? Yes he does. We are supposed to hook up tonight. Wow! You move fast! It's nothing like that girl! Stop, being so negative!

Knock, knock! Cynthia gets up to answer the door with a smile on her face. Yeah who is it! Hey lady I was just stopping by to invite you guys to a party we're throwing next week. I don't know you; why would we come to your party? Damn; it aint that serious redbone! Redbone? Look; my name is Quentin; my folks call me Q. I would appreciate it if you guys came through; only the coolest seniors will be there. Well Q; my name is Cynthia, not redbone and I'll think about it! What's there to think about; unless you aint cool; then I can understand that redbone. Your little party doesn't sound interesting nor does your invite.   And if judging by the way you look now, there wouldn't be much eye candy for me. I deal with chocolate delight not Hershey's kisses; now put that on ice to cool down.

Come on Cynthia; you and I would be like Reese's cups baby, my chocolate and your peanut butter. I'm gone leave these fliers with you along with these two V.I.P passes! When you two get there; just show these to the girl at the door and she'll let you guys in V.I.P with us. I will be looking forward to seeing you, so please don't disappoint me. You're cute and feisty; I like that in a woman.

Really Quentin, you are a funny character; cute is for puppies, I need for your flirting to be upgraded. Maybe I will come. You'll be there redbone and your roommate too; besides it's the coolest party on campus. I'm sure you wouldn't want to miss it. As far as me upgrading my flirting; I just did but you wouldn't know that unless you follow through on this invitation. You two have a good evening; I need to pass out the rest of these fliers. But it was nice talking with you Cynthia.

She stands at the door with her mouth dropped because she can't believe that this man abruptly just ended the conversation. Cynthia turns around hearing the sound of laughing in the background. What's so funny? Girl he just gave you the business; close your mouth before you catch a fly! Girl I let him finish the conversation. Yeah right; not from how I saw it; you got that man all interested. You can't say he didn't impress you Cynt!; I know he did because you would not be looking all shook right now. Girl anyway; we were talking about your little date tonight before he interrupted. Cynthia closes the door then returns to other side of the room and sits on her bed. What you gonna wear? Where are you going? Well, I was thinking of wearing my purple sun dress, you know the one that shows off my figure. We are supposed to be going to some place called Strokers; to get a couple of drinks and play pool.

Girl no, then you should wear your go get him skirt. You mean the black and white one? Yep; show off them legs and put on those white six inch, stilettos heels. Are you going to play the helpless damsel? Does he think you can't play? I may, I don't want him to think that I'm too fragile, but at the same time, I do want him to get a little close.

Chantel gets up and walks over to the closet and starts looking through her things. She brings out a couple of outfits and places them on the bed. Cynthia gets up and walks over to the selection. Put these two on and let me see what they look like on you. Chantel walks into their bathroom and closes the door while continuing their conversation. But for real, you know that Q guy was handsome. Can't you see that chocolate man melting all over you; he looks like he works out and he kinda resembles Omar Epps. Yeah but those glasses make him look funny. Stop it Cynt; I don't know why you are fighting it. Girl his game is weak, he just thinks it's on; someone is gassing his head up. Anyway what time is this guy of yours coming to get you?

The bathroom door opens; Chantel walks out then starts to model her out fit in front of the mirror, mounted on the back of their room door. His name is Donnie, and we are supposed to be meeting up at 8 tonight. Well, that should give you plenty of time to get ready. What are you going to do with your hair? I was thinking of an up do; with these tear drop earrings; it will draw attention to my shoulders.

So what are your plans for tonight; Cynt? I have a test tomorrow so I'm going to do some last minute studying at the library. The last test I had didn't go so well, so I definitely need to pass it but I'm going off campus first though, to get something to eat with a few of my friends. Where you going? Girl I'm in the mood for some waffle house; those smothered and covered hash browns are calling my name. Cynthia's phone rings. Hey Chant; it's my grandmother I have to take this call; I'll be in the hallway. Ok Cynt!

Chantel hears the sound of loud music outside of her window then walks over to investigate. She opens the window which sat just over, Atlanta; Universities common grounds; you could see most of the campus from her dorm room. Chant lifts the pane then takes in the smell of freshly cut grass in the air, along with the sound of loud music and sees other young adults sitting under the tree studying. The tall oak tree that sits in the middle of the grounds was now in bloom; several people sat under it on blankets with their books in hand. To the far right side on the upper level walk way, a couple sat cakin.

Chant's attention now turned to the parking lot closest to the entrance of the school; she sees a group of people that she knows then shouts out.

You guys know you can't dance, yall need to stop it! A man's voice yells back at her. What up Chantel; you gone come down and show us! No, I don't want to show you up in front of these strangers. Could you turn that music down though; you see people over there trying to study. You know; old man James is going to come around there and give you a ticket for being too loud anyway.

I don't think so Chant; I believe he will join in until he starts complaining about his hips. Ha-ha! She laughs at the thought of old man James doing the two step. I'll pass on that invite man, I'll see you around; turn that music down though! Alright; later Chantel, tell Cynt I said what's up! Alright man; later!

Damn Donnie; did you see that man? See what Q? That bow legged chic that just came in. Nah; where is she Q? In the fast food line man! Oh damn; she must be a freshman; I never seen her around campus. Me either D; I'll be back; I'm gone give her a flier for the party. Alright Q; see if she has some friends too bruh! Oh you already know!

What up Donnie; where's that fool going? What up Marcus; he's about to give that girl a flier. Oh that's what's poppin; what's on the menu today? The same thing they had yesterday bruh. Pizza, Burgers, Meat loaf, Rice and Veggies! Damn when are they gonna change the menu? Stop tripping Marcus; this is a College cafeteria bruh not a restaurant. Yeah whatever; what's new with you man? Aint much Marc; ready to graduate and get in the real world and make some real money! I hear that Donnie; I don't know when I'm getting out of AU! Damn boy; you still haven't declared a major? Hell nah man; I'm here for the woman; it' just so many. I can declare a major later; I'm 22; I got plenty of time. Marc; I'm graduating this year; so is Quentin and Harold. You bullshitting bruh; chasing skirt gone have you left behind man. You need to stop being a ho and get serious.

Donnie; I got this man; I know you're only trying to look out for me but we've been friends since elementary; when have I not took care of business. Alright; I hear you Marc; just don't mess your life up. I won't D; I promise you.

What up fellas? Hey Harold; where are you coming from? We had a team meeting knuckle head and you missed it! Damn Harold; I forgot all about it bruh; I had a job interview. Dude; I know you're just playing Basketball to stay in shape but you have to take this serious Donnie. Harold you're the all star athlete, not me; I'll be alright. Marc will you talk to your best friend man! Marcus, an average sized guy; fair skinned, curly hair and a natural, ladies-man; grew up with Donnie in Las Vegas. A handsome fellow; who never had any problems getting a woman, was used to being a player, even at an early age.

What's up fellas; there's gonna be a lot of girls at the party boy! What up Q! Hey Harold; I'm surprised you're not at the gym or running somewhere; Mr. All-star! Go ahead with all that Quentin; a brother has to eat don't he? I'm just messing with you man; how you been though? I'm good Q; how about yourself? On that hustle boy; like always; you're coming to the party right. Oh no doubt; you know I'm in the house shawty. Harold an Atlanta native; grew up in Decatur and came to AU on a full scholarship; an all-around athlete in Football, Basketball and Baseball; everyone that knows him; know he's destined to be pro.

Oh fellas; I met this girl in the laundry room today. Damn; she must be fine Donnie; she got you that excited? Whatever Marcus! So how does she look man; is she one of those slim model chics, like you like? Yes she is Q! Oh shit; she aint gone last! Why you say that Harold? Because; models go where the money is and your ass aint got none! Ha-ha! Ha-ha! Ok, so yall fools just gone laugh at a brother when he's trying to tell yall about a girl.

Go ahead shawty; how she look? First of all, she aint no model; she's a law student here and will be graduating this year. Ok shawty; that's why your ass aint come to the team meeting; huh? No Harold; I had an interview bruh. Man how does she look? Hold on Q; I'm about to tell yall. Alright; ol girl is like 5'8", slim, light skin, some long silky hair and got a tight ass body. I can't wait to wax that ass, boy. She sounds fine as hell D! She is Marc; wait until you see her. So when are yall hooking up then man? Tonight Q! Damn, you're moving fast playa. Hey; I had to jump on it quick boy; a fine chick with a law degree. I can't waste no time Q! Well, I met this girl today too man but she's playing hard to get. That's how you like him right Q; hard to get. Yep but she aint got no game; she think she does though. Quentin; your ass aint got no game; you need to take some notes from Mr. Marcus; I'm the ladies-man bruh. Marc you be hitting anything though man; I got class; you just wanna cut. Q; I'll take them eight to eighty, dumb, cripple and crazy. Ha-ha! See you just a damn ho boy! Oh man whore! Shit Harold; yall just mad because I be getting all the ass!

You need to be worried about getting your degree, fool; sleeping with all these skanks you gone be a poor broke ho! Why I got to be a poor ho D? Ha-ha! Alright that's enough yall; what's up with that girl though Q; what's her name? I think she said her name was Cathy or Cynthia, Donnie; something like that. Does she have a room-mate? I saw a girl in there but I didn't talk to her. Ok that's what's up; we need to link Harold up with somebody. Did she look ok? Oh she was straight; kind of look like that girl you described Donnie. Nah; it aint the one I met Q. What she have on Quentin? Some shorts, sandals; nothing special D! What's your girl's Major Q? I think a lawyer; I didn't ask! Man yall tripping; hold on a minute let me call Jason. Who is Jason, Harold? He plays Corner Back on the football team with me; he's the dorm manager over at the senior dorms. Cool, call him up Harold? Hold on Donnie; give me a sec!

Ring-Ring! Hello! Yo Jay; what up! Hey Harold; what up? Hey shawty; we're looking for two girls in your dorm; their names are Chantel and Cynthia or Cathy. Oh that's Chantel and Cynthia; the law students on the 4th floor. Thanks shawty, appreciate it! You're welcome Harold. Hey Donnie; your girl and Quentin's are room-mates. Hell nah; you serious? Yep; Jason just told me. Damn that's what's up right there partner; we gone double date then. Hold on Quentin; let me get my first date out of the way first then we'll get to that. I'm picking Chantel up later for a date; I'll ask her about Cynthia for you. That's what's up D; find out everything you can. Oh you already know Q; I got you bruh. Oh snap; hold on fellas; look at these two walking to the table. Where Marcus? Right there D; coming this way!

Hey fellas, which one of you guys is Q? That's me lil momma; what's up? My home girl said that you were the man. That depends on what you're talking about lil momma. Me and my girl need two twenties; can you help us? Sure; meet me outside of the cafeteria by the bathroom. Ok we can do that. Cool but I need that $40 right now though. I'm gone walk by and drop it in your purse. How do we know you're not gone play us. Lil momma; if you think I'm gone try and play you for $40; you can take your business to Bankhead or something. Ok here you go; we'll be waiting. Thanks; see you in a minute.

Damn Quentin; your ass is getting too popular with that weed bruh. Did you even know those girls? Donnie; it's only weed man; everybody on campus smokes; they probably got my name from one of my loyal customers. That's just what you call good business D. Man you act like you're running a legal business; weed is illegal fool. Marcus stop hating playa; you got your women and I got my weed. I don't hate on you for being a womanizer, so don't be judging me. Man; just don't get caught shawty; that's all I'm saying. I don't want folk in jail. Don't worry Harold; I'm careful bruh; yall take it easy. I'm about to serve these two chickens and head to class. Later fellas! Later Q!

Hey Quentin; don't forget to invite them to the party! Oh yeah; no doubt; got it Marc! Hey you guys want some of this pizza; I'm gone be late for my International Business class. I'll take it Donnie; did you want some Marcus? Yeah Harold; I'll take a slice, I aint got no class to be in anyway. Alright yall take it easy and Marcus do you even go to class anymore bruh? Ha-ha! Why you had to go there Donnie; yes I go to class man! Ha-ha! Harold that shit aint funny! Come on man and let's eat this pizza; I have to leave in 15 minutes. So what are you gonna do when we graduate Marc; you're gonna be at AU all by yourself shawty.

I'm gone be your manager man; so if you get rich; I'm getting rich. Ha-ha! Shawty; you crazy! I might be crazy Harold but I'm serious man. You need somebody that you can trust in your corner. Not those fake suits, whose waiting to stick their paws in your pockets. Let me think about it shawty; that might work. You know it's a good idea Harold; I got your back, no matter what! You do have a point Marc; I'll see what my dad has to say about it. Man that's my folk; you know he's gone be with it! We'll see Marc; we'll see!

Chantel is putting the last of her make up on; when she hears the phone ring, she places the tube of eye liner in the container then lays it on the side of the sink. Hello! Hey Chant; its Nadia and Tamara. Chant had met the two of them when she first got to Atlanta while partying at 112. The three of them had struck up a conversation while standing outside waiting in line. Tam and Nadia noticed that she was there by herself so they took her in as a sister and they have been friends ever since.

Nadia, a single 24 year old mother of 1 child, working for Barton Security as a supervisor, was no stranger to hard work; nothing ever came easy for her, especially when it came to love. Nadia's father had left her mother for a woman half his age and in a blink of an eye he was gone. Tamara on the other hand was of a mixed background; which always made her feel different, having blue eyes and brown wavy hair, with natural blonde highlights. Tam a Massage Therapist, quiet by nature, most people wouldn't even know she was there because she tends to keep to herself. Tam while traveling on a senior class cruise to the Bahamas; ran into Nadia while lying on the pool deck. After conversing a little; they discovered they had a few things in common and became friends. One year later she went to visit Tam for Christmas and found out that they shared the same Dad. Talk about a Christmas to remember!

Girl what you doing? Let's go out! If you guys would have called earlier maybe, but I have a date tonight. You have a boo; and didn't tell us Chant? No, no boo yet, there is potential though, if he acts right. Where is he taking you? Some place called Strokers, Tam. Hey Nadia! Yeah Tam? Isn't that the club on 78? I believe so. I don't know if this is correct information but I thought that was a strip club. He better not be taking me to some strip club! I can look at my own self in the mirror naked. Chant calm down girl; I told you I'm not for sure. Well; I will fill you guys in tomorrow; I have to finish getting ready. Ok later girl!

Chantel looks at the clock over on her short night stand to check the time. Damn; I have 15 minutes. She runs into the bathroom, finishes putting on her make up then reaches over for her stilettos; as she is putting them on there is a knock at the door. Hold on; I will be there in a sec. Chantel sprays her scent of sex and the city perfume then primps in the mirror one last time then opens the door.

Hey Sexy; I told you I would find you; didn't I! How did you manage to find me? You watched me when I left; you think you are so slick don't you? Ha-ha! No way! Well you look nice; A great clean up from what I saw earlier. I'm loving those white air force ones that you are rocking. Okay; I feel like I am over doing it with the heels though. Thank you and I have my ways but I'm here like I promised. These ones are new; I only take them out for special occasions. Keep those heels on; you look good enough to eat right now. Okay; flattery huh. Let me grab my purse and keys and I'll be ready. Hey I was wondering; some friends of mine said they heard Strokers is a strip club; is that wrong information?

Nah it's a pool hall, every one hangs out there. I was knocking for a minute; I heard you talking to someone, who was that; your girlfriend? Damn you can hear! What; was your ears pressed up to the door? That was my friend Nadia; she was asking if I wanted to go out with her and her sister. What if I said it was a guy? You nosey! Ha-ha! That's your business but you're with me now; so later for him. How do your friends look; maybe I can introduce them to my boys sometimes?

Yeah, not sure about that yet! Nadia is not about any bullshit. She has a child that she is raising by herself; none of your college boys will be able to handle that and she would see right through the games. Nadia can have any man that she wants; very beautiful, many who come across her thinks that she is of Native American descent. Plus I don't even know your boys myself, so good luck on that one. I wouldn't just go around hooking people up I don't know myself.

I hear you Chantel but my boys are cool; but I don't know if they're ready for the kid thing. Oh here's my car, the brown 89' Camry right there. You have to get in on the driver's side because the passenger's door is broke. Are you joking? You're kidding right? Look I am not high on a horse or anything but you are gonna get this fixed, right? I guess opening the car door for me is out of the question on this one? I thought you were a baller? Hell to the naw; I'm just a college student. Ha-ha! Yeah I'm getting it fix as soon as I get this job. You're too funny because I play ball don't mean I'm a baller baby. I'm living off my change check just like most students on campus. When I graduate though; I'm gone buy you one of those new Benz's.

What makes you think we are going to be together when we graduate? You are so sure of yourself huh? I will be making enough money to buy my own. I hope this door was not your fault due to bad driving. It was like that when I bought the car, put your seat belt on; I don't need a ticket. Donnie closes the driver's door, starts the car; then reaches in the back seat; turns back around then hands Chantel his box. Here you go; play this boom box if you want to hear some music. I have that new Mase tape in the player now; do you like Mase? If not, there some Jodeci and Jagged Edge tapes in the back seat on the floor.

Wait a minute, where the hell did you buy this car from? People are going to know this is not a car radio! Damn; what the hell did I get into messing around with you? How far is this place because this boom box is heavy, I can't feel my toes anymore.

Ha-ha! You can put it on the back seat Chantel, you don't have to hold it. I got this car from Old Man James my freshman year; I only paid $800 for it. We don't have far to go, though! Shit! It looks like you paid $5, a rip off, if you ask me.

Donnie takes the 78 east exit off of 285 then heads 1 mile down to Exit 3; Brockett Road. He makes a right then a quick left into the parking lot. Hundreds of cars crowd the parking lot as they find a parking spot in the far corner at the end of the building. The bright pink neon sign above; illuminate the lot as they enter the building. Loud music bounce off the tinted club windows as Donnie and Chantel walks through the double glass doors. Hundreds of naked woman; patrons and smoke, fill the building. Six pool tables sit off to the right of the entrance as two strippers entertain the crowd from its center stage.

Hey; welcome to Strokers; it's $10 a-piece. Alright; here you go baby; where can we order some wings? Just ask any waitress honey and they can help you. Thanks baby! Come on Chantel; I'm gone order us some wings and something to drink. Can you get a pool table; I'll be right back. Wait a minute! You must have fell and bumped your head, because you are out of your rabbit ass mind. I didn't sign up to see ass and tits! How can I enjoy some wings with the smell of pussy and cigarettes in the air?

You flat out lied to me; I asked if this was a strip club. Find a pool table my ass, you find your right mind and take me somewhere else. Chantel this is a pool hall; it just so happen to have strippers. Why do you think they call it Strokers? Just chill and enjoy yourself; the wings are good; trust me. Besides I already paid $20 to get in here; so you'll be alright sexy. Do you want me to buy you a table dance?

Damn were you built on stupid? Let me break it down a little more for you sweetie. I don't care if you spent $20 to get in here; it is not my fault that you chose to ignore me when I said I didn't want to go to a strip club. Simply put; naked people under a building shaking their ass for money equals strip club. I didn't ask you what it used to be. Wait, did you ask if I wanted a table dance? You keep playing with me, you are going to miss any type of chance you thought you were going to get from me. Take me some-where else! Look Chantel, this is Atlanta; strip clubs are what's happening. Let's just get some wings to go then we can leave. Will that work; I have a taste for some wings. Donnie- While you're thinking about it, I'm going to the bathroom; I'll be right back. Chantel asks a waitress where she could find the restroom, while in the stall finishing her business, she hears two strippers coming in.

"Girl I know, you got to make it wet, I use lubricant for the extra shine." "Let me get a swig of that Hennessey, my buzz is coming down and I am up next." "Okay girl you better shake that ass up there; go get that money." Then there was silence as the two girls walked out. Chant washes her hands then walks out, and passes by a crowded table of men; who are being entertained by one of the dancers. The stripper, see Chant passing then turns around and asks her if she wants a lap dance. Do you want a lap dance boo? Did I ask you for one; that would be something you should think about! Chant reaches Donnie with fire in her eyes; if looks could kill he would be the first on her list.

Damn; what's wrong with you Chantel; here I ordered you an Erk and Jerk. I think you need it! Chantel snatches the drink from his hands.

Are you really not going to take me home? I would throw this drink on you; if I didn't need it! Girl you need to calm down; it aint that serious. We'll leave as soon as the wings come; if you really want to!

Hey bartender; can I get two double shots of Jose' please! Sure babe; coming right up! Chantel I have some ones; did you want to tip the girl on stage? No I do not want to tip the girl on the stage, although; I will give you a good tip! If you keep playing, those same deck of cards; you're going to wish you folded them because it's going to be game over for you. Ha-ha! Girl you crazy! Here's your shots babe! Thanks! Did you want to pay for them now or start a tab? You can start a tab. Ok cool! Here Chant; take a shot with me! Yeah I'll take a shot with you, I hope that you don't think you are going to get me drunk. I do know how to hold my liquor; I don't babysit so try and keep up. Ok; hear you go Sag Nasty! Bartender; another round please! Sure babe; is that Erk and Jerk or Jose'? Jose'; two doubles! Ok; got you! Thanks!

So; you think you can hang huh? I hope you're sure about that; because we're about to see lady. Yeah we are going to see! I am a petite person so when we are ready to go; I will get the bouncer to peel you from up under the table, sounds like a deal Sin-City. Ha-ha! Well drink up woman; this is only the second round! What you procrastinating for? Bartender; keep them shots coming! Ok babe; you got it! Excuse me for a sec Donnie.

Chantel turns to the bartender. Are you serving pacifiers; did you just hand him a bottle? No; I don't think so! You see me sitting here; do you not? Let the word baby come out your mouth again, believe me; it will not be good for you. Since you want to call people baby, you can get the ass whooping that comes along with it!

The bartender looks at Chantel in disbelief; picks up their two shots and- Splash! Take that you sassy bitch; I'll say what the hell I want; who do you think you are! Chant stands there with a shocked look on her face. You aint seen sassy yet bitch!. Chantel grabs the beer bottle from a stranger sitting next to her, jumps over the counter and beats the bartender over the head with it. She then picks her up and shoves her into the cash register. Now close the tab bitch! Conversation over! Oh shit; Chant get your ass over here!

Donnie runs around to the bar entrance and grabs her by the arm as security hastily approaches them. Hey yall have to go; come on let's go! Alright man; we're coming; come on Sag Nasty! Damn girl; you done got us kicked out of Strokers; I aint even got my damn wings yet! Hey bruh; can I get my wings? No man; keep walking! Ha-ha! Wait until I tell my boys about this Chantel; wow you're a trip. Why you had to jump on the bartender like that?

Security escorts the couple outside of the club and into the parking lot; pass the line of patrons that stood there in line waiting to get inside. Sag Nasty; you a G! Shit I felt disrespected, oh, and I can take care of myself perfectly fine. Where are we going to now? Nowhere woman; I'm taking your gangster ass home; getting kicked out of one club is enough for one night. Where did we park the hoopty, I knew that you couldn't hang. I tell you what; let me go find it first so I can get in and hide in the back until we drive off!

No you stay here; I'll find it. It's about to rain anyway; wouldn't want your hair to get wet. Donnie leaves Chantel standing at the entrance by the patrons and outside security guards. Who stood watch, assuring that the two left the premises.

Three minutes later he pulls the Camry in front of the entrance; stops the car; places it in park; gets out and stands there holding the drivers door open. Hey Chantel; come on let's go before it starts raining! Chant turns her head as if she was looking at someone she knew then starts walking toward the side of the building. Oh hey; girl I didn't see you standing there! She keeps walking towards the side of the building while waiving at her imaginary friend. Donnie jumps in the car and starts driving in the direction she's going. Once they get to the side of the building where there is no one standing, Chantel stops walking as Donnie gets out of the car. Who were you talking to and walking towards? Nobody Sin-City!

Ha-ha! Wow; really; you are too damn funny woman; come on, get in and let's get back to campus! Fine! Let me take my heels off since I have to crawl through. You okay to drive? It is raining and it looks like your driver side wiper is on its last leg; cutting into the glass. Wait a minute my arm is wet, and it's not the liquor; hell naw! Is this rain coming through the roof!

Yeah my bad; I got a leak on that side. Reach under your seat and there should be a towel under it. Oh and it gets worse if it rains harder; just wanted you to know. We're not far from campus; it's only water; you'll be alright. Well while I'm at it; do you have a life jacket to match? You don't have a trash bag and some tape? You should make that your next investment Donnie.

It's only water; that's easy for you to say D, sitting over there all nice and dry! Ha-ha! I'm sorry Chantel; it's a hoopty baby; what did you expect? Man; wait until Cynthia hears about this date. What you saying Sag Nasty; you didn't have fun? I did but it was crazy! I'm not really that bad in public.

The rain slows up as they enter the campus gates. I guess you will probably think again before blackmailing someone else. I'm going to turn it in now; I need to put my hand in some ice anyway. Alright that's cool gangster;

let me let you out; I'm taking it in too. Don't forget to turn the boom box off! Ha-ha! Oh you got jokes huh; I got it! Donnie and Chantel laughs at each other, exits the hoopty and heads to the dorm.

2. Unconditional Love.

Knock-Knock! Knock-Knock! Wait a minute; here I come! Cynthia opens up the door dressed in red boy shorts and a halter top, with her robe; only covering her shoulders. Well hello there; how can I help you? Hey; you must be Cynthia; I'm Donnie. Is Chantel in? Oh so you are Donnie; she's not here right now, she stepped out for a minute. Would you like to come in and wait? I'm not sure if that's cool; when is she supposed to be back? I don't want to intrude. She'll be back in 15 minutes, believe me you are not intruding; come in. Cynthia steps aside, moves her robe then places her hand on her hip, revealing her body. Are you sure it's ok, Cynthia? It's okay; I don't bite. Donnie reluctantly enters the room as his white Jordan slippers squeak just a little from his wet feet because of a recent shower. His white Tee hangs mid-way over his brown khaki shorts, while his cologne scents up the dorm room.

Cynthia takes a whiff of the cologne passing under her nose; while licking her lips. She closes the door behind her. Have a seat; can I get you a beer while you're waiting? Do you drink ice house? Yeah that's cool; I can use a cold beer. So; where are you from Cynthia? I'm from Virginia. She closes the door to the miniature refrigerator sitting in the corner, then walks over to Donnie and hands him his beer. Thanks Cynt; can I call you Cynt? You can call me anything you want. Cynthia takes a seat next to Donnie, crosses and uncovers her legs. Donnie starts to feel a little uncomfortable as she gets closer to him. Sooo, how long have you known Chantel? We've known each other for only a year; we met last year because we had a class together. Cynthia moves closer to Donnie; smiles and places her hand on his knee. Heyyyy; you know my boy really likes you. He hasn't stopped talking about you since he gave you those fliers the other day! You should give him a chance; he's cool.

What was his name; P, J? Oh, it was Q right! I barely remember him; he was okay. Over confident if you ask me. I like a man with confidence but just the right confidence. You seem like a girl that knows what she wants; Quentin has that same attitude. If that makes him over confident then you're no different than he is Cynt. Trust me; he's a good guy; you will be glad you befriended him.

Besides; a sexy lady like you shouldn't be single anyway. I know my brother and you're his type; go ahead and give him a chance. Cynthia places her hands up to her hair; pulls it back from her face then looks at Donnie. You really think I'm sexy? Chantel is a lucky girl because you are sexy as well. Well thank you Cynthia; so are you gonna take Quentin up on his offer or not? We're all going to be at the party in a few weeks; it would be nice if you joined us. I guess I can; especially if you are going to be there. I hope it's going to be hot that day, so I can show some skin. Cool; I'll tell him you're coming! Hey it's been like 20 minutes and she isn't here yet. I'm about to leave; can you please tell her I came by. Thanks for the beer and I enjoyed talking to you Cynthia; you're gonna get somebody in trouble with that body of yours. She smiles at Donnie. Man; is it hot in here to you?

Cynthia stands up fanning herself and removes the robe, dropping it to the floor; showing off her body to Donnie. Really, you think my body is nice; thank you! Cynt turns around with her ass towards his face still conversing. It was nice talking to you as well; I'll let her know you dropped by. Cynthia bends down and picks her robe up off the floor.

Hmmm, yeah it was nice. I'll tell Q we spoke; did you want his number before I leave? No, but I can give you my number to give to him. Cynthia grabs a pen and paper, writes down her number then hands it to him while holding on to his hand. Cool; I'll give it to him; he'll like that. I'm out Cynt; don't forget to tell Chant I came by! Cynthia walks him to the door. And if I don't? Ha-Ha! Just joking with you sexy man. See you later. Alright Cynthia; you're a trip; have a good day.

Donnie had finally left the room after 25 minutes but the smell of his Cool Water cologne still lingered as Cynthia sat there in her robe drinking her cold beer, day dreaming about what just happened as jealousy and envy kicked in. She looked up from her dream as the mechanical sound of the room door unlocking caught her attention.

Damn girl; it smells good in here! Did you have company; you got a man or something I don't know about? Girl, now you know if someone were here, I would have put our sign up on the door. I've just been sitting here watching TV, and drinking beer. It sure smells like a man in here Cynt. Yeah I smell it too, I ran into one of my friends today in the hallway; he gave me a hug after we finished talking; it was probably him. Chantel kept it to herself but was thinking that the scent smelled familiar; she was sure it was the same cologne that Donnie had on last night. Did he come in and have a beer with you? No, why you ask me that Chant? Oh just because I see two cans, and only one has lip gloss on it. Oh that; I drank a beer before I put this gloss on. Chant; stop with the interrogation; tell me how your date went last night.

You wouldn't believe me if I told you. Try me! Now Cynt; I am not an uppity chick but I had to get in the car first off through the driver's side! Stop playing girl! Really! Does it look like I am playing? That is not the worst thing about the car; I had to hold a boom box to play the music, he had no radio. That sounds horrible Chant! Where did you end up going to, how was that at least? Don't get me started on where we went? Was it that Strokers club? Yes, and it was a strip club. I have never wanted to hurt somebody so bad in my life. Did you stay though? I had to; how was I going to get back home? Anyway, I got over the fact that we were there; only because we started to drink. Oh; so he was trying to get you drunk; so you could forget; typical male move!

Well I started to relax a little, until I got sick of the bartender disrespecting me by calling him baby; numerous of times. No she didn't Chant; what did you do? I told her about herself then she threw a drink on me. That heifer did what girl? You heard me; after that no conversation left; I straight jumped over the counter and introduced her to an empty bottle! In the end of course; we got kicked out. I didn't know you had it in you Chant! Oh, I don't like to fight Cynt but I have no problem with beating a bitch ass for what's mine. Damn; I know that's right Chantel; I don't blame you girl. Let me get you a beer, we're gone drink to that!

"What's up A.U; it's April 18th; 2000 baby; and tonight it goes down!" "It's our 10th Annual; Southern Basketball Classic" "It's your favorite Campus DJ; Dj Diamond and I'm here at the gym live!" "If you're not here; you better hurry because seats are filling up fast." "Tonight we take on the Tennessee Tigers; the band is jamming and the AU alumni, family and friends are in the hizz house!"

The gymnasium was packed to capacity as alumni and patrons pour in to be seated for the Annual Southern Classic. Quentin, Marcus, Chantel, Cynthia, Tamara, Thomas, Ted, Richard, and Nadia sit in the bleachers as Sylvia, Latrice and Sage walk up the steps to join them in cheering on Harold and Donnie tonight. Hey Unc; what's been happening man? Hey Q; how you been young fella? Good man; I can't complain. Ted; Donnie's Uncle visited Atlanta off and on while helping him learn the Real Estate Investment business. Glad to hear that Marcus! What up Marc; you still pimpin boy! Hell yeah Thomas; how long are you gone be here playa? Probably about two weeks Marc; you have to hook me up with some of those chics man. I got you Thomas; don't even trip.

Thomas; Donnie's cousin from Florida; didn't believe in working on anyone's job and had to have his weed every day, no matter what and any woman he was with had to believe the same thing. Well what's up young man; how's school? What up Poppa Rich; everything is cool man. Your son has been doing his thing though. I know how Donnie is doing Marcus; I asked about you. He told me you still haven't declared a major yet; it's been year's son; what are you waiting on?

I don't know Poppa Rich; I've been just partying man and living life. Marc you're not gone have a life and none of those women you're whoring around with; if you don't get your education. How are you going to support them with no job! I'm gone be like you Poppa Rich and own my own company. Oh really and what kind of company is that going to be Marcus; without an education? Poppa Rich; I'm gone be managing my man Harold; he's going pro! Marcus what the hell do you know about managing somebody boy; you need to learn how to manage yourself first son. I hear you Poppa Rich; I'll get it together, I promise. Ok young man; if you say so!

Hey Poppa Rich! What's up Quentin? Come over here and let me introduce you to Donnie's friend; Chantel. Sure; no problem! Chantel this is Donnie's father; Richard. Poppa Rich; this is Chantel. How are you, young lady; it's nice to meet you; Donnie has told me so much about you. Hi Mr. Richard; he told you a lot about me, I hope it was good but it is good to finally meet you. It was all good Daughter-in-law; sit here beside me so we can talk some more. Sage, Latrice and Sylvia had finally reached the top of the bleachers to join the group. Hey Chant! Hey ladies, come on up here, we have some empty seats. Damn Chantel; who are your friends? Slow your roll Q; let me introduce you to them. Latrice, Sage and Sylvia; this is Quentin. The three ladies all together say hello while Cynthia turns her head towards them; rolls her eyes and sucks her teeth.

Nice to meet you ladies; let me introduce you all to the fellas! This is Donnie's dad; Poppa Rich. This is his brother Ted; whose Donnie's Uncle and his cousin Thomas, and this is my boy, Marcus. Hey ladies! Hi fellas! Ted reaches out to shake Latrice's hand. How are you Ms. Latrice; come over here and sit with me. Not trying to be difficult but is there a particular reason why I should sit next to you, and nowhere else? Yes because it's the best seat in the house, and you, my lady, deserves the best. Why Mr. Ted; I thank you so much for considering me, when It comes to me deserving the best; because I do. See; I knew you had class; come on over here. Man do you believe that! What's that Marcus? Ted just pulled that bad ass chick! Man my Uncle invented the game boy; you're still a player tryna crush a lot! Ha-Ha! Kiss my ass Thomas; watch me in action bruh!

Marcus walks down one row to where Sylvia and Sage are sitting. Hey ladies; I'm glad you guys came through. Can I join you? Sylvia looks Marcus up and down and sees dollar signs; she had already taken a guess at how much his attire cost; from his Roca wear outfit, Timberland boots, Platinum Chain and Movado watch. You sure can cutie! Marcus slid in between her and Sage as Harold and Donnie ran up and down the court trying to keep the lead on the competition. Harold ran point guard as his team mates ran down court on a fast break. Donnie ran up the left side then cut across the paint as Harold threw a nice alley hoop for a tie breaking dunk. Yay Donnie!

The crowd screams as the game intensifies. Cynthia stands up; jumps and yells in excitement as Chantel, Tamara, Nadia and Poppa Rich looks over at her. Tamara tugs on Chant's arm. What the hell; someone is a little too happy over there, you need to check that shit! Chant; don't make me flatten her, take care of that! Nadia chill girl, it's nothing! Cynthia sits back down in her seat; Tamara reaches behind Nadia's back, ready to pull on Cynthia's hair. Chant, pulls her back. Girl stop! I just got kicked out of one place for fighting; Donnie would be mad if I got kicked out of the gym. Cynt is cool, she is just being supportive.

Thomas now sitting on the top bleacher all alone; looks down at the bleacher in front of them and notices Quentin, Cynthia, Nadia,

Tamara, Chantel and Poppa Rich sitting together. He looks to his left and see Ted and Latrice sitting alone; while Marcus and Sylvia sat off to the right of Q and the group. Thomas had noticed the tension brewing between the girls and Cynthia then decided to walk down and have a seat between Nadia and Cynt.

Excuse me; can you slide over please! Boy what are you doing? Look; Donnie's my cousin and I want to watch the game just like you guys but everybody is sitting with a group and I wasn't. So I said screw it and came down to sit by the prettiest lady in the building. I don't believe we've met; Hi; I'm Thomas! Hi; I'm Nadia. Nadia moves her hair from over her eyes and tucks it behind her ears. Are you sure you were speaking to me?

Thomas looks at Nadia with his gray eyes; curly afro, goatee, straight teeth and light skin then smiles. Yes Ma'am I was; why you say that; don't you think you're pretty Nadia?

What I think is unimportant; but thanks for the compliment. Umm, really! Well; what are you doing after the game? I was thinking about just going home and curling up to a good book; is there a reason why you ask?

Really; what book are you reading; I dig girls that read? Oh, I love to read; I am just starting on Moby Dick. Ha-ha! Are you trying to push me off or something; Moby Dick; I read that in 8th grade! No, just decided to do some light reading; I enjoyed it as well as a child. I just recently finished a book called Jewels before I started Moby Dick. Cool; I just finished A Devil in A Blue Dress. Did you ever try to read while on that natural herb; it's an unforgettable experience; it feels like you're a character in the book! No I haven't; is that even safe? From the sound of it, you're very familiar with it.

Ha-ha! Yeah it's natural from Mother Earth; of course it's safe. Yay! Come on HAROLD! Q and the others; stand to their feet as the game reaches the middle of fourth quarter. Harold steels the rock from his opponent then rushes down the court; stands behind the three point line then launches a jumper. Thump! All iron; the ball bounces off the rim then back to him. Harold slices through the defenders; leaps from the free throw line and in for a slam dunk. Yay! Yay! The crowd went wild as the band play, loudly in the background. The opposing team passes the ball in as Donnie ran pass the defender; swiping at the rock.

Yay! Yay! The crowd jumps to their feet and yells again as Q and the group stands up to celebrate while Cynthia stands atop the bleachers! Damn, Cynthia you fucking somebody out there? If I didn't know better I would believe you feigning for someone. What did you say, Chant; catch your tongue girl; why the hell would you say that anyway? Because; you look suspect over there Cynt; don't let your mouth write a check your ass can't cash! Tamara steps in between the two of them; Poppa Rich grabs Chant then puts her on the other side of him.

Ted turns to Latrice with a grin on his face. So what is it that you do for a living Trice? I'm a lawyer, why you ask? Sounds like some serious hours of work; always thinking and researching on different cases; when do you get the chance to relax? Well that's what I'm doing now. No! I mean really relax woman, this right here is not a way to relax and unwind. Then I guess I would say; not often then. You never answered my question Ted; why do you ask? I was asking because a lady like you needs to be pampered. Oh! You think so huh? Yeah I do and I want to be the one to do that for you.

Really Ted, what makes you think I can't pamper myself? I know you can woman, but you should not have to Mrs. Lawyer. Ted smiles and winks at her as the sound of the buzzer goes off, ending the time out called by the visiting team; the two of them turn their attention to the game. Donnie is at the free throw line waiting to take his shot, due to the foul that he had gotten; while he was trying to make a shot from the 3 point line, right before the break. Donnie makes his third shot; all you could hear was the swish of the ball going through the net, pulling them ahead by three.

The crowd goes wild, standing to their feet, clapping with excitement. That's my baby! Chantel shouts while looking over at Cynthia. The sound of Pops laughing rings out while everyone takes a seat. Chant feels a tap on her left shoulder and turns toward pop. Now Chant I just wanted to tell you, don't let any foolishness come in between you and my son. Pops tilts his head in the direction of Cynthia. I know pops, I won't; something just don't seem right though. The fans for the home team starts to chant in the back ground, in unison. Air ball! Air ball! Responding to a missed 3 point shot by the opposing team. Chantel leans over to her right and whispers in Tamara's ear. Girl; Thomas has Nadia in a trance over there, she better watch out!

The two girls start to laugh. Thomas and Nadia realize that they're being watch then move in a little closer; while deep in their conversation. So you wanna try it Nadia? We can have our own little burn session. I don't know Thomas; I guess, as long as it is not dangerous. Okay let's exchange numbers then so we can hook up. Nadia smiles with disbelief, flattered by all of the attention he is giving her; while Thomas reaches for his phone.

Everyone turns their attention to the game; the clock has only 24 seconds left with the opposing team in possession of the ball. The Tennessee Tigers toss the ball in to their point guard as Atlanta University sets into their defensive positions. The opposing team went up for a 3 point shot but gets blocked by

Harold. He gets the ball, looks up and finds Donnie going for a fast break with only 4 seconds remaining on the clock. Harold tosses Donnie an alley hoop; he finishes with a slam dunk; winning the game by 5 points. The crowd goes wild; standing to their feet, some rushing to the court as the fans goes crazy.

Ring-Ring! Ring-Ring! Hello; who's speaking? What's up Donnie; this is Marcus. Hey man what's going on? Get the boys together man; we're having a pool party today. Marc; what the hell are you talking about? D I'm at Sylvia's crib; this broad has a tight ass house bruh. I'm talking about a two story brick house; pool in the back with a damn water fall, 5 bedrooms, 3 baths and shit. Marcus; stop playing man! Donnie you know I'm not messing with you player. Call the boys and tell Harold to bring his special BBQ sauce; I'm about to light up the grill and Sylvia's calling all the girls.

Ok Marc; what's the address? Oh; it's 2569 Bentley Crest lane; see you in a bit playa. Alright Marcus; I'll pick up some beer too. Cool, that's what's up!

Sylvia walks into the kitchen to grab a bottle of water; she had just finished working out in her personal gym located in the left wing of her two story colonial white mansion. With sweat running down the side of her face, she wipes her brow with her towel and places it in the laundry-shoot that runs to the basement area of the house, where the maids pick up the clothes for the weekly washing. She turns to see Marcus sitting at the kitchen table eating on some leftover chicken served last night, from her father's celebration, she had thrown in his honor; due to a new Oil Rig deal he signed with a foreign partner.

Did you make yourself at home? Sure did; you could easily get lost in this place Sylvia. Okay good; sorry I had to leave you for a minute, I have a daily routine that I have to keep; I am trying to stay fit. Did you call your boys and let them know about the party? Yeah I did; they will be here shortly. Good; now I need to call the girls and let them know. Sylvia walks over to the island counter were she had placed her phone and calls up Chantel. Hello! Hey Chant; this is Sylvia. Oh! Hey girl what's going on? I need you to call up the girls; I'm going to have a pool party today. Now that sounds like fun; who's all coming?

Well; I had Marcus- Marcus! Stop playing Sylvia, you and him? Did not see that coming at all- Let me finish Chant, Damn! He just came by to see me, nothing serious. Oh! And you guys just decided to have a pool party. You can't lie to me girl, sounds like a love connection. Anyway Chant; you're coming right? Yeah, of course I will be there. Marc has already called the guys. Are you going to invite that chick? What chick is that Sylvia? The one you are rooming with. Yeah I can, it'll give her a chance to get her head from under my man's ass. Besides, I know Q is going to be there; maybe they can hook up. She needs to and quickly. Sylvia and Chant starts to laugh. Ok; I will call up the girls; what time do we need to be there? Be here around 4 O'clock. Cool; do you want us to bring anything? No; just bring yourselves. Are you sure? Yeah! Ok later!

Hey Sylvia; do you have any charcoals? Yeah my father has some in the garage. Cool, that's what's up; I'll go clean the grill while you season the meat. Oh no honey, I am going to take a shower first; then I can season the meat. But I sure hope that you know what you're doing on that grill? Don't be ashamed if you know nothing about it; speak now or forever hold your peace. Hey I know enough to get started; my man Harold is the professional on the grill. He's bringing his special BBQ sauce too; so don't worry baby, it will be straight. You need to hurry up and wash though so we can get some time in before everybody gets here. Here we go with that Marc; seems like everybody and their mother has a special damn sauce. I'll take my shower when I want and on my time, stop trying to boss me around; we will have plenty of time to talk before they arrive; you can, swim though, right? I will not be in the mood to save you.

Marcus stands up from the table; removes his wife beater then walks over to Sylvia. Smack! Ouch; what are you doing? You know you like me smacking that ass. And who said anything about talking woman; bring your fine ass over here. Marc grabs Sylvia by the waist from behind then pulls her close to his chest then whispers in her ear. Just for your information; I'm a certified life guard baby, I don't drown. But I do have that inner tube for you to grab on to; so nobody is drowning on my watch. Umm, oh really.

Sylvia now in awe from what just happened to her; feels her heart racing as if she were in a marathon. The thought of this man's body pressed up to hers turned her on in the worst way, she begins to feel weak and that is not something she is used to. Sylvia grabs a hold of his shoulders and caresses the shapes of his muscles, moves close to his ear, pushes him up against the refrigerator and whispers. You may be a certified life guard, but nothing and I mean nothing could have you ready for this test. Ding-Dong! Ding-Dong! God Dammit! Ha-Ha! You better get the door Marc; I'm jumping in the shower. Ding-Dong! That shit aint funny Sylvia; you're lucky the bells ringing. Ding-Dong! I'm coming, dammit! Marcus makes his way to the door as Sylvia heads upstairs to the shower.

What's up shawty? Damn Harold; you 20 minutes too early bruh. What you talking about Marcus; we need to get the grill going boy; so we can get this food poppin. Man; I was about to bend ol girl over the counter just now, then here you come. Shawty you fuck too much; move your ass out of the way; let me see the crib. Harold, you aint gone be pushing me around, boy; did you bring the sauce? I got it shawty; now give me a tour and you can leave that door open too. Harold you tripping; I aint leaving these people house open! Marc; Donnie and Chantel are right behind me shawty; you tripping. What up playa, playa! Hey Donnie; I didn't even see you guys. Come in bruh! Hey Chantel! What's up Marcus? I'm good Chant; your girl is straight; is all your friends cool like this? Marc; here's the beers bruh! Thanks Donnie! Where's my girl Marcus? Oh; she's in the shower Chant. Wow; so how have you been since the last I saw you? You and Sylvia seem like you are hitting it off pretty well, by the sounds of things.

Your girl is alright Chantel; are your other girlfriends coming too? Yeah, they should be here shortly, and why are you asking about my other girls? I thought you and Sylvia were hitting it off. Yeah we friends but its not serious. She's single and I am too; so until then I'm gone be a man baby; know what I'm saying Chant? Yeah well, first of all, I'm not your baby, that title belongs to your boy Donnie; there is a difference between being single and being an in your face hoe; that is my girl; so if you don't plan on being original and respectful to her, then you don't need to be walking all up and through her house.

Don't ask me about any other of my female friends; this is not a Marcus buffet plate, get your mind right. Donnie; get your girl bruh; she's tripping; I'll be out back on the grill. What are you talking about Marc? Nothing man; she just found out that I was a ho, that's all. You better let her know D; I'm trying to cut bruh. It can be her sister; her cousin, her friend, shit; I'll cut her momma too. Ha-ha! Marc; take your whoring ass to the grill fool.

Hey Chantel, don't mind Marcus baby; he's just being himself. We done tried to change that fool but aint no help for him baby. You need to get your man; I don't see how anyone would want somebody like that. He is going to make me spray; some ho be gone; on my girls when they get here; so they can be protected against that shit! Donnie he doesn't want me to get a bottle trust and believe me. Baby it's not gone matter what you tell them; they will still give him the drawers. I'll put that on everything I love. I hate to say it, but my boy got game.

Whatever man, you don't know my girls like I do; they would never fall for such foolishness. He is too sure of himself; his ego needs to be deflated and my girls will be the ones to do it. Hello! Hello! Is anybody home! There's your girls right now Chant! Tamara and Nadia walks in, dressed in sun dresses, sandals and sun visors. Chantel; what's up baby! We're in the house girl; it's time to party!

Hey girls, what's up? Hey Donnie; we're good; where is Chantel; I know we heard her voice. Oh she just went in the kitchen to season the meat. Thanks Donnie; that was a good game the other night. Thanks Nadia! Yeah you and Harold did your thing; is he here? Yes he is Tamara; he's out back by the grill with Marcus. Wow; everybody is here, huh? Hey Tam and Nadia; I'm in the kitchen girls! We'll talk later Donnie; we're going to help Chant.

The two ladies make their way to the kitchen with Chantel. So Chant; where is your friend Cynt? Oh she is supposed to be on her way, she stopped by the store to grab some cards so we can have a little game of spades. Don't start Tam; you can't be going buck wild upside people's heads. Nadia; will you tell your sister to behave tonight; this is all about us having some fun. I am not going to do anything that would put me in jail, don't worry Chant. Anyways girls; I trust my baby. It's not about if you trust Donnie or not; it's about how far, she will go. Okay ladies getting too far ahead of ourselves here, she doesn't want my man; besides; Q has a thing for Cynt, let him tame her.

The door-bell rings as the three are deep in their conversation. Cynthia walks into the kitchen wearing a two piece red and black bathing suit with half of her ass out and nothing to cover herself. Hello ladies! I am so ready for this party. Cynt; takes her shades, lifts them up off her eyes then places them in her hair. Nadia and Tamara turn their heads and roll their eyes. Tamara says hi to Cynt in a low voice; walks past Chantel and whispers. Look at this bitch; you could pick your teeth with that outfit. Chant looks at Cynt with her nose frowned up as if she got a whiff of bad tuna. Wow girl; that's all you brought. Yeah Chant; this is a pool party right, what do you think? Cynt turns around to model off her swim suit. It's cute, I guess. Nadia smiles and under her breathe says. Yeah; cute if you are a stripper! Surprised that Nadia said it loud enough for Cynt to hear; Chant grabs a plate full of seasoned meat and asked Nadia to help her carry it to the grill as Sylvia makes her way to the kitchen.

There she is; what's up girl! Hey Tamara; how are you girl? I am great Sylvia; thanks for asking. You're welcome; where's your sister? She just went out back with Chant and them! What are they doing out there; cooking? No child; they took some meat out to Marcus and Harold. Oh; I was about to say; that's Marc and Harold's job. Well, where's the alcohol girl? There's some wine coolers in the fridge Cynthia, help yourself. Thanks Sylvia! You're welcome girl and I love that bathing suit too. Thanks Sylvia; I got it from Lenox. I have to get me one; did they have it in blue?

Yep; blue; yellow; purple and green! Ding-Dong! Ding-Dong! I'll be back girls; let me see who this is.

Hey Sage; what's up girl; I'm glad you made it. Sylvia; you know I wouldn't miss a pool party at my girls house. Come on in child; the girls are in the kitchen and some of the guys are out back cooking on the grill. What's up Sylvia; we got the Hennessy baby and the Goose! Hey Thomas and Q; come on inside; everybody's here. Thanks Sylvia; where you want these drinks? Just put them on the counter guys; while you're at it Q, can you turn on the music in the living room, just turn it up and leave the door open. What up Q; what took you so long boy? I had to pick up some drinks Donnie, where's Marc and Harold?

Out back grilling, I'm headed out there now. Alright bro; I'll be out in a minute. Donnie kisses Chant on the cheek as he walks up to the grill. Hey baby, you got your hands full, do you need help? I'm okay Donnie; Nadia and I are going to take the meat that's done into the house then help in the kitchen. Nadia and Chantel walks towards the patio doors, on their way, they pass by Cynthia. I'll be right back to help yall in the kitchen Chant; I'm just going to speak to everyone. Cynthia takes in the sight of the area once she gets by the pool, she thinks to herself; this is the type of layout she wants and will have. From the patio doors lay a walk way to the pool; this pool was not like anything that she had seen before. Instead of an ordinary cement wall for the barriers, there were mounted boulders with lush green grass surrounding; there also stood a waterfall in the center of the pool, which had a tunnel that you could swim under and come out of from different directions.

Cynthia reaches the grill as she meets Donnie, Marc and Harold with a smile. Hello guys! Smells really delicious over here! The three men say hello to Cynt. You did a really great job at the last game. Both guys start to say thanks to Cynt; but Harold unexpectedly gets cut off when she turns directly to Donnie as if she were only talking to him. Donnie sensing her tension begins to feel uncomfortable yet again. Yeah well, me and Harold make it do, what it do. Yeah you do. Cynthia gives him a slight wink. Chantel walks over to the kitchen window that over-looks the back yard; then crosses her arms in disbelief at Cynt making flirtatious body language toward her man. Chant! Chant! Oh, what's up Tamara? What are you looking at out there girl; I've been calling you for two minutes. At that sneaky roommate of mine; what's up? Forget that skank; come help me with this potato salad.

Well what's up lady; you're looking good in that two piece. How come you haven't called me yet? Hey Q; I meant to but I've been busy with these classes. Thanks for the compliment though; how have you been Sir? I've been good but we really need to hook up though. Damn, what have you been eating, ham hocks! Those are some pretty thick legs you got woman. Umm-hmm, I love me a thick red bone. Quentin; stop acting up shawty! I'm not acting up Harold; she is thick bruh! Don't mind him Cynthia; he can be off the chain sometimes.

Harold; chill bruh; I got this man. So when are we hooking up Cynt? Maybe we need to revisit the manners class, Q. I am a lady; do you truly believe all of this you so thick, you loving red bone bullshit; is really going to give you any play? You can either come correct or you will watch these same pretty thick legs walk away. Q, pump the brakes and gear it in reverse, and like the little engine that could try, try again. Whooooo! She told you Quentin! Shut up Harold! And for you Ms. Cynthia; I was just having some fun with your pretty, insecure ass. I saw you over here trying to hit on my partner Donnie; so I thought I would break the tension before someone's feelings got hurt.

My boy Donnie was trying to play it cool because he's a Gentleman but I will tell it like it is baby girl. Manners is something I pride myself on; when I feel that you earn that type of respect, then and only then will you get it Cynthia. Don't get me wrong; you're sexy and got a good future ahead of you but you aint perfect with your fine ass.

Daaaaammmmmmnnnn Quentin; why you went in on her like that bruh? It's all good Harold; I just had to let her know who I was man; you dig. Dig that shawty! Cynthia, now in awe of what just happened, remain standing there in front of the grill with her hands rested on her thick red hips, and starring at Q.

I'm sorry Sir but you clearly do not know a thing about having manners, at least having the right kind of manners has fallen off of your radar Q. You could have started off by asking how I'm doing or what have I been up to since you saw me last; you chose to however, comment on my physique, a man should always know that if you want to get to the lady, you must first entertain her mind.

I am glad that you do realize that; which I have always known; my future does look bright, there is a blurry spot, and that blurry spot is whether you are in it; right now as it seems you are not. Never assume that you know what is going on because assuming makes an ass of you, I was not flirting with Donnie; I don't know what you thought. I do know that Donnie is with Chant. I will be nice and be the bigger person in this situation and ask for you to act as if you have some type of sense.

Excuse me fellas; I'll be back in a few; me and Cynt are going to have a little talk. Come on Ms. Cynthia; let's have a seat pool side and start this thing over. The couple slowly walks a few more feet away from Marcus, Harold and Donnie to have some personal space. Several round; stone marble tables, with huge umbrellas and stone benches surrounded pool side and complimented the stone wall ambiance as the water from the waterfall constantly clashed against the still blue chlorine water. Cynthia takes a seat at the first table as Q sat himself directly across from her. She then took a second look at him and starts to realize just how sexy he really is. So what is your major Q? I'm an; English major. Okay, that is a good career move. So I have to ask; why does it seem like you always have an attitude?

See Q; now you trying to start again, I don't always have an attitude, you have only seen me a couple of times; I just have a low tolerance for bullshit. It gives me an allergic reaction. Ok, I can understand that; I hate BS also. You're kind of cool Cynt; we should continue this conversation over dinner on a real date. What do you think about that? I would like to continue it now but everybody is about to come outside in a few and it won't be as intimate. I don't know Quentin, it has been a rocky start but that may be a possibility. We will see how the rest of the night goes. What up folks! Thomas is in this mutha; where the smoke at? Hey cuz; what's poppin? This party is poppin Donnie, yall got the grill smoking, the ladies inside, I just want to know where the weed at! Marcus what's up playboy? Hey Thomas; it's all good bruh. What up shawty, how long are you gone be in the A? I aint in no rush Harold; I'm gone chill up here with Nadia for a bit. Cool, grab a beer and come chill with us cuz. Where they at Donnie? Oh, look in that cooler inside by the sliding door. Alright, did you guys want another one? Yeah bring 4 back, Q might want one too. Man that fool over there cakin, he aint worried about no beer. Just bring it Thomas! Alright Donnie; I got you.

Harold you need to be hollering at Sage bruh, she's single and works at a bank. Which one is that Donnie? She's in the house; I'll get Chantel to introduce you to her. Is she fine D? Man; what you think! I don't know Donnie; you be tripping sometimes with them eyes of yours shawty. Trust me Harold; she's straight. Ok;

that's what it is; tell Chant to hook a brother up then. Don't worry; I'll make it happen; flip them burgers though before you burn them Harold. Yeah; don't burn the meat man. Marcus I'm the grill master out here brother, and Donnie let me do this, I aint burning up nothing!

Chantel places the dish of potato salad in the refrigerator to keep it cool until dinner is served; she turns to Tamara with a disturbed look on her face. Tam, I hope that she is not that stupid to try and step on my toes. Girl you and me both, she is wrong for being all up in Donnie's face like that. You should have seen her Tam, smiling all up in his face like she was in a pageant.

You didn't check her Chant, I told you that you should have handled that from the jump. Chant; leans up against the counter by the sink. Nadia grabs the silverware out of the top drawer by the stove and places them on the table. You need to give her some kind of a hint that you are watching her; but you have to make it subtle Chant. Oh, I will give her subtle.

Cynthia interrupts Q in the middle of his sentence. I have to go to the bathroom, I will be right back. Meanwhile; Chantel makes her way to the door to go out and talk to Donnie and see's Cynthia as she is passing by the window. A smile crosses Chants face as she opens the door to the patio. She pretends to wipe off her dress while looking down, just as Cynt is passing by. Swoosh! Chant nudges her into the pool. Oh damn! Cynt, I didn't see you girl; I am so sorry; are you okay? Cynthia, now splashing in the water with her hair covering her eyes, quickly responds. I can't believe you did that Chant! I didn't mean to girl. Q see's Cynt struggling in the water then dives in to save her. I can't swim, help! Everyone comes running out of the house from all of the commotion, to see Cynthia being dragged out of the pool. Tamara, Nadia, and Sage turn their heads quickly to shield their laughter.

I will get you a towel Cynt. Chant passes by the ladies in the door way with a grin on her face. You go girl, that's what I'm talking about. That's a damn shame bruh. What's that Marcus? Your girl, pushing Cynthia in the pool like that! It was probably a mistake Marc. Yeah right Donnie; that's the same chick that you said jumped across the bar at Strokers. Damn D; your girl be going in like that man? It was just that one time Harold; she's cool. I don't know about you cuz but I like mine a little feisty. Thomas you like yours crazy not feisty; there's a difference.

Ha-ha! Marc, Harold, Donnie and Thomas stands over the grill laughing while Quentin pulls Cynthia out of the pool. Tamara pulls off her sun dress then jumps in the pool, just to show she could swim as the other girls continue to chuckle at Cynthia. Daaaaammnn;

did yall see that! Yeah Marc! Watch the grill Donnie; I'm going for a swim. Marcus pulls off his wife beater then dives in the pool with Tamara as she swam by. Boy that fool is gone be a whore forever! You may be right about that Thomas; Marcus is a straight hound; that boy see fresh meat and he can't help himself. Tamara's long hair draped to the back of her neck as she swam towards the waterfall that fell off the tunnel. Marcus stroked and stroked until he caught up with her then matches her stride. Hey; slow down baby. Hey, I thought you were tending the grill, what are you doing in here?

I can't let a beautiful woman like you swim alone, besides one almost drowned, we can't have another. So where's your man? The two now stop under the tunnel as the water drapes the entrance. I don't have one, aren't you dating my girl Sylvia? Nah; we're just friends, no commitments. You're fine as hell though; why don't you have a man Tamara? I don't have time Marcus; I travel a lot with my job. Really; what kind of job is that? I'm a massage therapist. Oh that's cool; I do a little massaging myself. Are you shooting me lines Marcus? No; I'm serious, turn around and let me show you.

Loud roaring echoed through the tunnel from the water pouring above into the shallow pool. Tam reluctantly turns around and faces the wet stone wall inside of the caved tunnel. Marcus places his hands on the small of her back then runs his finger-tips along the sides of her spine, until he reaches the crooks of her neck. Ohh! Tamara moans from sheer excitement. Does that feel good to you? Yeah, it's ok. Ummmm! How about that? Ummm! You didn't answer me yet Tamara? Do you like it? Ummmm-hmmmmm.

Marcus brought his right hand up from under her legs then pulls the left side of her bottom string with his left. Stop! What are you doing Marcus? Shhhhhhh! I got this baby. Ohhhh!

Marc leans in closer and softly nibbles on the base of her neck. Tam reaches up for the wet walls with both arms as he slid off his shorts, thrust both her feet apart then. Ummmmm! Oh; you like that; don't you? Ummmm-hmmmm. Tam arches her back then thrust backwards against Marc as he thrust forward. Ummmmm! Ummmm! Marcus backs away from her then slides under water. Ohhhh! Ohhhh! Tam moans louder and louder as her voice echoed through the tunnel and past the raging water fall.

Hey, what the; did you hear that Donnie? Yeah I heard it Harold! Oh my God! Ohhhhh! God help me! Oh it feels so good! What is that noise; did you hear it Chantel? No; what are you guys talking about Nadia? Nothing; I thought I heard someone screaming. Ummmm! I can't! No more! No more! Tamara dives under water to get away as Marc comes up for air.

Hey Marc! Marc! Donnie yells out as Tam swam back towards the others on the other side of the waterfall. Marcus could see everyone poolside through the water as it formed a wall over the tunnel. He pulls up his shorts then swam fast as he could to the opposite side of the tunnel, jumps out, runs through the bushes then jumps the 6 foot tall cast iron fence.

Latrice hangs up the phone after finishing up a conference call with her colleagues; she sits back in her black leather chair and takes her glasses off her face then places them in her hair. It's back to work for her; she still smiles from the thought of the weekend get-away that she and Ted had in Barbados. A sense of accomplishment comes over her, while she glances about her office, she breathes in deep, inhaling the sweet smell of her favorite perfume; Sex in the City. She gets up from her desk, then walk over to the bookshelf located on the left hand side of the grey, stone fire place. People thought she was crazy for wanting a fire place in her office but she insisted on having it. Man, this case is really trying me!

Latrice shakes her head, thinking of all the research that she still has to do. Tippy toeing to reach the top shelf, she grabs the blue paper back law book from up above; Trice opens the book, sifting through the pages, while walking back to her desk, she makes sure not to trip on the black bear skinned rug at the base of the fire place that sat directly in front of her grand cherry wood desk.

Umm! That does not look right. Pausing at the front, she notices that her gold plated name tag was slanted. She reaches over and fixes it. The office was immaculate by far, out of the norm for a law firm, the walls were covered with photos of famous black leaders, and the mantles were covered with sophisticated antiques that she had collected while on various trips. Latrice walks around the side of her desk, takes a seat then places the open book down.

Trice remembers that she wanted to ask Chantel about the pool party that she had recently missed. Hmmmm, I wonder if Chant is in already. Chantel and Cynthia are working for Trice for their internship; so it made it much more-easy for them; on one hand, Latrice needed the help and the two girls needed the experience. Buzz! Hey Chant; can you and Cynthia come to my office for a second? Sure; we'll be there in a minute. Thanks Chant!

The door knob to the office twists open, Chant and Cynthia walks through. Hey ladies. How have you been? Chantel reaches over and gives Trice a hug. I am doing good Trice. I didn't realize that you were in the office yet. Yeah I got in this morning at 5; the plane landed around 2; which gave me about 1 hour to sleep, and the rest goes to hell. Cynt, how are you girl? Cynt glances over at Chant while she passes by, to give Latrice a hug. Latrice, Chantel and Cynthia take a seat; Trice in her large black leather chair and the two girls on the opposite side of the desk; both facing their boss. I am so sorry that I missed the party; how was it? Chantel smiles a little, feeling the tension Cynt was throwing her way then answers. Trice it was a blast girl; everyone was there except you and Ted of course. I would have wanted to be in your shoes any day Trice. Why you stay that Cynt? Let's just say, it was all watered down at the beginning.

Latrice starts to laugh franticly. Cynt, you are crazy girl. Cynt however didn't find it at all amusing; she cuts her eyes over to Chantel; who clears her throat, in order to let Trice know to stop laughing. Trice picks up on the signal quickly. You know what ladies, I would love to hear this in more details later, right now I am trying two cases and if I don't leave now, I will be late. Latrice grabs her brief case, glasses and her law book then exits out of the office.

Chantel turns slightly to Cynt. What was that look for? I told you that I was sorry. Yeah I heard you say that, but your actions suggest different. Cynt, stop being that way girl; Donnie told me to tell you hi anyway. Cynt sits up in the chair as if someone had splashed cold water on her while she was sleep. Really, I mean oh, that's nice; tell him I said hi. Okay I will. Well since we are on hour lunch break, I am going to head out to the mall and pick up his favorite cologne, it was... Chant starts to snap her fingers in the air, pretending that she couldn't remember ummmm, it was- Cool water! Cynt blurts out.

Really, how would you know that Cynt? Girl that was a lucky guess! Yeah I'm sure it was Cynt, kind of like that day when I got home and smelled it in our room; you know that day when you had the two beers? Chant, that cologne is very popular! Yes, yes it is Cynt, how are you and Q coming along?

We are doing well, he seems to be nice so far; a change from when we first saw him. Changes how Cynt, for the better would you say? I saw the way he jumped in to save you, I would have dived in after you but he was in before I knew it. Yeah that was pretty nice of him right, he still think he's all that? Cynt please, you know that he's all of that; I don't know why you are trying to fight it, it's not like you have someone else that's on your mind; do you? No Chant, been too busy to have people on my mind. So do you guys plan on going out? Yeah he asked me, not sure where or when we are going, but it will be sometime soon. Well that's good Cynt, I think you guys would make a cute couple. I don't know about that girl but I will give it an honest try.

I see that you and Donnie are hot and heavy. Yeah, he is all of that and a bag of chips girl, so glad we hooked up, he just might be the one if he keeps acting right. Let me tell you; I wish a chick would push up on him. Chant, no one is thinking about your man; stop being so paranoid. That's how I like it, no one thinking about my man but me.

Cynthia gets up from her seat then walks around the desk. She straightens her white blouse, tucks it back in her black skirt then walks over to the large picture of Maya Angelou that hung by the fire place, looks in the glass then proceeds to fix her hair. Girl this is the life; I can't wait to graduate Chantel. I want my office to be just like this one; Latrice has it going on! Cynt makes her way to Trice's large black leather chair, takes a seat then props her legs up on the huge cherry wood desk. See, I belong here Chant; don't I look good?

No, you don't look good in that chair. Not trying to be the mean one here but I would look better sitting there. Now that is not right Chant! You right but it's the truth Cynt and the truth hurts. I have another bit of truth; you need to get your feet off of her desk before she goes ham on you. Chant, she is not going to know unless you tell her; you need to loosen up sometimes. I am loose right now but you need to chill and get up out of her seat.

Hello! Hello! A deep male voice echoes down the law firm hallway. Hello; is anyone here? Shhhhh. Did you hear that Chantel? Hear what? Someone's in here! Hello; oh there you guys are! Hi; have a delivery for Ms. Latrice; can one of you sign for it? Cynt stands up from the desk. Ummmm, hmmmm sure! The tall 6'4", white male stood in the doorway of Latrice's office holding a package and clip board waiting for a signature. Where do you need me to sign handsome? You just brightened my day when you walked through the door; do you like chocolate? I sure hope you do, because I have plenty to give. My name is Cynthia, what's yours?

Hi Cynthia, I'm Robert and I love chocolate; can you sign right here for me please? Sure; no problem. Thanks! Hold on Robert; why are you leaving so Fast? I have several stops to make Cynthia. Well; do you want my number? Sure write it down for me. You don't have a girlfriend do you, kids, wife, I'm just saying. Oh; I have two baby mommas and I stay with my friend Janet for now but we're just friends. Ha-ha! What are you laughing at Chantel? Nothing girl, go ahead and give dude your number so he can get back to work already. You know what Robert; just give me your number and I'll call you. Cool, no problem; take my card. Thanks Robert; have a great day. Thanks Cynthia; you too.

Ha-ha! Ha-ha! Chantel and Cynthia laugh continuously after the delivery guy leaves. Girl why you aint give him your number! Shut up

Chantel, don't even start with me. We need to hurry up and finish this work before it's time to go Cynthia. Bring your ass on out of here and come up front and help me! Hold on a second; let me fix Latrice's desk; I don't want her to be tripping. Yeah you better; I told your butt not to be putting your feet up on it anyway.

Cynt and Chantel, enters the hallway and makes their way back up front. Girl did you hear that screaming at the pool the other day. I swear it sounded like your girl Tamara. Yeah I heard it but what makes you think it was her and why would she be screaming? Chantel you can be slow sometimes child; you're trying to tell me that you didn't see her and Marc swimming together before they went in that damn tunnel. I know you are not calling me slow, what exactly are you trying to say? I hope that you are not trying to imply that they were together; you always have something negative to say. You need to be worried about your affairs. What you mean by that Chant?

Exactly what I said; worry about yours and not about someone else's. I'm just saying; it is kind of funny that the two of them seemed to disappear for a minute. How would you even know; you and Q were in the corner caking anyway. We were not caking; we were right by the tunnel Girl, sounded like someone was getting it in to me.

Hush your mouth Cynt, if you start a fire and it spreads; I am not going to be the one who sprays the water on it when it turns into a wild inferno. I know what it is Cynt; you just need to get some, your well has to be making a crackling sound when you walk. Don't you worry about if my well is half empty or half full! Oh, I am not worried; I am getting mines; but for you it's written all over your face; you're not! Chantel why are you always so damn mean! Shitting me; I am not mean; I just see through the bull.

Well; mark my words girl; Marcus done tap that ass! Shut up Cynthia; Marcus is with Sylvia and besides, Tamara is our friend, she wouldn't do that. See; I'm done talking to you about this situation; just ask Quentin when you see him. And what is he gone say? He's gonna tell your crazy ass what we saw; that whore ass Marc took his shirt off and jumped in the pool as soon as he seen Tam in there by herself.

You don't have to believe me; I know what I saw Chant. Hell; you can even ask your man; Donnie was at the grill when it happened! Girl, I am not about to entertain the idea, I know my girls. Tam wouldn't fall for any of his antics. Child please, if a woman hasn't been getting any, she will jump, it's just nature. Maybe that is your nature Cynt, but it's not everyone else's; just drop the subject girl.

Okay if you say so; I'm hungry; you want to order some take out? Sure; what are we getting? I don't care; Japanese or pizza; what do you feel like Chant? I'll take pizza; I don't want to get too much to eat; not trying to catch the itis. Yeah we definitely don't want that, I'm sure you don't want everyone to hear your snoring problem. Please Cynt, the only one that snores is you, and I hope that you get that under control before you and Q get together.

You think you are funny Chant. Cynthia goes through their stash of menus and finds the number to Pizza Hut. So what did you want on it girl; sausage, pepperoni and what else? Extra cheese! Ok cool; your ass is going to be sick from eating so much damn cheese all the time Chant. Cynthia picks up the office phone then places the order as Chant continues to file through Latrice's case load. Ok it will be here in 30 minutes, so tell me Chant; is it good? What girl? Donnie girl!

I don't see how good my man is, would be any of your business. Damn, chick slow down; you stated that you were getting it in and inquiring minds want to know. You been sexing? Chant spill it. I'm not spilling shit; you never tell how good your man is to another woman because she will want to try it. Let's just say this Cynt, you don't have to have sex to get to the climax that you want. Bam! Cynthia slams her hand on the receptionist desk. Word; say that again Chantel!

3. BFF.

The Atlanta Skyline, lit up the I-75/85 corridor as Harold exited off onto Peachtree Street. High above; The Westin Hotel towered over downtown amidst the Atlanta Merchandise Mart and adjacent venues as he approached 529 N.E. Harold anxiously parks his car then hurries up to the entrance to meet his date. The Blue and Yellow sign above; read Gladys and Ron's; Chicken and Waffles; several patrons wait outside the entrance and in the foyer for their names to be called. Harold makes his way through the crowd to see if Sage was inside already. He gazes over the caramel colored seats, Mahogany tables and walls but to no avail. There was no sign of her. Welcome to Gladys and Ron's Sir; how may I help you? Oh I was looking for someone; she's supposed to be meeting me here. Ok; do you see her? No I don't; I guess I need a table. Sure; I can help you with that sir, it's currently a 15 minute wait. That's fine; put me down for two. No problem and what's your name Sir. You can just call me Harold. Alright Harold; I will call you when your table is available. Thanks!

He makes his way back outside with the other patrons, constantly checking his watch; their date was set for 7 pm and it was now 10 minutes pass the hour. But still there was no sign of her. Hey bruh, you got a light? No shawty; I don't smoke. Ok thanks bruh; you look familiar though, do I know you? I don't think so shawty. Yeah I know you man; you play for AU; don't you? Yeah I do. That's what's up; I'm Mike, bruh, nice to meet you. Nice to meet you too Mike. So what's up Harold; you ready to go pro next year? As ready as I'm gone get. Who you want to play for? It don't matter to me man; whoever wants to cut the check. Shit I dig that man! "Rogers your table is ready!" "Michael Rogers; party of two, your table is ready." Alright bruh, that's me; it was good talking to you; keep ballin. No doubt Mike, be easy. Damn, this girl got me twisted; shawty all late and shit. Harold stood there impatiently, pacing back and forth, walking up and down the sidewalk, constantly checking his watch and stalking every car that rolls by while talking to his self.

Sage pulls down the sun visor to her black 2002 Chrysler Sebring then looks in the mirror to make sure that her make up still looked good; she reaches for her Louis Vuitton hand bag, pulls out her lip gloss and touches up her lips. Hesitation at this point weighing on her heavily, as she takes a deep breath; it's been a long time since she has been on date. The plan for Sage was to write all men off, because in her mind none of them could be trusted. While looking in the mirror she spoke aloud. This is going to be a waste of my time! After all; the only reason she agreed to this date anyway, was to appease her friend Chantel.

For Sage, she would never allow herself to fall into the same devastation she was thrown into with her ex fiancé; no one should ever be subjected to that type of pain. Well, let's get this over with she says while looking at herself! Sage places the tube of gloss back in her bag, push the visor up then steps out of the car. It's now quiet outside, the clicking of her heels against the cement path echoes as she makes her way to the front of the building. Sage turns the corner, glances through the front entrance and sees Harold. Hey, how are you; sorry I am late.

Hey; I was beginning to think you stood a brother up. "Harold your table is ready!" Well, I guess you're right on time; come on, our table is ready. Right this way guys; I have a booth for you all, is that ok? Yeah that's good shawty; appreciate it. I noticed you pointed out that you thought I was standing you up; how long have you been waiting on me? About 25 minutes. Well, if I really didn't want to meet you, I'm grown enough to cancel. The two follow the Hostess to their booth. Here you are guys; your waitress will be here shortly. Thanks! So, how was your day ma'am; I like your outfit; you look sharp. I'm not that much older than you, I would appreciate it, if you do not address me as ma'am. Thank you for the compliment; you clean up well yourself. I have never been here before; is there anything that you can recommend Harold? Yep; the chicken and waffles shawty! What else?

I will be as nice as I can when I say this to you, so please don't take me as being rude Harold. I am a manger of a bank; which means; I supervise people on a day to day basis. I work long hours and make sure that my customer's money is well taken care of; a shawty, is a short term for a girl, I by far have graduated from that title. It would be pleasing to me however instead of using the term shawty; you can call me lady. Sage picks up the menu that the waitress places on the table then clears her throat. Umm; ummm. I will look at the menu myself, I'm sure there other things besides waffles and chicken. Well; my bad, Ms. Sage; I'm just use to girls in tight jeans; not really slacks and blouses. So excuse me if I seem a little excited. You're very attractive and I'm feeling you. But it doesn't matter what you order off that menu, can't none of it touch my BBQ Ribs and chicken you had at the pool party the other day! I'm just sayin.

If I remember properly Harold, myself and the other ladies did the seasoning to the meat, all you had to do was make sure it didn't burn; from the look of the piece of rib I got, it was closer to very well done and a little on the crunchy side. I know what I will order, these smothered pork chops look good. Sage closes the menu then places it back on the table and looks up at Harold. Like I said; I am a lady, it's not what you are used to, it's how well you can adapt to change when you are faced with it. The waitress walks up to the table to greet them, with a pencil and a pad ready to take their order.

Hi, my name is Geneva; are you guys ready to order? Hi Geneva, I wanted to ask you a question; do you serve alcoholic beverages? Sage turns to the direction of Harold and says in a low voice. It is going to be a long night. Oh, no we do not carry alcohol here ma'am; sorry. It's okay, just thought that I would ask; I'll have the smothered pork chops with mashed potatoes, side of greens and a sweet tea. Okay got it! The waitress turns to Harold. What would you be having Sir?

Let me have the Chicken and Waffles with lemonade. Ok sir; I have the Chicken and Waffles with a lemonade and The Smothered Pork Chops, Mashed Potatoes, Greens and sweet tea for the lady. Yep, that's it Geneva. Ok; I'll be back with your drinks in a sec. So, how come a pretty successful lady like you, don't have a man? You haven't gotten caught up in this Atlanta girl on girl dating scene; have you? Sage looks at Harold in disgust; as the look of rage is piercing through her eyes, her thoughts go back, reminiscing about the heart break she had been through.

No one in her immediate circle knew of the pain that she was put through, when she caught her now ex fiancé cheating. Three years of her life was wasted on someone that she had completely and utterly given all of herself to. Sage knew that she worked a lot but she didn't realize that it was a problem in her relationship; all the lines of communication were severed. The bank that she was working at as a teller had closed down early because of an attempted robbery; shaken up, she went to visit her fiancé', having a key to his home, Sage figured she could go there and wait for him to get off of work.

When she reached his home and turned the door knob to his front door she found him having sex with his so called best friend Jacob, from grade school; talk about down low.

Why the hell would you ask a question like that Harold? My being single at this point is considered none of your business.

My bad Sage; I didn't mean to offend you. I'm going pro this year and I'm trying to find that special someone before all of that happens. Lord knows all the gold diggers will be out when that day comes. So please forgive me for being so aggressive. I'm sitting over here looking at you and how gorgeous you are and I want you to myself. I just feel some resistance coming from you and I was trying to break the ice.

Well, Harold; I sure hope that you find your special; express someone. I do understand that you want to be able to share something real with someone real, but remember things like that take time. Words do not empress me at all; I have been told by many about my appearance; yet nothing substantial has come about. Sage becomes bored with Harold, picks up her Samsung cell phone and starts to play her scrabble game.

Ok folks; here's your food; enjoy. Thanks Geneva! Ummm! Chicken and Waffles! The waitress places their plates in front of them. Will there be anything else I can get you? No we're okay for now. Okay, I will be back to check on you two in a bit. Oh, Geneva! On second thought; can I get a box to go? Sure thing ma'am, give me just a second. Damn Shawty; you're just gone leave; what's the problem? Did I do something wrong? Here you go ma'am, did you want a box too sir? No I'm good; Sage what's the business? I have to cut this short, I have more important things to take care of in the morning. That shawty bit; is a word you just cannot let go of, can you? This right here is a waste of my time; I am a banker not a teacher, I do not have time to teach you the ropes on how to treat a woman. Sage; wait!

I appreciate you spending your valuable time with a young college boy like me, maybe one day; I will return the favor. Please forgive me! Sage's body comes to a complete halt, something about the way the sentence rolled from his lips; made her feel wanted. Warm sensations came over her as she turns to face him. Sage tilts her head in disbelief, she starts to question herself; was this the same guy she was just talking to? Something deep down inside, starts to tell her to give this man a chance. Sage's frown turns into a smile as she spoke. Maybe, you can return the favor Harold. Sage turns around then continues to walk to the front door and out of the restaurant.

Ring! Ring! Hello! Hey Nadia; what time is your lunch baby? In ten minutes; why you ask Thomas? I'm picking up some Jamaican beef patties and cream soda; did you want any? No, don't really like them like that, can you pick me up some curry chicken and white rice please? Damn baby; how long is your break? That's a lot of food woman, are you sure you got time to eat all that? I have an hour lunch sweetie, that's plenty of time to eat it. Is that going to be a problem, I'm just very hungry. No it's no problem; I'm walking in the restaurant now. I'll call you when I get to your job. Okay sweetie, I will talk to you soon.

Hi; welcome to Golden Crust; what can I get for you today brethren? Hey bro; let me get two beef patties, some of that curry chicken over white rice and throw in some of that coco bread and a few plantains. Alright; did you want anything to drink with this? Yeah, add two sodas bro. Ok, you can get the sodas out of the cooler while I'm fixing your plate. That's what's up; how much I owe you? That's gonna be, $18.87 brethren. Cool, here you go, keep the change. Thanks; did you want a bag? Nah, I'm good, those boxes will be enough; I'm only going around the block. All set then my friend, come back soon. Yep!

Ring! Ring! Hello! Hey, I'm outside! Nadia! Okay Thomas; give me a second; I need to let one of my co-workers know that I'm going to lunch. Cool, I'm in the black Navigator with the Florida plates. Thomas opens the glove box and pulls out a pack of swisher sweets, takes one from the pack, licks it, then splits it down the middle. He reaches in his jean pocket then pulls out a purple bag of weed, sprinkles it in the blunt then rolls it up while waiting on Nadia. Tap-Tap! Someone taps on the passenger window. Hey what are you doing in there? Unlock the door for me so I can get in. Thomas a little startled, gathers himself then unlocks the door. Nadia opens up the door and climbs in the front seat with him.

What is that smell? Hey baby; this is some purp, you want a hit?

I don't know Thomas. Come on girl, it's good for you. Maybe later; I'm hungry. Alright you can try it after we eat. He passes her the curry chicken and rice while he eats his beef patties. This is the best Jamaican joint in the A right here. It is good; where did you get it? Golden Krust right there on South Hairston. Oh around the corner? Yep. So Thomas; what do you do? I see you're stuttin in this Navi, I know it's a magnet for women, how do I know that you don't already have a lady?

I do a little bit of this and a little bit of that. Mostly making runs for my uncle though, picking up orders for his investment company. But I aint got no lady; you're my lady, that's why I'm in the A girl. Wow, that sounds like a great job; sounds like you have a lot of freedom, not having anyone looking over your back is a plus. And I didn't know that I was your girl? Let me try some of that, what did you call it; purple? Hold on baby; have you smoked weed before? This aint no regular shit now. No I haven't smoked weed before, but I love to try what you have; I 'm sure I will be okay, I am a big girl.

Thomas picks up the blunt from the ash-trey; lights it, inhales, then blows the smoke in Nadia's face. She coughs continuously as the smoke fills the Navi. Are you alright baby, you sure you're ready to hit this purp? Yes I am; go ahead and pass it! Nadia takes the blunt from Thomas and puts it to her lips then pulls from it one time. Thomas tells her with instruction to hold it in, don't blow it out yet; so she follows his advice. Nadia holds the smoke in until she cannot take it anymore. She let out multiple coughs as she starts to feel a little bit different. Hey Thomas; I like this feeling, this is crazy. Nadia you a hype; go ahead and finish that one, I'll roll another. Oh, I meant to tell you that I have to head back to Miami tonight; I got business to handle.

When will you be coming back Thomas; wait a minute; did you see that? In a few days; no, I didn't see anything; what are you talking about? Don't start tripping on me girl, what time is your break over, you need to take your ass back to work. Give me that damn blunt! No, I am not tripping, you sure you didn't see that? The smoke was changing colors. Thomas confused, looks at Nadia with concern.

Thomas; look, look they are forming shapes. There is a dragon, ummm now there is a dog, wow and an alligator. Nadia couldn't believe what she was feeling; she turns to Thomas then points to the window to show him what she's seeing. Nad, you need to get it together it's time for you to clock back in. If you go back in there like that; they're gone fire your ass. Roll the window down and get some fresh air; here drink this soda. Okay, roll down the windows;

damn I'm hungry again. Did I eat all of my food; Ooo! I want a peanut butter and jelly sandwich.

You better get back inside Nadia and you only have a little bit of food left in here. I have to hit the road, are you going to be ok? Yep, I will be good to go, but my heart is racing; what's that all about? Is this real; am I really sitting here? You're fine; just enjoy the high and act normal; no matter what your damn mind is telling you to do or say! Just act normal! Can you do that Nadia? Yeah; I'm good baby. Ok give me a kiss and be careful stepping out the Navi. Muah! Alright see you later boo; drive safe.

Nadia walks in through the glass double doors, carefully makes her way over to the help desk then takes her seat behind the four surveillance monitors at her station then places her leftover curry chicken in the trash. Nadia bids the last employees in the building goodnight; as they walk out of the building. Glancing over to the top monitor, she sees it flicker on and off; pausing for a second she turns and takes a second look. Nah! That can't be!

Nadia now starring at her monitor, notice what seems to be a giant white rabbit, dancing up and down the halls. Paranoid she picks up the phone to call her sister Tamara. Hello! Girl what you doing? I'm in the bed Nadia; what's up? Sis; I'm going crazy in here! What the heck are you talking about girl? I'm seeing rabbits in the hallway at work; big white ones too! Nadia; I'm going to bed, your ass tripping. Tam no! Don't hang up! Girl I have to work in the morning; stop playing games. Sis I'm serious; I smoked some purp with Thomas on my break, I was seeing alligators, dogs, dragons and yellow smoke. Damn fool; you need to take your ass home. Call your boss and tell him you're sick, so you can leave. Call me in the morning, I'm going to sleep. I'll have to hear this story later; with your crazy ass. Ok, bye sis!

Nadia picks up the phone and dials her boss's cell number. Hey John; this is Nadia. Hey Nad; everything okay over there? Yeah, everything is okay at the job but I'm not feeling too well, I think I may have a stomach virus; I need to leave for the day. Okay Nad, I'll send Tyrone to cover your shift for you. Thanks John. The munchies came over her as she sat waiting for Tyrone. Nadia looked under the counter, in the small fridge and all around her desk for her curry chicken. God dammit; I know it's here somewhere! Where in the hell did I put my food, I'm starving! Hey Nad; you ok! Oh hey Ty; I was just looking for my food. Where did you put it? On the counter I thought! Well, I don't see it; you better head home and get some rest. Damn, that food was good too! Are you sure that food didn't get you sick; boss said you had a stomach virus. Oh shit! What Nad! Look! Look at what! That big ass rabbit on monitor two! Ha-ha! Nad you stupid; go home; I'll see you tomorrow. Alright Ty; thanks for covering for me. No problem buddy, get some rest. But you don't see that Ty! Bye Nad! Ok later Tyrone.

Hey Chant, can I have one of those Icehouse beers yall keep in the fridge, please Ma'am? Chantel, frowns up her face in confusion; I'm sorry; what did you need baby? One of those Icehouse beers, why are you looking like that; are yall out or something? How did you know there was some icehouse beers in there; you must be psychic. Curious, she logs off of her laptop; walks over to the fridge, pulls out two bottles and pops the tops. Here is your ice cold beer baby, is there anything else that you know of in here that you need me to get?

Well, I wasn't gonna say anything about it because I didn't want you to feel some kind of way. I came to see you a while back but you weren't here. Cynthia answered the door then invited me in. I waited for a few minutes; hoping that you would have walked in. But you didn't; that's when Cynt offered me a beer. We talked a little bit but I had to leave once she started getting aggressive and touching my leg and shit. I didn't want to start any drama between yall, so I kept it quiet. So there it is; it's nothing to get upset about though.

Wait; that chicken head did what? What do you mean nothing to get upset about; she had her hands on your leg and you didn't feel the need to tell me Donnie? Okay so no, let's turn the table here; say for instance your boy Q became a little aggressive with me, touched my leg, no better yet, grabbed a hand full of my ass? What would you have wanted me to do, keep it to myself and not tell you? My guess Donnie; would be that you would want for me to tell you, so you could beat the bricks off him. I don't know; did you and Cynt fuck?

Man that's why I didn't wanna tell your crazy ass; I aint bone that girl. Look, I aint got time to argue with you Chant; I was gone skip practice and give you some today but I changed my mind. Donnie stands up and walks towards the door. Really Donnie, I'm sorry, was you giving me some today supposed to be a privilege? That's what guilty people do, they walk away. You probably did bone, your cologne was all up in the air that day; did you spray it to keep the stench of sex from lingering? You're full of shit right now; I can call Cynt and let her know you're going to need company tonight! I'm going to practice; you need to take a chill pill. I aint even gone entertain this stupid ass conversation! Donnie exits the dorm room to head to practice and bumps into Cynthia as she walks in. Excuse me Sir; how are you today?

Move out of my way Cynthia! Damn, my bad nigga! Chantel; what's wrong with your boyfriend, is he on his period or something?

Cynthia, closes the door behind her, sits on the love seat directly in front of their 52inch big screen television. Chantel; begins to twist her long silky hair and places it into a perfect bun. What do you mean, what is wrong with my man Cynt? I saw him in the hallway and he was acting all different and shit.

Chant, walks over to the door; turns the lock then double checks it, making sure no one could get in. Cynt; I think that its' time we have a talk; there has been something on my mind for quite some time. Cynthia turns to face Chant, lifting her left eyebrow in confusion. What's up Chant? Chantel with ease and comfort like a lioness on the prowl; picks up the chair from the computer desk then places it under the door knob.

You know Cynt; I just caught wind of a bit of information. What kind of info are you talking about Chant? Remember when I asked you about the beers and the cologne when I got back to the room that day? Yeah girl; why are we revisiting that day? Cynthia; watches as Chant takes her earrings out of each ear and slip on a couple of rings.

Cynthia starts to realize that maybe the truth of her encounter with Donnie in the dorm room might have come out; so she gets up and walks to the opposite side of the room from Chantel.

You lied to me Cynt, you had your hands on my man and he was all up and through here. Who told you some mess like that Chant? It came straight from the horse's mouth; my man Donnie! Girl who are you going to believe; me or him? We have been friends longer than you could claim him being your man. Cynt; you are trifling; you are always so negative, you always want what you cannot have and you think that everybody wants you! Really Bitch; is that how you feel? Nothing happened with us, you act like a little girl any way Chant! He should be with a real woman! Yeah I tried to seduce him and what the fuck do you think you're going to do about it? Huh Bitch; if you feeling froggish; jump Chantel!

Chant; rushes in like a running back, executing a well thought out play; grabs Cynt's hair and lights up the left side of her face. Cynt manages to unwind herself from Chants grasp and tosses her across the room. Chant, picks her-self up after tripping over the foot stool that sat in front of the sofa then rushes at Cynthia again, throwing an upper cut, straight to her nose.

The two tussle for what seems like thirty minutes, none stop. Finally, very tired of the Warfare in the room; Chant musters everything in her and manages to get behind Cynt, kicks her in the back of the knee; making her fall straight to the ground. You fucked with the wrong Chick Cynthia; what's mine is mine; I don't share! The two girls breathe with all intensity while Cynt still lying on the floor, pulls together the strength to speak. Chant; I'm sorry, I was just jealous.

Save that sad depressing song for someone else. Chant grabs her purse, now dangling off the side of the turned over computer stand, puts her shoes on , fixes her hair, unlocks the door and turns to Cynt still lying on the floor. Your check has been bounced, insufficient funds! Chant walks out of the door then slams it behind her.

The sound of idle chatter fills the air as Nadia and Tamara stand in line to place their order at Starbucks. I'm so glad we were able to meet up Tam. Me too sis, I think we should try more often to connect. The Barista finishes up with the customer in front of the two sisters then greets Nadia. What can I get for you? I will have a Frappuccino with a blueberry muffin. Tam; hearing Nadia's decision, orders the same. Okay your order will be up in the next five minutes. Nadia pays for their orders and they walk over to the nearest chairs seated by the window.

So what have you been up to Nad? Nothing much, just been really busy with work. How about you Tam; how have you been? I've been good; a lot on my mind is all. Really, what's going on? Nad if I told you, you would not believe me. Tam, I'm your sister, you can tell me anything; what is bothering you? Number 137; your order is ready! That's us; hold that thought Tam; let me get that. Nadia excuses her-self from the table, grabs the two drinks and muffins then walks back to the table. Sorry, what were you saying? You remember at the pool party, a couple of weeks ago?

Yeah Tam, Why? Well I might have done something that I should not have Nad. What you mean Tam? Remember when everyone thought they heard noises coming from the tunnel in the pool? Yeah what about it? Well that was me and Marcus, and let me tell you, the things he did to me, makes me want more. No, no, no, Tam! Yes Nadia, I had a moment of weakness. I have not been able to stop thinking about it ever since. No, Tam you need to stop thinking about it. Why, I think he likes me Nadia. Tam, he and Sylvia are messing around! Ugh-um! What! Tam starts to choke off the piece of muffin that she just put in her mouth. He told me that they were just friends; who told you they were messing around? Chant told me so. That lying son of a Bitch, someone should clip off his balls and feed them to him! Tam, you let him hit; really! Tam sips on her Frappuccino then pushes her muffin to the side. I can't even finish this, I feel sick to my stomach.

Nadia, feeling and hearing the stress in her sister's voice, grabs her phone and starts to call Chant. Who are you calling Nad? I'm calling Chantel; to see if we can meet up with her, maybe I heard her incorrectly, let's find out the truth. Ring! Ring!

Hello! Hey Chant; me and Tam are out and about today, are you busy? No Nad, I was just finishing up my paper; I'm almost done though, what's up? Me and Tam need to meet up with you, are you going to busy around two? No, I won't; you guys come my way? Yeah Chant; we can do that. Is everything okay? Of course but we do have to talk though. Okay see you then ladies. Nadia hangs up the phone then places it on the table. Don't worry Tam, we will get to the bottom of this. I sure hope so sis.

The campus at AU was busy as normal, students hung around by the library and mingled with each other in between classes while the day rolled on. Marcus and one of his female classmates; stroll the sidewalk in route to the cafeteria. So what's up baby; how come you aint call a brother yet? Marc you a damn man whore, I don't have time for you and your harem of woman boy. Damn baby girl, it's not even like that; I just have a lot of female friends; I don't even be cutting them girls. Yeah that's what your mouth say Marcus. I tell you what; let me take you to the Shark Bar tonight and we can talk about it over some drinks. I'll think about it Marcus. See; now we're talking baby girl. Hey Marcus! Hey Chantel, what's up sis? Nothing much, about to meet Nadia in a minute! That's what's up!

I'm gone Marcus! Hold on baby girl where you going? Leaving you to talk to your friend! Hold on baby; Chant's my man's girl. Whatever Marcus; bye! Hey; are we still on for tonight? Bye Marcus! Damn, aint that a bitch! What's wrong Marc? This damn girl thinks I'm messing with you. Umm-umm-umm. That's what you get for being such a ladies man. Don't start Chant!

It's now 2 in the afternoon as Tamara and Nadia walk up behind Marc and Chant. Hey Chantel; what's up girl? Oh shit; I didn't see yall walk up. Hey Marcus! Hey Tamara; how you doing baby; I was about to call you! Marc, stop lying. Aint nobody lying Chantel, stop hating. Tamara crosses her arms and starts to roll her eyes at Marcus. Looks like you made some unsuspecting soul pissed at you; what did you do to her? Nah, she just mad because I told her I was taking you to the Shark Bar tonight. Oh really, when were you going to ask me that Marcus? I just told you, I was about to call you. Chant places her hands on her hips, looks at Marcus and shakes her head. Boy you are something else. Chill Chantel, come here Tam, where's my hug baby? Damn, you smell good too, so do you want to go or what?

Wait, pump your brakes Marcus; you should be concerned about how your lady, Sylvia smells. I am not your baby; you think you have so much game; I have no time for your little antics. I don't play with Barbie dolls, and I do not play house; so whatever games you are trying to play, keep them to yourself Marc.

I'm not playing games Tam; Sylvia is just my masseuse, we fooled around a little but other than that, it's nothing. You can call her and ask her if you don't believe me. Besides; Sylvia is always on the road and never home; I need my woman to be close to me. I don't know what you heard; but she aint my chick. Now are you coming to the Shark Bar with me tonight; you can bring Nadia and Chantel if you want. I don't want any trouble Marc; if Sylvia calls me and says different, I'm gone cut your ass.

Ha-ha! Come on baby; why you want to cut a brother. It's all good, I promise, she's just my masseuse. Hey girls, ya'll want to go to the Shark Bar tonight with Marcus? Chantel instantly without skipping a beat shrugs her shoulders. Marc, I am going to have to pass on that invitation, not trying to be a part of your train wreck.

Nadia staring off to the side; pretending not to be a part of the conversation; abruptly blurts out to Marc. I have a prior engagement; sorry I cannot go as well. Tamara, last of the girls to make a decision; shakes her head from the ideal of how much his head has been gassed up. Tamara grins in Marc's direction. See I told you Marc, you think that you have game. You need your women close, hmmm! Just for the sake of me wanting a drink, because it has been a long day; I will go with you. Don't think there is anything else to it, other than just a drink. Hey that's all I want baby, be ready at 8! Alright sir, go on about your business, me and the girls need to talk. Alright; I'm gone; see you later!

As the school year; quickly comes to an end. Chant sits in class listening to her professor as her cell phone vibrates. She picks up and answers with a whisper. Hello. Hey Baby! Donnie, I'm still in class, what's up? I'm picking you up after; meet me out front. Ok bye. I'm glad you're back with us Chantel. I'm sorry Professor. Ok everyone; make sure you study the Brown vs Board of Education case tonight; there's going to be a quiz on it tomorrow followed by a Q and A. Class is dismissed, see you all Friday. Chant picks up her text books from her desk then places them in her book bag. I'm sorry professor, it was a very important call; it will not happen again. Ok Miss Chantel, see you Friday. Picking up her book bag from the floor, she then places it on her shoulders and walks out the door.

As she makes her way outside she spots Donnie waiting in the parking lot in front of Hall B, sitting on the hood of his Camry while Outkast; Atliens is playing on his boom box that sits in the back seat. Instantly a smile traces her lips at the sight of him.

Hey baby, so where are we going Donnie? You know you made me embarrassed in class right; it's okay though because I was ready to hear your voice anyway. Chantel walks over to him and plants a kiss on his lips. Hey, I didn't mean to embarrass you but I planned a nice dinner for us; I hope you're hungry. Come on and get in so we can go. He holds her by the hand then escorts her to the driver's side, so she can slide in.

I appreciate you being a gentleman and all but you do not have to hold my hand while getting in through the driver's side Donnie. Sure hope it doesn't rain tonight, did you bring the plastic bag to cover the window D? Chantel looks back at him and shoots him a devilish grin, followed by laughter. Oh you got jokes; yeah the bag and towel are under the seat. Ha-ha! So, are you ready for your finals Ma'am? Yeah, I 'm as ready as I can be; I am so tired of studying. How do you think you will do on the exams Sir? Hand me some aluminum foil for this antenna Donnie, the boom box is not sounding that well. Girl you know I don't have no damn aluminum foil, hold that sucker out the window. That might help. Yeah it would also help if the window went down Donnie. You have everything else up in here smart ass; figure it would be on your list of survival tools.

Nah I don't but it's all gonna change soon. I'm about to ace these finals so I can graduate and get to the paper. Hey look in my back pack and hand me that $5 so I can pay for parking. They turn off Peachtree and ride by The Westin to enter the parking garage. Is that where we are going, the Westin? I heard that it's a nice place. Eww Donnie; you got me going through this bag with these sweaty ass shirts and shorts!

Chantel frowns up her face while digging, finds the money and hands it to him. Now I have sweat all over my hand. Chant, takes her hands and wipes them on Donnie. You can have this funk back too. Yep, you just were funkdafied baby; baptized in the funk! Ha-ha!

Donnie opens his door, pays the attendant and parks the car. What's wrong Chant; that was funny; come on we can't be late. The couple; exit the garage and walks down the sidewalk towards the Westin. Chant, grabs a hold of his hands. I hope that I'm not under dressed for this; I could have done something else to my hair or changed my clothes. It's not fair you looking all fresh to def over there and I look like Jill on crack. You look fine baby, come on. Donnie and Chantel stand at the corner of Peachtree and Ellis as traffic pass. The sound of Clydesdales galloping got louder as Chantel turns to see what the noise was. Hey Donnie; look!

I know baby, that's our Horse and Carriage. Really baby! Chant's mouth drops open with excitement. You did this for me? Chant's face all aglow with happiness; stares deep in her man's eyes, thinking to herself, how she could have become so lucky to have him in her life. Sir, Ma'am, if I may! The Carriage driver; assist the couple as they step up into the White and Purple carriage. As the Clydesdales gallop through the city; Donnie and Chant soak it all in while enjoying the night air under the Atlanta Skyline. Yeah; I thought this would be a goodtime to discuss our future, we will be leaving College soon and I want us to be prepared.

Oh I'm sorry; did I hear you right, I thought you said our future; statements like that suggest that we are going to be together. The words we and our; are commitment words. So that my dear must be established first, don't you think? I do understand that Chant, and I'm ready to commit to you. If you don't feel the same about me, now is the time to say so. I will respect your feelings either way. All I know is I'm ready to get my life started and I want Chantel by my side. With me going into the

Real Estate investment company, and you into Law! We will make a great couple, not to mention our feelings for each other. So you tell me Ma'am; the ball is in your court.

Well, that sounds like music to my ears; I wouldn't just beat two women's asses over a man that I am not committed too. So yes, I am yours, you better know how to handle me though. So does that mean that you are not going to do anything with your talent for basketball?

Oh I can handle you, that aint no problem. As far as basketball; that's just something I did to stay in shape. My man Harold asked me to play on the team because we played together since AAU and it made for good team chemistry. My dream is Commercial Real Estate investment; my uncle has been in the business for 25 years and I am opening a branch here in Atlanta. That's my entire reason for attending AU and not going to USC; meeting you has made it that more special.

I can see us now; fat crib, two Benzes and some motorcycles too. You're making the right decision baby; you won't regret it. I know you're ready to get in the court room; are you still gonna be with Latrice's firm? Yeah I'm going to finish up internship with her; she already let me know that she wants me to be a part of her team; that will give me some experience as a prosecuting attorney. Once I am established and have some time under my belt, I will be branching off and opening my own law firm. I have wanted to do this since I was little; it is refreshing to see my dreams becoming a reality. You can keep the motorcycles for yourself, I do not like them; I do have my eyes on a Lexus though.

I'll buy you a bike anyway; you'll probably change your mind once I start riding out. The Lexus is a good car; we can switch up sometime. Damn I can't believe we're finally about to graduate; this feels good. I'm ready to eat now; are you hungry? I am very hungry, what are you in the mood to eat Donnie? Speaking of hungry, your friend Marcus sure has an appetite for women, especially my friends. Why you say that; didn't I tell you he had game! Nooo, you didn't want to believe me; now look. Go ahead and tell me; how many of your girls he cuttin?

You don't have to throw my words back at me, I remember what I said Donnie. Marcus has my girls Tamara and Sylvia wrapped around his little fingers. I am not trying to be in no mess around this. Get your boy baby. I see you are over there thinking all of this is funny. He, he Hell! Chant, I aint getting in that, let them do their thing. Marcus knows what he's doing. Donnie; you aint right! Sir, Ma'am, we're back at your destination; enjoy your dinner at the Sun Dial. Thanks man.

The driver, assist Donnie and Chant as they step down from the carriage. She wraps her left arm around Donnie's waist as he places his right arm around her shoulders. The Clydesdales gallop away from the Westin as the couple walk up the steps then heads to their romantic dinner.

4. Graduation.

Cars constantly turn into the ESPN Zone in Buckhead as Valet's rush to service everyone. Hundreds of AU students crowd the front entrance and waiting area while Harold and the rest of the Team speak with management about reserving four sections of the restaurant. Tonight is NFL Draft night and Harold along with some of his team mates has entered the draft. Quentin excited by the news post fliers all over campus and invites everyone he could tell. After some discussion and a few hundred dollars; management gives in then sections off three adjoining areas for the draft party. Several flat screen TV's, leather couches, and a private bar make up the area that comes with 6 waitresses and two bartenders. Q walks over to the waiting area to share the news and with those outside as well. Their section rapidly fills with AU students, Alumni, Family and Friends. Chantel and Nadia decide to go over to the bar and order two shots.

What can I get you ladies? We'll have two shots of Patron. Coming right up! The bartender grabs the bottle of Patron and two shot glasses from behind the counter, pours the drinks then hands it to them. That will be 24 dollars; is there something special you guys are celebrating? Yeah, graduating soon! Well congratulations to you. Thank you. Chantel reaches into her Black Hand bag, pulls out her wallet and pays the bartender. Nadia picks up her shot glass and holds it in the air. Chant; let's toast to a successful life, full of happiness and good health. Chant lifts her glass. I'll drink to that Nadia. The two of them take their shots then place their glasses back on the bar counter. As the ladies start walking back to the table they spot Cynthia coming in the door. Chants face instantly turns sour.

Look at this Bitch! She really has some nerves; coming in here Nadia? Chant, leave her be; I'm sure after the business you gave her; she's not going that route with you again. Cynt now within arms-length of the two ladies, over hear the two talking about her. I'm not a bitch Chant. You're right Cynthia; you're not a bitch, you a black eyed bitch! Nadia starts to laugh frantically holding on to her side in disbelief. Cynt rolls her eyes in Nadia's direction. I don't have time for this Chant; I told you that I was sorry. Ladies, ladies calm down we're here to have a good time.

I'm calm Thomas; tell Q to get his girl though. Come on Chant behave; and where's my drink Nadia? Oh, my bad Boo; we just had a shot between two friends. I will order you something when the waitress or waiter gets here, matter of fact where is ours? Chant; flags down the waiter passing by the table. Hey do you know who our waiter is? That would be me. I'm sorry for the delay; it's been very busy tonight. No worries sir! Thomas baby; what do you want? Let me get a shot of goose baby and a Corona. Ladies, did you all want anything? Yep! Nadia and Chantel reply simultaneously. Well, what yall want? We'll take two Hpnotiq's mixed with Hennessey. Damn, you two are about to be wasted huh. That's it man, put it on my tab too. No problem Sir; I have a shot of Goose, Corona and two Hpnotiq's with Hennessey.

Donnie, Quentin, Harold, Marcus and Cynthia sit together at another table with AU teammates and alumni, taking shots and eating hot wings as they all wait for an hour to pass to watch the draft. Harold tap's on his glass with is fork to get everyone attention. Ok; listen up everybody! Listen up! I like to thank all of you for being here for me tonight, for my draft party. Coach wanted me to declare for the NBA Draft but yall know this Decatur soldier likes the grid iron shawty! Don't get me wrong; I love basketball too but I rather be cracking skulls on that green; you heard me. So cheers to yall shawty and to the AU Class of 2001! Cheers! The crowd cheer and toast Harold as he stands at the head of the table.

Hey Marc, Chantel told me about Sylvia and Tam. What about them Donnie? Boy, she said you got them wrapped around your finger. You know how I do D; I put's it down. Once I laid this pipe on them, it was all over my nigga. I told Chant a few months ago that her girls weren't ready. Oh yeah; what did she say D? She told me that her girls could see through your game, and see you coming a mile away. Donnie, you should've told your lady that I was a beast in the game bruh. Marc I told her once; it was up to her to tell her girls after that. That's what's up; here she comes now with Nadia. Donnie and Marc lean back against the table as Chantel and Nadia approach.

Chantel, walks up to Donnie and glances over in Cynt's direction then looks back at Donnie.

Hey baby, I know you are spending time with the guys but don't you want to come over here with me, away from satin's snare? Chantel puts her arms around Donnie's neck then plants a kiss on him. Cynt rises up as if she wants to rebuttal Chants comment, but Nadia interrupts by clearing her throat. Umm-hmm, down dragon! Cynthia pauses then cuts her eyes over towards Nadia. We don't need any problems do we Cynt?

Donnie follows Chantel and Nadia away from Harold's section over to Thomas's table. What's up cuz? Aint nothing Thomas; what you drinking on! Some Goose and this Corona, you want me to get you something? I'll get it cuz; I want some of them wings anyway. Hey Chant, walk with me to the bar. Donnie pulls Chantel by the loop on her seven jeans and guides her with him. Your ass looking kind of fat in these sevens baby! Don't make me kill a fool in here tonight. You're looking sexy as hell too baby. You better be glad we have on lookers around us, or you would be in a lot of trouble. You know I can get all kind of Janet Jackson on you. Chantel starts singing to him in his ear. "Anytime, anyplace I don't care who's around." I am trying to be on my best behavior tonight; how am I doing so far? Oh yeah and do you know if Tam and Marc talked to each other yet? You're doing good baby and Marc aint said nothing about it. Ok; so what's up; are your parents coming down early for the graduation; I'm so excited to finally meet your mom, Donnie.

Yeah, she's coming in a few days early; my dad is coming the night before. How about yours, do you think they're ready to meet me? Hey folks; how can I help you? Yeah man; let me get 20 wings; mild with lemon pepper. Sure; I'll put that in for you; I can bring it to your table if you like. No that's fine; we'll just wait here at the bar. Ok it should only take a few minutes. Thanks man! Well Chant; are they? I'm sure my parents are going to love meeting you baby. My mom and dad will not be able to make it till the morning of graduation but they will be staying an extra day, so you will have time to talk with them. Do these wings come with fries D; I need to soak up some of this liquor.

I find it hard to believe that you and Marc have not talked, you guys being all close and things. But don't worry about it; I know that you guys have your man code; I don't even know why I asked. Chantel; if you slow down a minute, I can answer you! No don't worry about it; did you get the tickets for the step show? I can't wait for the concert! Chant, now you know we don't need tickets; Q is promoting the show; so we all good baby.

Here are your wings guys! Thanks man! No problem, enjoy your night. Chant and Donnie walks over to the table to join Nadia and Thomas. Damn cuz, those wings smelling good as hell; how many you get? I got 20 cuz. Shit

I'm about to order me some; Nadia you want some wings baby? Sure Thomas; I want mine extra hot though. Hey waiter; come here bruh! Yes Sir; how can I help you? Can I get 20 wings, extra hot and add 10 teriyaki ones too. Ok; I have 20 extra hot, and 10 teriyaki! Yep that's it. Alright, it will be a few minutes. Here Nadia; you want to try some of these mild with lemon pepper? Thanks Donnie. Umm, these are good; I have never had the lemon kind before. Cynt walks up to the table and touches Chant on her arm lightly. Hey Chant can I talk to you for a moment? I guess so Cynthia; I'll be back guys! Ok! The two ladies walk towards the entrance and make their way outside.

Chant takes a seat on the bench by the entrance and Cynt takes a seat beside her. Chant, I want to apologize again for the way that I acted with your man; it should have never happened, we are friends and I over stepped my boundaries in the worst way; I let my jealousy over take me, and I lost sight of the friendship that we have in the mix of it. Cynt, I don't know how you are used to rolling with your friends but how I was raised, you never try and take what doesn't belong to you; that shit you did; even though it didn't go far, is what I call a tragedy. I don't know if I could ever trust you again. I understand Chantel but I hope you can try to forgive me; I don't want to lose the friendship that we have. I will try Cynt, I can't promise anything though. Thanks Chant, that's all I could ask for. You need to give Q a chance though, he's really feeling you Cynthia. Yeah I know; I'm feeling him as well.

The two girls decide to call a truce. In agreement they stand up and walk back into the building then take a seat at the table. Donnie touches Chant's hand and smiles at her. Is everything okay Chant? Yeah everything is okay; we finally talked. Donnie caresses her hand. That's good to hear baby.

Harold stands up to address his people. Everyone listen up; the draft is about to start and my agent is on the phone keeping me posted, so keep the noise down a little for me. Thanks I appreciate it! Everyone directs their attention to the flat screen TV's up above. "Welcome back to the 2001 NFL Draft, just in case you missed it; Minnesota picked running back; Dj Brown from Alabama as their first pick." "The Saints selected Full back Michael White from Ohio State as their second pick."

Yeah boy I'm about to be paid! Marcus shut up; you're not getting drafted. No, I'm not Cynthia but I'm going to be Harold's manager; so don't hate on a brother. Shhh. Be quiet yall! Harold continues to speak with his agent. Why you aint enter the draft Donnie? Oh you got jokes Thomas; you know I don't play football. Man I'm talking about the NBA. Nah; I'm good, I'm about to open up this Real Estate Invest Branch with Uncle Ted. Yeah he was telling me about that; have you found a location yet? Nah cuz; I've been concentrating on graduating; you should come run the new office with me. I don't know Donnie; I aint the office type cuz. Man you can work the field; making sure the properties are up to code and all that. I probably can handle that; I'll let you know. Harold jumps up and stands on the table. I just got confirmation yall; I'm about to be picked right now! Everyone look at the screen; check it out!

"With the 5th pick; the Cowboys select; All Conference Corner Back from Atlanta University; Harold Washington." Hell; fuck yeah! I'm a Cowboy shawty! Yay! The AU students, Alumni, Friends and Family; jump for joy at the news while celebrating Harold's new success as bottles of champagne pop amidst the celebration.

"What's up AU, this is your boy Bobby Ray broadcasting live from the center of the campus commons." "We got the flatbed juiced up and ready for today's concert." "So get your coolers and blankets ready for the 2001 Senior Class Concert and Step show." "My folks Lil Jon and The Eastside Boyz along with 112 will be performing live today!" "And you know the step show is going to be crazy!" Those Que dawgs, Alpha's, Kappa's, Delta's, AKA's and all the frats will be going in baby!" "I will be here with you all day, the V 100 grill is blazing with them burgers, hot dogs and some of those juicy Turkey legs." "So what are you waiting for; come on out here and join the festivities!"

Yo Marc, I'm about to meet Q down at the concert; you coming? Yeah Donnie; I'm waiting on your cousin; we're gone smoke a swisher before we come down. Alright man, tell Thomas to bring my cooler out of his truck. Ok Donnie! Thanks Marcus and don't forget to lock this door too bruh. I aint gone forget man! Yeah you always say that but leave it wide open. Go ahead D; I got it.

Nadia and Tam reach Cynt and Chantel's dorm room, after wading through all of the commotion of student's making their way to the commons area; to join in the festivities. Knock! Knock! Who is it? Hey Cynt, it's me and Tam. Come in guys, the door is open. Tamara twists the knob and pushes the door open. You ladies aren't ready yet? Okay, Nadia now you know we have to look extra sexy out there; we have an image to uphold.

Chant, turns back to the mirror and puts the final touches of lip gloss on. Tam looks around the room and only sees Chantel. So where is Cynt, I just heard her voice. She's in the bathroom fixing up her hair. The bathroom door opens up and Cynthia walks through with both hands in her hair, trying to place the last bobby pin in her bun. I'm almost done; my hair will not do what it's supposed to, I'll be right back, I need the mirror again.

Tamara walks over to the couch to take a seat. See, black folks can never be on time. Chantel turns to Tam and laughs; while she's putting on her shoes. Tamara looks directly at Chantel with a grin. What's so funny about what I just said Chant? You, because you forget you're talking about half yourself anyway, and that's not nice. Alright ladies, do we have everything, I know that the guys are bringing the coolers and drinks. Yeah we're good! Great, this is going to be a night to remember. Cynthia; pops her head out of the bathroom door again. Okay I'm ready ladies. Let's get it started!

The drums sound through-out the court yard as the AU Drum line parade through the crowd while playing; Petey Pablo's Raise up. The commons area has now begin to fill, students gather in front of the flatbed while others sit on their blankets they place on the lawn as Bobby Ray starts to speak. "Listen up AU; my man Harold Washington wants to say something." Harold steps up on the flatbed and takes the mic from Bobby Ray. What's up A.U Dog's! Are yall ready to party shawty! The crowd responds with cheers as the drum line continue to march through the commons. Donnie and Quentin makes their way through the crowd to find Chant, Cynt, Nadia and Tam sitting together on their blanket as Thomas and Marc places the cooler down behind them. Hey baby, I see the gang is all here! Hey Thomas, I missed you! Nadia runs over to Thomas and wraps her arms completely around him, her face lights up like a kid in a candy store.

Did you bring a blanket for me and you to sit on baby? Chantel stops temporarily in her tracks as she takes a breath while looking at Donnie. Hey Donnie, I don't get a hug over here? Chant cracks a smile in his direction, while poking fun of Nadia. Ha-ha. Chant you got jokes; don't be mad because I'm not ashamed to show some love to my baby. I'm just kidding Nadia, you are right though; come here Donnie, let me lay one on you boo!

"Alright people; I got your boy Harold up here; we're celebrating his success as a NFL rookie along with the graduating class of 2001." "Right now we need your undivided attention, because coming to the stage is the Kings of Crunk baby!" "Let's hear it for my folks; Lil Jon and them Eastside Boyz, performing that Bia-Bia!"

"Yea! What up AU!" "Yeah!" "Come on AU let me hear it!" "Why you acting like ah-" The excited crowd jumps and yells out. Bia-Bia! Bia-Bia! Hey cuz; can you take me and Chantel's picture? Yeah let me hold the camera Donnie; where yall want to take it at? Thanks Thomas, get us right here while we're on the blanket. Come on Chant; let's take this picture baby. Donnie and Chantel sit up on their blanket, hug each other and smile for Thomas. Click-Click! That looks good cuz, give me two more poses. Click-Click! This is a good one too D. For real, let me see it! Hold on cuz, let me get this last one. Click-Click! Nah, you weren't smiling in this one Chant; the other two are good though. Thanks Thomas! You're welcome cuz. Donnie takes the camera from Thomas then shows the digital pictures to Chantel. So what do you think baby?

I don't know baby, my hair is sticking up on the side. Chant points to the top corner of the picture. See I told you Donnie. Donnie looks at Chantel and laughs. Girl stop tripping that was a smudge on the frame. Oh, okay well it's good; I like this picture then. Look, I like the Eastside Boyz and all but I am ready for some 112. They'll be on in a few but we're getting crunk right now baby. Yo D; you want a beer bro? Yeah Q, let me get one! Here you go; what about you Marc; you want one? Yeah pass me one. "Aite AU, I see the ladies are out here representing; this next cut is for yall shawty! Yeah!" "I like them guls with them gold's in they mouth" "That be them guls from the motherfuckin' south." "I like them guls with them big ass butts." "That be them guls that'll let a nigga cut."

Nadia, Thomas, Cynthia, Quentin, Donnie, Chantel, Marcus and Tamara all stand to their feet and starts Bankhead bouncing along with the crowd. The energy is electric as the entire commons area now filled with students; friends and alumni enjoy Lil Jon's crunk performance. "Yeah, sing it AU!" The crowd participates while dancing along. "It's some guls in this house." "It's some guls in this house." "If you see them point them out." "If you see them point them out!" Yeah, ATL Shawty!

"Yeah AU; yall crunk now baby!" "This is your V 100 Dj; Bobby Ray, and we got the kings of crunk right here on the stage rocking with the AU Dogs!" Yeahhhhhhh! See Chant, that's how we get crunk in the south baby. Now; do you still want to hear 112? Yeah this is off da chain. It still doesn't compare to the up top hip hop. Hey Q can you pass me one of those beers, you guys are being stingy. Cynt, cosigns with Chantel. Yeah Chant; these guys act as if us ladies can't hang with them. Cynt grabs a beer from Q, stands in front of him and starts to drop it like it's hot to the music. Chantel, Nadia and Tamara start to cheer on Cynt. Go head it's ya birthday, get it girl!

What up Shawty; I see yall over here getting crunk. Hey Harold! Hey ladies; how are yall doing? We're good Cowboy! Cool; what's up fellas, can a brother have one of those beers shawty? Here you go playa! Thanks Donnie. Now back to you baby; what you mean by the south aint got nothing on them up top niggas? Can't nobody do it like the A-Town baby. Peace up! A-Town down! Whatever Donnie; but you know NYC is the Hip Hop Mecca!

"AU!" "Get your mind right people; it's about time to bless the stage with them brothers known as the Sons of Blood and Thunder or simply, The Omega Psi Phi Fraternity better known as those almighty Que Doggs!" Frats and Sa Ra's, it's time to represent your clicks baby! Barks; Sighs and Chants emerge from the crowd as Bobby Ray introduces the first Steppers of the day. "Ok AU; let's hear it for the Ques!" George Clinton's Atomic Dog starts to play as the fellas of purple and old gold enter the stage. "The Atomic Dog, the atomic dog"

Nadia and Tamara start to step along with the music as the frat performs their routine. Oh shit; get it girls.

Oh you ain't know Q, Delta in the house. Chantel, turns to Tamara in disbelief. You are a Delta Tamara? Tam turns to Chant and smiles then holds up the diamond. There're a lot of things that most people don't know about me. Tam turns her face towards Marcus and winks at him. Chant shakes her head as she watches Tam flirting with Marc. Tam, girl stop! Chantel brings her attention back to the show and then looks at Donnie. They rockin my favorite color up there Donnie; why didn't you join a fraternity?

Nah I'm good on that frat stuff; show me the money baby. Marcus wasn't you going to join one year bro? Man, those fools told me that I wasn't going to be able to get none for two weeks! That closed the deal for me D; I got to have my women bruh. Yeah ho's always do! Don't go there Q! I'm just saying Marc; that's all you do man. What are you going to do about graduating; we're out of here in a few days. I dropped out Q. Why fool; you got like a half year before you finish. I'm gone manage Harold, we already discussed it. What! You heard me Donnie. Harold is this true? What's that D? Are you gone let this fool manage you bruh? Yeah man, he's family; I'll trust him before those suits in the game. You got a point Harold, just make sure he has his mind on your money and not on all of that random pussy that's gone be around. We got it Donnie, don't worry shawty. Ok Harold; if you say so.

"Alright AU; we're gonna take a short break from the step show to bring on 112 then we'll be back with more of the Frats and Sa Ra's." "Let's hear it for Slim and the gang, 112!"

"Girl if I told you I love you." "It doesn't mean that I don't care, oooh." "And when I tell you I need you." "Don't you think I'll never be there."

Donnie holds Chantel from behind as they sway back and forth with the music while she sings along. Yeah; you're singing that joint, aint you baby? Chantel; grabs a hold of Donnie's hands nestle around her waist line and holds on tight. Yeah baby this song is dedicated to you. Q and Cynt, stand up and face one another. Cynthia; places her arms around Q's neck then brings her face closer to him, Quentin places his arms around her waist as their eyes locked into one another with the look of seduction; while the music plays. "Cupid doesn't lie, but we don't know unless we give it a try".

Tam starts to feel a little left out watching the couples in their one on one trance and instantly looks over and catches Marcus staring at her. Tam decides that for at least for the moment she would give in and ask him to dance. Marcus being the playboy he is; beats her to it and holds out his hand towards Tam. You want to dance? Sure Marc, but don't get any ideas though; keep your hands at a safe distance. The two start to dance slowly to the rhythm of the music. Tam, lost in her desires for him, feels her body melt against his. Then thinks to herself; maybe she wants him to ignore her wishes; just this once while everyone around them seem to sway to the music while enjoying this special moment.

Every chair in the library is filled as students gather and cram to study for finals. Donnie, Chantel, Quentin, Harold and Cynthia occupy a table off in the far right corner of the AU library. The aroma of fresh Starbucks coffee; permeate the air as they study the pages of their notes and text books. Harold pulls out a narrow piece of paper then writes down the answers and definitions from his study notes while sparingly taking a sip from his silver flask then pours some in his coffee. Man, I don't see why I need to take these damn tasks, I'm already rich. I'm a professional football player shawty; you know what I'm saying Donnie.

Hold your voice down man and you need to take them because anything can happen on that field brother. What's gone happen shawty! I'm in perfect condition! Harold stands to his feet and pounds on his chest. Would you please hold it down Harold! You hold it down Cynthia; I can say what the hell I want! Come on Harold, calm down man. I'm calm Q but you need to get your chic shawty.

Who are you calling a chic Harold! My name is Cynthia and don't you forget it. Sit down shawty before I have Chantel bust your ass again girl! Excuse me! You heard me Cynt; I heard about Chant beating you down. Hell, everybody knows about it! Cynthia gets up and runs out of the library, Chantel jumps up then follows behind her.

Cynthia runs through the tall glass double doors of the library's entrance with tears running down her face from embarrassment; shame reeked through her pores and anger poured from her heart. Cynt, Cynt! Chantel calls out to her hysterically. Stop, Cynt! Cynt finds a bench not too far from the door and takes a seat, whipping the tears from her eyes.

I am so sorry Cynt! Chant catches up to her and takes a seat next to her. You told people about what happened? What kind of shit is that Chant? You beat my ass, is that what you told everybody? Cynt I was mad, and this was before we talked. Harold never should have said that to you in front of everyone. And yeah, even though you put up a good fight I did beat that ass, but that is neither here nor there. Are you okay though Cynthia? I will be okay. Harold is such a Dick! He's just drunk Cynt, and not being himself. Are we cool roomie? Yeah, I'm not mad at you Chant but I'm still upset at Harold.

That was messed up Harold; why you do that girl like that man? I wasn't lying Donnie; Chant did bust that head. Look, let's just put that shit behind us and worry about your drunk ass. I aint drunk Q; your shawty was tripping. Both of yall need to chill out and you need to stop drinking Harold. You have bigger responsibilities now dawg and if you keep this up, you're not gone be in the league long. This is not a problem Donnie; I can stop drinking anytime. Well, you need to get it together brother, I see you writing cheat notes over there too. What this; I always write cheat notes man; I've been doing it since High School shawty, the only thing that matters is how I perform on that football field or the Basketball Ball court. So you telling us that you cheated your way all the way to college. Q that's just the books, I got a full scholarship to play ball, I earned that. Yeah none the less, just apologize to my girl when she comes back in. I'll do it for you Quentin but that's the only reason shawty.

Cynt and Chantel walk back through the library doors passing by Harold without saying a word. Chant takes her seat next to Donnie. Dead air fills the air with a touch of awkwardness lingering like smog rolling over the London harbor, early in the morning. Chantel, looks over to Harold then whispers. You need to apologize to her. There was no need for that to roll off of your lips. Harold surprised to see Chantel taking up for Cynt blurts out. Chant; it is not your place to tell me what I should and should not do. Anger darts across Chants face as she stands up to square off with Harold.

It became my business when you decided to put my name in it; you think that you are so untouchable with your draft pick that you think you can treat anyone how you feel. Your drunken ass, need to go sit down somewhere. We came in here to study but you come up in here to talk all kinds of shit. You don't have to give a damn about school and anyone else's feelings; but some of us do give a damn! You can also choose to be the dumb ass athlete with no brains, only relying on bronze and that is fine but do that shit on your time and not mine!

Look I apologize if I hurt anyone; I was celebrating for the past few days and I haven't gone a day without a drink since. It's the alcohol talking. I'm sorry for saying those things Cynthia and Chantel we're cool, I meant no disrespect sis. You good Harold just put that damn flask up and stop drinking long enough to sober up and pass your exams bro. Thanks Q; I appreciate the love shawty. We need to go study at the dorm fellas; old man James is standing at the door ready to put us out. Ok I'm coming Donnie; hold on. Cynthia, Chantel, will you two accept my apology?

Cynthia looks at Harold disgusted as If the devil was standing on her shoulder, telling her to let him know where he and his apology can kiss it but she reluctantly answers. Yeah, Harold I accept your apology; we're cool. Chant nods her head up and down in agreement. Harold you know we are cool, no love lost.

Thank you girls, I got love for yall shawty! Alright Harold, bring your drunken ass on before you do something else. Quentin, help me walk this fool back to the dorm. Come on I got him, let's go Donnie. Hey Chant, call me later, me and Q are taking Harold up to the dorm. Ok; Cynthia and I are going to stay here so we can finish studying. Donnie holds Harold's left arm while Q holds his right as they walk him back to their dorm room. Come on buddy, you need to sleep this off we have a long few days ahead. I love you guys, man! Yeah, yeah just keep walking.

The arena fill to capacity while ushers continue to guide new arrival family members to their seats; red and white banners and flags celebrating the school colors surround the building in recognition of the senior class, while smiles fill the faces of their loved ones. Excitement is thick in the air as the school song is being played by the band seated in front of the stage while patient on lookers read their programs that were given to them on the way in. The joyous crowd impatiently waits for the empty chairs to be filled by the graduating class of 2001.

The commencement music starts playing over the intercom signaling everyone to rise to their feet; chants of the graduates names are blurted out from the crowd as the grads walk pass until the last member of the 2001 class is seated. Applause rings through-out the building echoing off of every wall. At the last minute; Marcus and his date rush to be seated before the Dean stands up to give his speech. Poppa Rich what's up man? Hey Marcus; how are you doing young man; you're about to miss the ceremony. We had to find a park sir! Oh do you remember Sylvia; you met her at the game I think. Oh yes, hello Miss Sylvia; how are you sir? I'm great young lady.

Hello Marcus; you haven't changed a bit! Wow, hey Ms. Anita; I didn't see you sitting over here. Sylvia this is Donnie's mom; Ms. Anita. Hello Ma'am; nice to meet you. Nice to meet you as well sugar. Marcus and Sylvia takes the two seats in between Donnie's divorced parents. Ms. Anita leans to her right and whispers to Marc. Young man why aren't you sitting up there with Donnie and Quentin? Oh I dropped out Ms. Anita; I took a job as my homeboy's sports manager; he got drafted into the NFL. Marcus; are sure about this son? Yes Ma'am. What did your folks have to say about it?

They were upset at first but eventually they came around. Well; I wish you the best of luck and just remember you can always come back to finish school. Yes ma'am. Ok here's the Dean; we'll speak later. Ok Ms. Anita. "Ladies and Gentlemen; today is the first day of the rest of your lives, some of you will go on to be great attorneys, business men and woman, professional athletes, Architects, Doctors and Educators. You will continue the long proud legacy of our Prestigious Atlanta University."

"Today your parents and love ones are smiling because of this long awaited accomplishment." "As you go out into the world and make your marks, remember what your professors have taught you as well as life's lessons."

"For those instances will be the ladder from which you climb during this journey called life." "So as you walk across this stage today, be joyous in your stride as you collect this hard earned Degree." "Will the Graduating Class of 2001 please stand and prepare to receive your reward." The Class of 01 march across the stage one by one as their names are called to receive their Degrees.

Camera's flash through-out the crowd, along with cheers and shouts during and after each name that was called as they shook the Deans hand while receiving their Degree's with the other. After the last senior leaves the stage; the entire crowd, stands then cheers louder and louder for the class of 2001. Graduating Caps now tossed in the air by the elated Graduates shadowed above as family and friends embraced their College Graduates.

Marcus and Sylvia stand and wait beside Donnie's parents for him and Chant to come over while Donnie is across the way with Chantel and her parents. Mom, dad I would like you to meet Donnie; Donnie this is my father Greg and mother Darlene. Oh sweetie; so this is the young man you are always talking about! Darlene reaches over and gives Donnie a hug. It's nice to meet you honey; I have heard nothing but good things about you. Chantel's father reaches over and shakes Donnie's hand. Congrats son! I look forward to knowing more about you; do you like fishing?

We can set up a day where we can go out on the boat , throw the line out and get away from these women. Chantel taps her father on the shoulder then smacks her teeth. Stop playing dad; you better watch out, mom is giving you that look. What, Chant I'm just playing with you guys; but seriously Donnie we should get together.

Tam still seated in her chair notices that Marcus is standing by Sylvia and can't believe what she is seeing. Chantel glances over at Tam and realize that she's agitated, watching Marc and Sylvia mingling with the crowd as if they were a couple. Tam builds up the nerve to go over and confront Marc; picks up her purse and proceeds to walk in the direction towards him. Chant, in fear of an all-out brawl between the two ladies, seizes the moment while her parents and Donnie are talking. Excuse me guys I will be right back; there is someone I need to speak with. Chant rushes over to Tam and stops her in her tracks.

Don't do it Tam, it's not worth the drama. Chant, this guy just played me to the left and he knows that he aint right. Let dogs lay where they are Tam; one day they will catch fleas. I can-not believe I let him get to me like that; look at Sylvia over there smiling her ass off, like she got the hottest shit. Tam, I don't think she knows about what he has done, don't blame her. Whatever, I hear you but this right here is bull shit. Come on Tam, this is one of the best days of my life thus far; please set it aside and support me, be my friend! You're right Chant, Congrats boo; I am okay. The two ladies smile and hug.

It was nice to meet you sir and I am looking forward to that fishing trip. Can you guys excuse me for a minute? Sure son go ahead. Hey Chant come with me baby; she'll be back Tam, I need to borrow her for a minute. That's cool Donnie; I'll be over there with my sister. Donnie and Chant approach his parents. Congratulations son, I'm so proud of you. Thanks mom! Good job son! Thanks pop! Mom I like for you to meet my girlfriend Chantel. Chantel this is my mother; Ms. Anita. Hello Ms. Anita; I've heard so much about you. Well,

I do hope it was good shuga. Donnie has the habit of making me the bad guy. If you let him tell it; I was always beating his behind. Mom that's because you was! Um-hm, that's because your butt was bad but mommy loves you. Aww, that's so sweet. You're a momma's boy D? Chant; don't start. Hello there young lady; congratulations! Thank you Poppa Rich; it's good to see you again. Good to see you too baby. Hey Donnie; I'll be back I'm going to thank Nadia and Tam for coming. Ok Chant; I'll be right here with my folks.

Hey Sylvia I'll be back baby, I'm going to holler at Harold real quick. Ok Marcus; I'm going to congratulate Chantel and speak to Nadia and Tam. Alright cool, let me know when you're ready to leave. Sure baby.

Oh hell Nadia, here she comes! Who Tam? Sylvia's coming our way! So what, she's cool people. You didn't just see her and Marc all coupled up over there? No way Tam, for real!

If I'm lying, I'm dying. Tam I don't think she knows about you and Marc. What if she did find out by him twisting things up, making it seem as if I knew about them? Tam I don't think that it is that deep. Tam's whole demeanor shifts, as Sylvia approaches. Sylvia senses and sees the stink eye that Tam has thrown in her direction.

Hey, Nadia and Tam; how have you to been doing? Nadia gives Sylvia a hug while Tam simply nods her head and gives her a half ass smile. Haven't seen you in a while Sylvia. Tam smirks at Sylvia before finally speaking to her. We've been doing well, a lot of things have been happening since we saw you last. Nadia butts in.

What she means is; life doesn't stop for anyone, we've been really busy working. Tam clears her throat and looks off into another direction. Nadia stays focused so she can clear the air, and smiles at Sylvia. I didn't know you and Marc were together Sylvia; you guys look so cute with each other. Yeah Nadia, we've been dating for a couple of months now. Tam's face turns red with anger. Sylvia turns in Tam's direction noticing her face looking flushed. You okay Tam?

Tam torn about the situation; starts to remember that she just told Chant that she would keep it drama free for her; at the same time, she was so pissed she needed to tell Sylvia, no, she wanted to tell her, about her four legged man. Nadia looks over at her sister, hoping that she would make the right decision. To Tam her decision was clear. Oh, I'm sorry; just all the excitement from the moment, has me on another level but I'm okay Sylvia thanks for asking.

5. Commencement.

Patron's become impatient during the Friday lunch rush over at Atlanta Bank and Trust as they wait in line for the next available teller. Harold don't take all day in there man, we need to get over to the Jaguar lot in Buckhead before 4:30 pm; don't forget you have an interview downtown with 88 Fanz Radio at 6 tonight and we can't be late. Alright Marcus, calm down shawty; I'm just going inside to speak with Sage real quick then open this new account.

Ok bruh; you got 20 minutes. Man chill; you're taking this manager job too damn serious. I'm about to fire your ass; don't start bugging like no broad shawty. Harold you wasting time talking all that shit; go handle your business so we can stay on schedule. Alright man, damn; I'll be right back! As Marcus waits out front, sitting in the green Blazer, Harold enters the bank, wide eyed and nervous in search of Sage. He glances over the tellers; but to no avail then he spots her over in the corner office, sitting behind a cherry oak desk while talking on the telephone.

Anxiously he makes his way over but gets interrupted by a young lady who is sitting at a desk just outside Sage's office. Excuse me sir; may I help you? Yes, I'm here to see Sage. Ok is she expecting you? Harold ignoring the young lady, waves to get Sage's attention. The young lady looks over at her just as Harold is waving to see that Sage waves him in. Ok, you can go in sir. Thanks! Harold stops for a second then tucks his Red polo shirt in his jeans, tightens his belt, gets his composure then enters her office.

She covers the phone with her hand then speaks to him in a low whisper. Hey you, I'm surprised to see you here, have a seat, I will be off this call in a second. Sure no problem. Harold's heart pounds rapidly against his chest while he waits for what seems like forever. Her office smells of Dolce & Gabbana women's perfume which complimented her natural bouncy hair, red lipstick, white silk blouse and black skirt.

Harold glances down to the bottom of her desk and see Sage's bare feet, neatly pedicured and polished with the same glossy red as her lipstick. Anxiety overcame him as he inhales her womanly presence, now stuck in a daydream wondering what it would be like for her to be his woman.

Well what brings you by mister? Harold! Oh I'm sorry Sage; I was day dreaming, what did you say? I was asking, what brings you by? Two things actually! Really, and what are they? The first is; I wanted to see you before I left for camp. And the second? I need to open a bank account. I'm sure I can help you with the second but as for the first; what makes you think I wanted to see you?

I don't know if you felt it but there was a vibe between us the last time we met. What kind of vibe; and you should be careful how you answer that question too; I might add. You know a good one, like we were meant to be with one another. Harold please, don't even try those lame college pick-up lines with me.

I'm not shooting you any pick-up lines shawty- Excuse me! I meant Sage; you can't tell me that you didn't feel it too. Well if I did; I wouldn't tell you; when are you leaving for camp? Why not? Because you're still calling me shawty! That was a mistake and I did correct it. Um-hmm, when are you leaving? In seven days. Wow, that is soon; did you really need a bank account or was that just an excuse to come see me.

Ha-Ha! You think you know me; don't you? No, I just know your type. Did you need one or not? No I don't need one but I can open a new one. What's wrong with the bank you're at now? You're not at that bank, that's what's wrong with it. Harold you are too much, I have to be getting back to work; is there anything else you want sir? Yes; promise me that you will go out with me when I come back to town.

I don't know about promising anything but we'll see what happens. Alright that works for me; I'll let you get back to work. Thank you sir! You have a good day Sage. You too Harold and be safe. Thank you and I will.

He makes his way across the lobby and outside to the blazer where Marc is patiently waiting. So are you finish; can we go get this new Jag now bro? Yep let's go Marc; what time did you say we have to be at the radio station again? Six O'clock Harold! Cool, let's pick up the car then hit Lenox Square; we need to get some new clothes shawty. Now you're talking Harold! Man that's gone be my woman, watch and see. Bruh you're a damn NFL player; why are you stuck on one woman? In a minute you will be able to have any girl you want.

I don't want any girl bro; I want that one; Sage! Alright but don't say I didn't warn you when all that new booty starts popping up at your hotel, at practice, at the club, in the kitchen. Ha-ha! Marc you're a damn fool. But I'm so serious though bruh. I'll let you have them; I'm good. Yeah whatever Harold; we'll see about that when that time comes. Man; get pussy off your mind and park this Blazer right here in front of the dealership so I can get my ride.

Slow your role Harold, I got this man. Now as your manager you should let me negotiate the price before you buy the car. Shawty I got money; I aint negotiating nothing but what kind of rims going on this new joint. Now come on and let's do this so we can hit the mall. Harold and Marcus enter the Hennessy; Jaguar Dealership and gets greeted as soon as they enter. Mr. Washington; congratulations on your new job sir! Thanks man. You're welcome; I'm Stanley we spoke over the phone. Oh yeah nice to meet you. Like-wise Mr. Washington!

If you come with me Sir; I have your car right around back here. I just had it waxed and detailed for you; and it's Cowboy blue; just as you requested. Damn, that baby is sharp! Yes Sir, this is your 2001 Jaguar XK Series – XK8; convertible. Harold jumps into the driver seat, starts the engine then lets down the top. Hey Stanley, can we leave that Blazer here for a few hours; me and Marcus need to hit Lenox Mall for a bit. Sure Harold that's no problem. Cool bruh; come on Marc let's test this baby out!

Marcus hops in the passenger seat and buckles up. Let's do it Harold! Vroom! Vroom! They peel off the lot then head towards Lenox, dipping in and out of traffic while ignoring the speed limits.

A few miles and a couple of red lights later they arrive in front of Lenox Mall, stopping at the Valet. What time is it Marc? 4:45 Harold! Cool we have an hour to do some shopping shawty. Welcome to Lenox Square gentlemen. Thanks bruh, take care of the Jag; it's brand new. It will be my pleasure Sir! Alright Marcus; let's do this. The two gentlemen enter Lenox without a spending budget and only name brands on their minds. Marc we got to hit the Rolex store first shawty then we can hit the Gucci and Louis joint after that.

Whatever you say Harold; it's your money bruh. Damn! What Marcus? Look at what's walking towards us! Oh let me get that door for you ladies. Oh thank you; you're so sweet.

You must not be from around here. Guys don't open doors for ladies anymore. Well, I was taught to always open the door for a lady. Well thank you. You're welcome; what are you ladies names? I'm Jasmine! And I'm Natalie. Nice to meet you; I'm Marcus and that's- Oh we know who that is!

You're Harold Washington; aren't you? Yes I am ladies; do we know each other? No; we saw you on TV during the NFL Draft. Oh really; do you guys watch football? Yes and you are going to be playing for my favorite team. Ha-ha! Is that right Natalie! Yep!

Well ladies; we were just going in to do a little shopping. Are you guys leaving? We were about to Marcus but I guess we can hang back for a few. That's what's up Jasmine. What are you guys going to get Harold? Just a few things like a watch, some shoes and maybe a pair of jeans or two. Ok we can come with you guys and help you pick out some things. Ok

Jasmine; come on then let's do it. Jas; you and Harold go ahead I'm going over to the Cheese Cake Factory, I'm starving. Yeah; yall two go ahead; I'm going with Natalie. Are you sure Marc? Yeah man, why you ask? Shawty I have that radio interview; remember! Oh damn; I forgot all about it. Yeah I see!

Look ladies; let's just all go to the Cheese Cake Factory, get some grub and get to know each other a little bit. Afterwards; me and Marcus need to head over to the radio station for an interview. We can get up with you guys tonight and hang out or something. Awe Harold; you guys don't have to cancel your shopping to come eat with us. We can go eat alone then meet you guys later tonight. No Jasmine; it's no problem, that mall will be here tomorrow. I'm sure of it, now let's go eat. I'm getting hungry now anyway. Ok wait for us right here while we put our bags in the truck. Sure no problem Natalie, did you want my help? I got it but thank you for asking Marcus; you're so sweet.

Man those freaks are fine as hell! I know Marc; that damn Natalie looks like Lisa Raye. I don't know about that Harold but she is fine though and Jasmine aint bad either nigga. Yeah; she straight enough to cut shawty! So you gone hit it tonight if she let you? Marcus; stop asking dumb questions! I'm just saying bruh because about an hour ago; you was all about Sage. Man I don't know what you're taking about shawty, stop tripping. Yeah I told your ass; pussy gone be coming out of the wood work; you're a pro baller now bruh. Get used to it! Ok guys we're ready; thank you for taking us too. Oh it's no problem girls; it's our pleasure. Jasmine grabs Harold by the arm as the four of them head towards the Cheese Cake Factory.

Yeah Marc, I can get use to this! What was that Harold? Oh nothing I was talking to

Marcus, Natalie. Yeah I heard you Harold and this is just the beginning!

Ted watch his image in the spotless glass double doors as he enters the high rise on 1 Glenn Lake Parkway; on the North East side of Atlanta. Gray and Wine marble tile floors decorate the enormous lobby as he and Latrice make their way across them in route to the elevators. Huge palm trees; beacon by rays of sun light from the above glass roof; align the inside walls while a security guard sits at his black marble desk; greeting everyone that passes by. Fresh; country scented, enzymes, filled the air from the chemical used to shine the floor the night before.

Hello folks, welcome to Glenn Lake Towers; can I help you guys find something? Do you know which floor you are going to? Yes young man we do but thanks for asking. Oh no problem sir; you two have a nice day. You do the same young man. This is a really nice building Ted; do you think Donnie likes it? He says he does but I'm the one footing the bill; so who cares. Aww; you don't mean that. Latrice; stop being so dramatic baby I'm only fooling around. Ding! Come on, let's grab this elevator Trice!

I'm right behind you Ted, keep walking honey. Oh I'm sorry; I thought that you were walking beside me. I was but I had to check my phone for messages real quick. Oh, did you have any? It's nothing that Chantel and Cynthia can't handle. Cool, how are they working out anyway? Both of them have very promising careers ahead of them. Wow, that's good to hear; I bet that makes your work easy. Boy you have no idea, how helpful those two has been. What floor are we going to Ted? Oh I'm sorry, press 29. Sure no problem, now how big did you say this place was?

It's about 6 thousand square feet with a large conference room and waiting area up front.

There's also a nice receptionist desk when you first walk in and 4 offices off to the right down the hallway with a picture window at the end. Is it a corner office? Yes it is. Is it carpet or tile? It's carpet Latirce. Ok and how much are they asking for rent? $4200 a month. It sounds good Ted but I will let you know what I think when I see it. Ok baby just make sure you look over the lease really good before I sign it.

No worries Ted; I got your back baby. The elevator door opens. Ok we're here Latrice; let's go. Donnie and Thomas should already be here with the property manager. Ted and Trice exit the elevator, walks to the left, makes a right then enters the first office on their left. Hey Unc! What's up Donnie! Ready to get to work man, me and Thomas have been waiting for 30 minutes. That's not long Donnie; stop complaining. How you doing Thomas? I'm good Unc, I just hope that I'm making the right decision by moving to Atlanta.

Nephew this will be the best move of your life, just wait and see. I hope so Uncle Ted. Hi fellas! Hey Latrice! Where's the property manager D? She's in the corner office at the end of the hall Unc, she had to take a call. Ok; so what do you think of the office? I love it; I can see us doing really well here. It's not the office that determines that Donnie; it's gonna be you and Thomas working your butts off. That's not what I meant Unc. I know what you meant nephew; I just wanted to make a point. Oh we know it's going to be hard work, we talked about it last night. Good; I'm glad to hear that. Well hello; you must be Ted!

Yes I am! Hello Ted; I'm Joyce; the Glenn Lake Property manager. Hi Joyce; nice to meet you; this is my girlfriend Latrice. Hey girl, nice to meet you. And you as well Joyce! So what do you guys think of the place; is it what you're looking for? I think it will work Joyce; my nephews seem to like it. Those two have great taste; we were in here chatting it up before you two came. I'm glad that you all got to know each other; do you have the lease for me? Yes I do; it's right here! Latrice reaches in to intercept the lease as Joyce hands it to Ted. I'll take that! Oh excuse me; I'm sorry Latrice. You're excuse; could you give us a few minutes while we go over this lease. We'll call you when we're ready to talk. Oh sure, no problem; I'll just take a smoke break while you guys are doing that. Yeah; you do that. Joyce takes a pause, looks at Latrice then addresses Ted. I'll be downstairs Ted; call me when you're ready. Ok Joyce.

Well, is there any funny business in it Trice? It's your traditional commercial lease; it looks pretty legit Ted, no crazy clauses or anything like that. If you guys are serious about this place then I see no problem with it. Donnie, Thomas this is a serious business; you two have to stick to the game plan and really focus. I'm ready Unc; I didn't graduate from College to lose. I admit; it is good to see that you guys are excited about the family business. I'm gone make us tons of money here in Atlanta, Uncle Ted; I can see it now! Hold your horses Donnie; I'm gone have you guys start off slow, so that you can build up your properties and get a chance to find your way around the city. You have a lot of networking to do in the private and public sector.

Exactly how are we supposed to do that Unc? Thomas I haven't been in this business for over 20 years for nothing son. Just be quiet a sec and I will tell you guys what to do. Alright; we're all ears. Ok the first thing we need to do is establish some passive income; some money that's going to keep coming in regardless. This is where we get signed on with the Government by putting our properties in its Section 8 and public assistance programs. Those are guaranteed checks every month.

Nephews you never have to worry about the Government not paying you. Wow that's cool.

Yes it is Donnie but there's more. I want you to contact HUD here in Atlanta and let them know that you will be running our Atlanta office. We're already a part of the HUD program in Texas as well as my other locations. It shouldn't be a problem getting with them here in Atlanta. I got a question Unc? What is it Thomas? How are we supposed to offer homes, if we don't have any to offer yet?

Well; that's what this is for! What's that Unc? It's a check for $250,000.00 Donnie. This is your seed money to get you started. Take this check; deposit it in your business bank account then you and Thomas start searching the low income neighborhoods for homes we can buy for cheap then fix up. Before you make an offer to buy, look at how much we will have to invest to make it livable then search the local market to see what price we can get for it. You two are still new at this so I want to approve every purchase before you get it! You guys got that!

Yeah we got it! Good! Donnie you need to get all your business license and Certifications to do business here in Atlanta. Thomas you will be on the payroll as one of our Inspectors and you will also be responsible for hiring contractors to do the jobs. But guys each house will come with a set budget and that will include labor. If you're not careful that $250,000.00 will disappear so fast you won't know where it went!

That's a lot of money Uncle Ted! It's really not Donnie, once you start investing and fixing everything. So is that how we're going to pay rent every month from the profit we make off the renovated homes? Eventually that's how it's going to be done Donnie but as a Graduating gift to you. Me and your father chipped in and paid your lease off for two years.

Oh shit! Oops I'm sorry Unc; I meant to say that's what's up! Yeah whatever Donnie; you meant it. Yeah he did Unc; I know I would have. Ted reaches in his back pocket, pulls out the check book, sits it on the window seal then writes it out for $108,000.00.

Silence; over-came the huge open office space as the sun set shadows of neighboring buildings on its empty egg shell white walls. Alright Thomas; go get Joyce so I can give her this check. Donnie you can sign the lease. Oh I got it baby; let me hold that check Thomas. Are you sure Trice? Yes, I got it Ted you two read over the contract and sign it; I'll get her. Ok baby; hurry back so we can go get some Chicken and Waffles. Boy your butt is going to look like a waffle in a minute. Ha-ha. Donnie and Thomas laughs at Ted as Trice heads downstairs to get Joyce.

While you two jokers are laughing; you need to figure out how you're going to furnish this office and hire a secretary. Huh! If you can huh! You can hear Donnie. Dang Unc, I didn't think about that; can't we just use- Nope don't even think about it Thomas. The rent and seed money is taking care of, now it's up to you and your cousin to get furniture and a secretary. Damn that's messed up Unc! No it's not Thomas; you guys can't have it all easy. Chill cousin we got this; thanks for everything Uncle Ted, we'll get the furniture and I already have a secretary in mind. Good; that's what I like to hear Donnie.

Well I see you like the place; Latrice just gave me the good news gentlemen; here are your keys and Congratulations! Thank you Joyce; here's the signed contract and thanks for everything. You're welcome Donnie and if you guys need anything; my card is attached to your copy of the lease. Ok cool. Well you all have a great day; I'm about to starve; I'm headed over to Gladys and Ron's to get me some of those delicious Chicken and Waffles. Ted smiles, looks at Joyce then points. You know I was just saying- Latrice interrupts him mid-sentence then approaches Joyce. Thank you again Joyce; enjoy your chicken and waffles! I sure will Trice. That's Latrice! Oh I'm sorry Latrice; bye guys! Bye! They all say in unison as she walks through the door way.

Beep! Beep! Quentin blows the horn on his classmate's small pick-up truck as he backs over the grass, to park in front of the Dormitory doors. God Dammit Quincy! Didn't I tell you blame kids not to drive on the grass! Aw, old man James I won't be long; I'm just helping Chantel and Cynthia; move their things out. I don't care who you're helping Quincy; move the blame truck son! Ok hold on old man! And my name is not Quincy either; it's Quentin! Dag nabbit; if I say it's Quincy then that's what I'm gone call you.

Whatever man; just hold your horses; we won't be long. I'm going around back to the gym and when I come back; you better not be here Quincy. Old man I've been here for the past four years and you're still calling me Quincy. Because that's what it is. You just need to retire Mr. James; give it up already. Who me! I don't give up on nothing; this here; is good, easy money.

Be gone when I get back; you here! Yeah, uh-huh; Mr. James! Q places the truck in park, shuts off the engine then walks to the rear to drop the tailgate. It's about time! A voice yells out from a window above. Hey Cynt; are yall ready? Yep; Chant is on the way down with a few boxes. Ok I'll be right up to help out.

Ok Q; hurry up; we have to be at the office in three hours. Alright I'm coming! Beep! Beep! Q turns around as he reaches the doors at the top of the steps to see who was blowing the horn. Hey Q! Nadia; Tam what are you guys doing here? We came to help our girls move. Damn all they have is some clothes and a few boxes. Ha-ha! Well; we can watch you move while we direct you. Ha-ha. What the hell ever Nadia;

you two got jokes. We're just playing Q, we came to help out. You say that now Tam but we'll see what happens. Quentin holds the door open for the ladies as they enter the dorm.

Well hello; everyone! Hi Chant; we came to help girl. Great Tam; all the boxes are packed and ready upstairs. Cool we'll go get some. Is the truck open Q? Yeah but just sit the boxes in the back. Boy; there are some expensive suits in this bag; it is not going on the back of no truck. There aint nowhere else for it to go Chantel. Just watch me Q; I'm sure there's room up front. Girl; that's the whole reason for borrowing the truck, so we can put everything in the back! Quentin just go upstairs and help the girls with the other boxes; I got this honey.

See; you women are too much; I'll be back down in a minute Chantel, just stay here and watch the truck until I come back. Ok hurry up. What's up ladies? Hey Cynthia how many boxes are left? Just those 5 over by the wall Tam; I appreciate you guys helping too. You're welcome Cynt; we weren't doing anything anyway. Nadia had me up since 6 this morning, doing her damn hair. Your butt wasn't complaining when I had breakfast waiting on you; were you Tam? Oh no; I'm not complaining sis and that breakfast was slamming.

Man; yall aint bring a box down yet! Cynt walks up to Quentin then gives him a hug. Aww Q; we was just talking baby; I'll make it up to you later. Umm; look at you two! What Nadia? Yall all lubby dubby and stuff. Girl this is my baby; my Professor. Yeah; ok professor! Must be the natural herbs professor, Chronic 420! Ha-ha! Good one Tam! I'm serious Nadia; you and Tam are looking at one of Clark's newest Professors. What! They both said in unison. Yep; my Quentin got the job yesterday. Well I'll be damn; congratulations Q! Thanks girls; now help me get the rest of these boxes down to the truck.

Yes Professor; whatever you say! Nadia stop it with your crazy ass. I'm just messing with him Cynt. Yeah I know; let's finish up so we can all go the Waffle House; I'm starving! Nadia, Tam and Cynt pick up the last three boxes, close the dorm room door then follows Q downstairs.

Ring-Ring! Hello! Hey Chant; what you doing baby? I'm still at the dorm loading this truck Donnie; are you still at work? Yep; we're about to check out some Houses over in East Point. Oh ok; I think we all are going to the Waffle House when we leave here. What time are you coming home today? I don't know yet baby but I'll call you as soon as I do. Alright here are the guys with the other boxes; I'll call you later D. Ok Chant; later.

Water still beaded on the back of Sylvia's neck as she dry off her body while looking in the mirror. She removes her white embroidered robe from behind the door, slips it on then pins her wet hair up on her head. Ding-Dong! Its 10 O'clock at night; who can that be at my door. She said out loud as she walks into the hallway then down the long flight of stairs. Ding-Dong! I'm coming! I'm coming; hold on a minute! Sylvia stood on her tip toes to peek through the peep hole. Oh my God; Marcus! What are you doing here; you didn't tell me you were coming! I know baby just open the door; I have a surprise for you. Alright hold on a second; let me unlock it. Ok, hurry up; it's raining.

Rain drops tap on the cement like fallen rocks as Marc stood there wet with both hands behind his back. Well, don't just stand there silly; come in out of the rain. In one swift motion he swung his hands in front of him. Oh wow! Are these for me! Yes baby! 18 fresh red roses, wrapped in gold foiled paper looked surreal under the soft white porch light and sparkling rain drops as he held them in his left hand while the cold bottle of Rose' in the other fogged up from the misty weather. Aww; thank you! There're so pretty! Get in here! Sylvia grabs the roses with her right hand then pulls Marcus inside the house by his wet shirt.

I didn't mean to come by so late without calling baby but it was important that I saw you. It's fine; is everything ok? Oh yeah, everything is fine; I just wanted to tell you in person that I will be going to Texas with Harold in a few days for training camp. How long are you going to be gone? It's going to be my job now Sylvia. I don't understand? Well I'm Harold's Manager; so that will require me to be on the road a lot. Sylvia makes her way into the kitchen then leans against the counter, pulls her hair down then strokes it as Marcus continue to speak. A few months at least baby; you can say the entire football season. That's a long time Marc. Yeah I know. Well, it's not like you and I are serious or anything; I'm sure I will be alright while you are on the road with Harold. Are you sure Sylvia? Yeah; why wouldn't I be? Good; I'm happy to hear that; get two glasses while I open this champagne.

Sure but what are we celebrating Marc? You baby, I don't ever want you to forget this night. Why me? Because out of all the women I've ever dated you are the realest, you don't question what I do or anything. Now I'm kind of nervous; what are you talking about Marcus? Sylvia leans against the counter while Marc opens the bottle of Rose'. Curiosity overcomes her as she watch him pour the bubbly into two champagne flutes. The soft roar of the refrigerator motor broke the uncomfortable silence in the kitchen as her curiosity risen.

Here you go Sylvia; let's make a toast to us. Wow; what does that mean Marc? Are you going to purpose or something? Ha-ha. Why are you laughing sir? I'm serious! Marcus leans in close to Syliva while holding the glass in his right hand then reaches around her waist with the other hand to retrieve the stereo remote. As he push the power button; Promise by Jagged Edge echo through the speakers and adds to mood in the luxurious kitchen. "Nothing is promised to me and you" "So why will we let this thing go."

See Sylvia; I know that I'm not going to be here in Atlanta for long, so I wanted to make my time left here with you special. This moment is for you; have a drink with me Sylvia. Quietly she looks into his eyes then takes a sip from the glass. Her robe now halfway open exposing her chiseled abs and perky breast added to the energy and excitement in the air as Promise continues to play in the background. "Should of known the things you said been right" "Forever is such a longtime." "We never even had a fight."

As Sylvia sip her champagne, sparkles gleam in her eyes all the while watching Marc's every move. The closer he got; the more reciprocal she became. Bling! Both glasses hit the floor as she abruptly starts to remove his shirt. The moment intensifies by the second; her robe falls to the floor as she reaches down to remove his pants. The music constantly plays in the background as Marcus lift her naked body up onto the island. His legs parts hers then with natural instinct Sylvia wraps her toned calves around his waist while leaning backwards and gripping the islands edge as Marc thrust forward. Oh baby; that feels so good. Yeah, you feel good too girl.

You can't leave me Marcus; not after this! I won't be gone long baby I promise. Ummm, yes, I love you right now boy! Oh yeah; you like this huh? Yeessss! Please don't stop Marc, keep going! You feel so good right now; oh my God! He reaches down, grips her waist then strokes harder. Oh God! Marcus! Marcus!

Marcus! One stroke, two strokes, three strokes! Ugggh! Yeah you like that, huh Sylvia? Ummmm yes, damn I'm going to miss this! Both their bodies collapse upon one another as the radio continues to play in the background. Sylvia now humble than ever before, held Marc by his head and looked deep into his eyes as he lay atop of her moist body, her legs still wrapped around his waist as they lay on the island. Deep inside she knew that he really wasn't hers but she kept it to herself and enjoyed the moment.

The fresh smell of new carpet fill the air over in the Buckhead apartment while one huge card board box sit in the middle of the dinning-area with one blue; bean bag chair on each side. Only shadows of buildings from the surroundings outside tattoo the empty white walls through the huge picture frame windows. In the center of the bedroom sat a blue blow up mattress covered by a red and black wool blanket. The shadows dance on the walls as the candle flickers from atop the card board box as Donnie sat there patiently while Chantel removes the chicken flavored Top Ramen noodles from the steaming pot.

Horns and engines from the traffic downstairs added to the already subtle atmosphere as she made her way over to the card board box. As the steam from the noodles rise from the bowls; Donnie opens two cokes, one for him and the other for the love in his life; Chantel. Total darkness, illuminated by apple, cinnamon candles, only fell around them, as spectrums of light beamed across their faces.

Well baby; this is our first meal in our new place. It smells good Chantel but how are we going to eat it? Oh snap Donnie; we don't have any forks! Ha-ha! You're kidding me right Chant? No baby! She jumps up then runs into the kitchen to check the obviously empty drawers. Donnie don't just sit there baby; help me find a fork, spoon, knife, something! Ok, I'll check my boxes, maybe there's one from the dorm room. We ordered out so much; it has to be one in there somewhere. Ok good idea; I'll check mine too!

No; come sit down Chant; I'll find something. Are you sure Donnie? Yeah baby, calm down, it's not the end of the world. Ok but hurry, the noodles are getting cold. Ha-ha! It's not funny D! Alright just chill girl. Chantel sits and wait patiently while watching the shadows dance from wall to wall, inhaling the apple cinnamon aroma then a smirk dawns her face as Donnie walks back in. Look; I found one! Yay; come on; let's eat! D takes a seat on the bean bag chair, places the fork in his bowl, twirls it a few times, picks it up full of noodles, holds his left hand under the fork then gradually feeds them to Chantel.

Hmmm; these are the best noodles I've ever had in my life Donnie. That's because it has that special season on them, huh baby? Ha-ha.

Yep; very special; here let me have the fork so I can feed you too. Donnie let's go of the fork as she reaches for it. While Chantel places the fork in her bowl to gather some noodles, Donnie reaches down under his bean bag chair then pulls out a small; purple, suede box with gold trimming then places it on the table by his bowl. Ok baby, open up, here's your noodles! She brings the fork close to his mouth then pauses. Donnie? Yeah baby, can I have my food? Donnie? Yes Chant? What is that? My mouth and it's waiting for those noodles. No silly, that purple box, it wasn't there a few minutes ago. Ummm-Hmmm. He clears his throat, picks up the purple box then gets down on one knee and faces her.

She drops the fork of noodles then places both hands over her mouth as Donnie begins to speak. Chantel ever since I met you in the laundry room that day; I knew that I wanted you to be in my life forever. I love your smile, the way you walk, the way you hold me; I even love you when you're angry. You have a good heart and you always stick to your word. Chantel I want you in my life forever; will you do me the honors of being my wife? Tears slowly fell from her eyes as she reach for his hands and pull them both close to her heart then looked into his eyes. Donnie I would love to be your wife; Yes! Hell yeah; aww baby, I'm so glad you said yes! I love you Chantel; we're going to be together forever!

6. TRUE LIFE.

Ok Cynthia, I need you to look sharp in this court room. This Judge is a real hard ass when it comes to repeat offenders. And our client has 4 offenses on his record already. So make sure that he's in place when court begins. So you want me to baby sit that grown ass man? Yes I do; is there a problem? Latrice you can't be serious. Oh; if you think I'm joking, just go back to the office and answer the phones or something. He's our client and it's our job to do what's necessary within the scope of our profession to provide him with the best representation.

Alright I'll go get him. Thank you and hurry up; we have 5 minutes before court is in session. Where is he Latrice? In the third room on the left; the officer was letting him change out of that God awful; orange jailhouse suit. I'm going in the court room; just bring him up front with you when you come in. Ok I'll be back in a second. Oh Cynthia! Yes Latrice? Make sure the officer is close behind; we don't need our client getting any crazy ideas about running! Got it Latrice!

The cherry oak wood; double doors swung open just as she was heading inside. Oh I'm sorry; excuse me Ma'am! I didn't see you there. It's no problem officer; I was just coming in. Latrice hastily walks into the semi crowded court room; the front bench off to her left filled with several inmates all dressed in orange jump suits and off to her right on the opposite bench sat their families, spouses and loved ones. A mixture of prosecutors, court stenographers, Fulton County police officers, bailiffs and clerks crowd the front of the court room as the D.A call inmate after inmate to her table to discuss plea deals and other options to close their cases. Latrice amidst all the commotion; quietly took her seat at her table off to the left in front of the inmates.

"All rise; for the Honorable Judge Walker!" The entire room rise as the judge enters. You may be seated; clerk whose first on the docket? Latrice franticly looks behind her to see where Cynt and their client were just as they enter the court room.

Your Honor; first on the docket we have Defense Attorney; Ms. Latrice representing Mr. Goines! Very well; Good Morning Ms. Latrice; I see you but where is Mr. Goines? He's right here sir; walking up now! Mr. Goines; you should know by now not to be late to court; after three times, one would assume you had it pegged by now son. Ms. Latrice your client is charged once again with burglary; and I see here that you are trying to get bail set. That is correct judge. Mr. Goines with his head held down; cautiously walks over by Latrice and stands there quietly as the judge reviews his file. Ring-Ring! Ring-Ring! The entire court room including the judge looks around to see whose phone was ringing. Ring-Ring!

Latrice turns to look over her left shoulder then see Cynt scrambling with her purse. Ring-Ring! Ring-Ring! Nervous, shaking, frantic and ashamed; Cynt reaches for her phone to turn it off! Excuse me Ma'am; you need to take care of that phone. Yes; you Honor! Ring-Ring! Ring-Ring! Bailiff; please escort that young lady out of my court room. Yes you Honor.

Ok Ma'am come on; let's go. Latrice, ashamed, shakes her head as the judge starts to read over Mr. Goines charges. Ring-Ring! Ring-Ring! Stay out here Ma'am and next time, turn that thing on vibrate; I know you're new to this; I'll let you slide this time but if it happens again; you owe me lunch. Ok thank you bailiff! Umm-hmm. No problem. Ring-

Ring! And answer that thing already. I am and thanks again. Ring- Hello!

Hey baby; what you doing? Q! I was in court; you got my boss and the judge mad at me! How did I do that? You called me when I was in there, that's why. That aint my fault woman; you should have had it on vibrate. Shut up Q; what you want this time of day? Oh; I was calling to see if you wanted to go over to Benihana's for lunch. What time is your lunch Quentin? In a hour baby. Sure, I might as well; you done got me in trouble anyway. I'm sorry Cynthia; I'll make it up to you; I promise. Yeah whatever; I'm going back in the courthouse, just pick me up from the office. Alright baby; see you later! Cynt turns her phone on vibrate; fixes her clothes, takes a deep breath, releases it then walks back into the courtroom.

Miss Latrice; Mr. Goines has continued to break the law after several run ins and brief stays here at the Fulton County jail. Right now

I don't think that he is a good candidate for bail. Maybe he needs to spend a little more time here with us this trip. But your honor- That's enough Miss Latrice; bail is denied! Disappointed; Latirce shakes her clients hand before the officer escorts him back to the tombs, grabs her brief case then head back to the office just as Cynthia is walking back in. Come on Cynt, bail was denied; let's go. Clerk; who's next on the docket!

Chantel I'm so proud of you girl. Why Sylvia; what did I do? You're living your dream and you stuck with it for all those years. Thank you Sylvia but I swear I came close to quitting those last few years; law school is brutal. Look at you now though; wasn't it all worth it? Did you see this check girlfriend; hell yes it was worth it! How much is it; let me see that thing. Hold on; let me park the car first. Ok, I sure hope it's enough to buy yall a new car; this thing has had it. Ha-ha. Hold on Sylvia; don't be talking about my baby's car now.

Child tell Donnie to drop this thing off at the junk yard, it's a wrap! Ha-ha. See you wrong girl! I'm just kidding; let me see that check. Alright here you go. Thank you; what took you so long. What the Hell! Girl what did you have to do for this? Practice Law girl; and that was just for one week. Damn; I need to take my ass to Law school. This is a damn check for $8,000.00; for one week! Are you serious! Yes Ma'am!

Turn this damn car off and let's go in this furniture store; I'm about to make you guys apartment look like a New York Penthouse. Now you're talking Sylvia; and don't be picking no expensive stuff now. Chant just let me do me; I got this covered. Alright but you can only spend $5000; I still need to get groceries and a washer and dryer. Baby that's plenty; come on let's go! Get out the car so I can crawl across the seat already. Oh you got jokes huh. No but Donnie can at least fix the passenger door so people can get out, sheesh!

Just come on here Sylvia; I'm not trying to be in here all day; I'm hungry. Me too Chant, let's get some Varsity afterwards. That's cool with me. We can go pick out that washer and dryer too while we're over here on Jimmy Carter by all the furniture stores. Nah Donnie can do that; I'm too hungry to be out here all day. Ok suit yourself Chant.

Hello ladies; I'm Charles; welcome to By Design; what can I help you ladies with today? Well Chuck; can I call you Chuck? Yes Ma'am that's fine. Good; I'm Sylvia and this is my friend Chantel; the Criminal Attorney. Hello Chantel. Hello Charles. Girl; call him Chuck; he said it was ok. Sylvia; stop acting up! I am not acting honey; now Chuck show us your new pieces; Chant just moved into a new apartment and all they have in that place are boxes and air mattresses. So we need help brother. Ha-ha. Ok ladies; I can assist you with that; right this way. Right behind you Chuck!

Oh Chant; guess who came by the other night girl. Who? Marcus and he brought flowers. Hmmm, what did he want? Um girl! Sylvia; don't walk off from me! Did you give him some? Sylvia, did you? Chant I couldn't help it; he was so romantic. Girl you are a trip; you're a little sneaky one. I have to keep my eye on you. Are you guys getting serious? I don't know about that; I'm no dummy. Marcus has his share of women; he claims I'm special but I'm not buying it. Humph! I can't tell! What's that supposed to mean Chantel?

Ok ladies; here are the new arrivals. This particular model comes in Black, Cream and Brown. As you can see it's a traditional three piece, more on the modern side. You have your Sofa, chair and love seat. What kind of material is this Chuck; it feels like suede. That's actually micro fiber Ms. Chantel. What the hake is micro fiber? It feels and looks like suede but is more easy to clean, a perfect material for a piece such as this; in my opinion. Does it come with pillows Chuck? As a matter of fact it does Ms. Sylvia. We keep them in back so that they don't lose their original state from normal ware and tare, after being on display.

This is ok Chuck; what do you have in leather? I have a few pieces Ms. Chantel. Hold on Chuck; I'm the designer, that's why she brought me. So never mind the leather for now, can I see the cream set like this micro fiber here? Sure, just follow me into the back and I can show you. Alright; lead the way young man. Pssst! What Chant? You never answered my question? What question? Are you and Marc getting serious? Now Chantel; I maybe a little naïve but can you give a sister some kind of credit; come on.

I'm just asking Syl; you do get all excited whenever you talk about him. Did you know that Harold hired him as his Manager? Yes I did; I'm still not too sure about that move though Sylvia. Me and you both, Chant! That alone gives me plenty of reason to keep him at a distance. I know Marcus is going to lose his mind with all that money and ass coming from everywhere. Ha-ha. Yep you're probably right about that girl. Probably! Chant please, you know it's true. Well at least you got your senses about you, now I'm not so worried. Why would you be worried about me; I'm a big girl. That's true Syl but Marcus is a true ladies man and I just don't want you getting hurt. I'm good Chantel; I know what I'm doing. Ok Ma'am; I heard you.

Alright ladies; this is the cream one. Wow! I love this Sylvia! I know; doesn't it look great. Oh God yes; I want it. How much is it Chuck? It's $2,300.89 Ms. Chantel. Great; I'll take it; how soon can you guys have it delivered? We can have it to you in a few days Ms. Chantel. Cool; let's do it. Sure; I can take your payment; at the counter up front. Ok we'll be there in a minute; we want to look at some of these pictures you have. Take your time ladies.

Thanks Chuck! Well that's going to look nice; do you think Donnie will like it? I'm sure he will girl; he trust my taste. Yeah whatever! What's that supposed to mean Sylvia? Nothing; I was just messing with you. How does it feel living with him? Chantel stops walking, smiles then holds her hand up to Sylvia's face. Oh my God; shut the front the door. Is that what I think it is? Yes girl!

Wow! Congratulations! Thank you Sylvia! That Donnie is about his business, I'm so happy for you girl. Forget these pictures let's go celebrate! Hold on Sylvia; let me pay for the furniture first. Oh I'm sorry; hurry up! Do you have a pen Chuck! Sure; is there anything else I can get for you before you guys leave. Oh shit; yes! I almost forgot! What did you forget Chant? The damn bed child! Ha-ha! Chant really. Don't really me; fashion slash interior designer; you didn't remember either. Chuck do you have any King size beds around $1500? Yes I have a few Ms. Chantel. Well pick out the best one and send it with the couch set. Sure no problem. Ok great; what's the damage? Let's see; your total is $2,300.89 plus $1,100 for the King size bed with my store discount. Aw thank you Chuck. You're welcome ladies; it's not a problem. That total comes to $3,400.89. Super, can I get that pen so I can write you a check? Oh yes; I'm sorry!

Thanks! Here you go, just make sure your guys deliver it to this address ok. Not a problem; I will see to it. Thank you ladies and have a wonderful day. You're welcome Chuck; now come on Chant; we're stopping by Pappadeaux's; my treat. Alright now Sylvia; sounds good to me; let's do it!

Knock-Knock! Hold on, hold on, I'm coming. Hurry your ass up Q; I got to take a leak boy! Fellas; what's up! Move man; I got to use the bathroom. Damn Donnie; aint you gone speak first! Man whatever! Ha-ha. What's up Thomas; why you aint take your cousin to a gas station or something if he had to pee that bad. Q aint no way in hell I was going to stop anywhere, out in that Atlanta traffic. I can't blame you for that man; it can be nerve wrecking. Anyway, what you been up to professor?

Just kicking it bruh, how is business at the Real Estate Investment Firm? It's coming along; we still need to buy a few more houses though. Aaah don't worry; it will happen; you guys are just in the beginning stages. Yeah I know but its hard work Q! What, did you think it would be easy? Nah; but not this damn commanding! What do you mean Thomas? Q have you ever cleaned out an old abandon house, the bathroom alone will have you thinking twice. Damn, I can't imagine that- Quentin what's up bruh; are you ready to get that butt spanked? Donnie; save it playa, you can't slap no bones boy. Well come over here, have a seat and put them on the table and let's handle business Mr. Professor.

Thomas; get your cousin before I hurt his feelings. I don't know about that Q; I got my paper on D! Oh, so that's how yall gone do me? I'm just speaking the truth Q. Thomas stop wolfing and grab some beers; while I clear off this table. Damn bruh you're a professor now, aren't you gone buy some new furniture? What for D; that chair can still hold you and my bed is too comfortable to be swapping it out! Alright, calm down Q I understand; loud and clear. Enough about my stuff; Cynthia told me about the ring man; why you aint tell a brother?

My bad Quentin; I was going to but when I heard her telling Cynt; I figured she would tell you. Yeah, yeah, congratulations boy; whens the big date? That fool aint got no date man; he only proposed because he seen how much loot Chantel was making. Thomas shut up, don't start no damn rumors. Donnie; I'm your blood, your first cousin, they might not know you but I know your ass. What's T talking about D?

Nothing; that fool just high! Nah Q; I'm just playing; Chant got cuz locked. He done threw in his player's card. Well; speaking of playing, you two cousins need to sit your asses down and wash these bones, time to spank some butt. Oh is that how you feel Professor? You heard me D, class is in session.

Thomas, Donnie and Quentin, take their seats at the oak wood kitchen table that sits by the Stove and Fridge in Q's mid-town studio apartment. The sound of the MARTA engine, purr as it pass right under his large picture window. His King size bed sat in the far right corner, unmade with the comforter hanging to the floor. Dust, blew across the 2,000 square feet of wood finished floors from the breeze that seep under the front door. Bruh you need to clean this place up. For what fool, aint nobody here but yall knuckle heads?

Donnie has a point Q, how does Cynthia come over to this dirty crib! Man; yall need to stop trying to change the subject and wash them bones. Alright, alright, how many we pulling? Six D! Hey Thomas; how's Nadia doing? She's good Q; we're going on a cruise tomorrow. What! What you mean, you going on a cruise T? Like I said Donnie, we're going to Jamaica for a few days. When did this happen cuz, we got four houses to renovate next week? Stop worrying D; I got that handled; my crew will take care of it. Alright Thomas, don't get fired while your ass is in Jamaica! Bam! Stop arguing and get behind that big six! Q slams down his domino in the center of the table.

Ok I see you playa! Oh yeah, what are you going to do about it D? Bam! Follow that truck; it got drugs in it! 6-3! Give me fifteen; baby! Write down my points Professor, don't cheat! I got you D, your play Thomas. Shit, let me slow this train up. Take this 6-2 and let me get 5 Professor. Ring-Ring! Oh-oh, is that your phone Thomas? Yeah it's Nadia. Get it then knuckle head; I'm gone write your 5 points down. Ring-Ring! Hey Baby, what's up? Nothing much, I just got to work and Tam just called me, she wants to drop the tickets off with you. Ok that's cool. Great; so where you at? I'm over at Q's playing some bones with him and Donnie. Well are you going to call her so you can go get the tickets? Nah, just tell her to bring them to Quentin's. Cool, I'll let her know and tell the guys I said hi. Ok Nadia see you tonight baby. Alright, love you Thomas. Love you too, bye!

Damn; what was that cuz? "Love you too bye!" Don't start with me Donnie! Ha-ha! Aint nothing funny Quentin; it's your play; lay it down! Thomas; why you say it so fast cuz? That wasn't fast D! Q wasn't that fast. Yeah it was kind of fast Thomas. Man forget yall fools; play your domino already Q!

So when you getting married T? Bruh; play your hand, stop worrying about my business.

Ooooh; do I sense some hostility from you young man. Nah but you better tighten this apartment up because Tam is coming over to drop off the tickets. She'll be alright; that's Marc's cut buddy anyway; it doesn't matter to me what she thinks about my crib. Man yall two sound like two hens going at it; I need a drink! Do you have any beers in here Q? No; all I have is some wine from the other night. Wine! Yes; wine D!

Yo hold this game up for a minute; I'm about to walk across the street to grab a six pack. I can't believe we're over here playing dominoes and your ass aint got no beer Q. Donnie I thought yall was bringing the party favors since I'm hosting the party. You got issues professor; I bet you got some weed though. Hell yeah; you want to smoke a blunt; I got two rolled up already. Hell nah; I'll be back in a few minutes. Donnie gets up from the table then heads towards the door. Yo cuz bring me a bag of plain lays back. Yeah whatever! Bam!

Hey don't be slamming my door boy! What's wrong with your cousin Thomas? I don't know Q but where are those blunts? Right here playa; you got a light? Hell yeah!

Chronic aroma fills the air as Thomas and Q inhale their Mary Jane. So, when you get to Jamaica T; make sure you smoke some of that ganja boy! Man you already know! But I'm curious Thomas; have you tried to stop smoking since you got that professor gig? I tried but as you can see; that's all it was bruh. Won't you get in trouble if they catch you? Maybe but they don't be drug testing people like that; that's college man; everyone is grown there. Yeah I guess so; it just seems like a risk. The way I see it T; it aint no big deal; it doesn't affect my job. It's not like I go to work high.

Q I feel you playa; there is no way I can go with-out smoking. Hell; Nadia even smokes with me from time to time. What; stop playing! Nah for real; she can't hang though! What you mean? Bruh she starts tripping when she smokes; I can't let her smoke that kush with me. I have to find her some Reggie. Ha-ha! Man; don't even get her started; she's going to be hooked on this shit just like us. You think so Q? Yep go ahead and stop; I really don't think that she can handle it Thomas. Maybe you're right Quentin; I just might let it go. Besides she has a kid to think about. Good idea brother. Knock-Knock! Damn; I thought I left the door unlock T! Me too! Knock-Knock! It's open Donnie; come in! It's not Donnie! Oh my bad; hold on! Thomas jumps up from the table, blunt in hand and opens the door. Hey Tam! Hey Q; is Thomas here? Yeah I'm over here! Come in Tam; we were just- I can see what yall doing and no thanks.

Hey sis; what's up? I'm dropping off these cruise tickets. Oh thanks; we appreciate it; where you coming from with your hair all tied up, wearing tights. I was at the gym Thomas; trying to keep this body right. Oh trust me; it's tight too, Tam! Alright don't start no trouble Q; the last thing I need is Cynt's crazy ass in my face. Who? Boy don't play; here you go Thomas; I'm gone let you guys get back to your smoking session. Thanks Tam; see you later! Alright T; see you guys around. Bye Tam! Bye Quentin. Damn boy; she's fine as wine; aint she? Yeah she hot Q; you know Marc still tapping that. Man; that aint no surprise Thomas! Pass me that blunt bruh! Oh here you go T; my bad.

Three nights and two days later, Thomas and Nadia arrive in sunny Miami.

"This is your Captain speaking; Welcome to the Princess Cruise; Jamaican Tour!" "We hope that you are making yourself at home." "Please enjoy our ship and all that it has to offer." "Dinner will be served at 6pm, 7pm and 8pm; please check your travel vouchers to see what time your dinner is reserved." "Just a reminder; you get three meal Vouchers a day so don't use all twelve of them in two days." "Once again this is Captain Burleson; please enjoy yourself and all the festivities that we have planned for your trip." "The casino will be open 24 hours for your entertainment pleasure."

Port of Miami; As the warm breeze blows across the sea; Nadia's white linen dress caresses her figure while Thomas grasp her waist from behind while they watch patrons down below, board the massive cruise ship. The smell of salt water, steam engines and loud fog horns add to the already exciting atmosphere. Wow this is so beautiful Thomas; look at how blue the water is. Yeah Nadia; it is pretty, aint it. Umm-hmm; I want to make love on the deck under the stars tonight. Oh really; the sea brings the bad girl out huh? Yep!

Well I'm down for it; if you are! I mean it Thomas; it will be so romantic. Ok we'll see what happens tonight. You promise! Yeah baby; I promise; anything for my girl. Damn it's a lot of people on this cruise; they're still boarding and we already been on here an hour. It's a big ship Thomas. This damn thing is a city; we can live on this sucker. Ha-ha. Thomas you're silly. I'm serious Nadia; come on let's go take a look around. Alright; lead the way sir.

Crisp, shiny gold panels align the walls, wooden walnut colored hand rails held the glass bannisters in place as they swirl along the royal blue carpeted stairwell that lead down from the 9th level and onto the cream and gold marbled tile floor. Sunrays bounce from window to window through-out the luxurious Cruise ship, mall shops that greet you at its entrance. Oh I think I'm in heaven; I don't ever want to leave this place Thomas. "Attention mates; this is your Captain speaking; we are set to leave port in 30 minutes; please make sure that you have all of your belongings and prepare for our lovely 4 day; 3 night; Island voyage."

Nadia do you have everything baby? Yeah I'm all set Thomas; just me; you and the clear blue sea! Girl you're a trip; the clear blue sea huh? Yep; and I want to ride the jet-ski's when we get out in the ocean. Can you even swim Nadia? What; I was the swim team captain in High School boy. Um-hmm; you probably swim like a rock. Ha-ha. That aint funny; I can swim. I know Nadia; I'm just teasing; let's put these bags in the cabin so we can grab us a few Margarita's.

Ooh baby; now you talking; did you bring some smoke with you? Nadia; aint no way in hell; I'm letting you smoke while we are on this ship! Do you remember what happened the last time I let you smoke some weed? That was just because it had been a while. Well it's gone be longer this time because I'm not trying to stop you from catching dragons and rabbits and shit. Ha-ha! You were buggin; so no way sister, not going to happen. You might try and fly off the dang ship! Whatever Thomas; that's not fair! Yes it is; now come on.

Hey nephew! Nephew! A loud male voice shouted out as he and Nadia made their way towards their cabin. Thomas! T stops; turns around to see who called him. Oh what's up Uncle Ted, Latrice! What are you guys doing on here? The same reason yall are. Hey Nadia! Hello Latrice, Ted. Man; Tam gave us these tickets because she couldn't make it. Well that was nice of her; I thought you had some houses to renovate this week? I do Unc but my crew is going to handle it for me. Alright nephew; I bet Donnie wasn't too pleased about it. No he wasn't but I wasn't about to pass this up. Shit I hear you nephew; come on; I'll help you with the bags. Nadia; why don't you go with Latrice and grab a drink! Sure that sounds great to me. Let's go Nadia; I can't wait to get my drink on!

Ring-Ring! Ring-Ring! Ring-Ring! "Hi you've reached Sage; sorry that I've missed your call. Please leave your name, number and reason for calling and I will return your call as soon as possible." Hey Sage; it's me Harold; I'm in town for a few nights; we're playing the Falcons Sunday as you know. I'm staying downtown at the Ritz in room 489; come by if you can; I would love to see you. Thanks; hope to see you later.

Knock-Knock! Yeah who is it! Knock-knock! Hold on a minute. Harold places the room phone back on the receiver than walks towards his room door as the knocking continue. Knock-knock! Who is it! It's Dana! And Missy! Who? Confused but curious; he opens the door. Hey Cowboy; your teammate sent us to your room. What teammate? You know that big guy down the hall? Who; Massey? Yeah that's him; so are you going to let us in; we're naked under these robes. Whoa! Never mind we'll let ourselves in; what do you have in here to drink? Dana; with her jet black hair, still wet from a prior shower rushes in then jumps on the bed. Harold now in shock but not really; stood there admiring her soft bronze skin, pedicured toes, pretty white teeth and gorgeous smile when he felt a hand on his family jewels. Whoa; hold on baby! What's wrong Harold; don't you want to share with us.

Baby, calm down for a minute! It's Missy, and I am calm; are you? Yeah let's just take it easy for a minute. Missy wraps her long arms around Harold's waist then grasp his Johnson with her right hand. The sweet smell of her perfume brushes under his nose as she rest her head on his right shoulder from behind. Oooh, what's this Harold; your friend doesn't seem to mind; I think he likes me. Grrrrrrr; it's big too Dana, come feel it. Ok ladies; that's enough; it's time for yall to leave my room shawty. How did you know I was staying here anyway? Ummm, it is big Missy! Hey come on now girls; I'll fuck both of yall, just chill for a minute shawty. You promise! Yes Missy; now go have a seat and let me get myself straight; you too Dana. Ok sexy; we're gone wait right here on the bed for you. Missy and Dana begin to remove one another's robes as they sit on the edge of the large; heavenly, king size bed. Harold flustered with embarrassment walks over to lock the room door while unzipping his pants. Knock-Knock! Knock-Knock! Oooh, are you expecting company Harold. Shhh; Dana be quiet! Knock-Knock! Who is it?

It's me! Me who? Open the door and see! I will but move your finger off the peep hole. Why; don't you know my voice? Nope! Suddenly the peep hole was clear; as he looked through to the other side; his heart dropped to his drawers. Now are you going to open up; I was only a few blocks away when you called. He stood there quiet as Sage continues to talk. Harold! I know you hear me! Sage reaches down, pushes the handle and feels the tension as Harold tries to close the door that he unknowingly opened while in dismay.

Harold, what's wrong with you; move out of the way and let me in. The door swings slightly open, just enough for her to look in. Hey baby; I'm glad you came by, can you come back later? Missy jumps up off the bed to see who's at the door. Hey Harold; who is it; are we having a four way! See; I knew it; you aint about nothing, just like I thought; another whore ass athlete! Sage; baby wait a minute; let me explain! Bap! Harold stood there in awe after the palm of here right hand smacked him in the face. Sage; come back! Lose my number; little boy!

7. Love Bites.

The Atlanta Skyline; brightens the late night sky outside Donnie and Chantel's bedroom window as they lay atop of their queen size air mattress. Streams of smoke from Egyptian musk; scented inscent's; float up from the window seal to the ceiling. Their naked bodies caress one another as they study each-other's eyes. As her lips part to accept his tongue into her moist lip glossed mouth, the mood is perfect as the notorious boom box from the back seat of the Camry plays the soundtrack to this romantic moment. "Hello out there; Hotlanta; you're listening to the Quiet Storm with Dj Cool Cal." "This next song is a request from my AU Alum, Donnie; this goes out to his lady Chantel." "Enjoy this brother; it's one of my favorites." "Lover's here's I Belong to You;

by Brian McKnight." "I want you to myself." "I don't want to have to share you with nobody else." "I want you baby." "Come to me."

Donnie this is a lovely song. Shhh; just listen Chantel. He sticks his tongue back in her mouth to silence her and enjoy the moment. The air mattress squeaked continuously as their gyrating naked bodies pull the white sheets away from its surface. Do you love me D? Yes baby; I love you more than you'll ever know. Do you trust me? Yes Chantel; I trust you. Good; take off that condom. Are you sure baby? Yeah, we're engaged aren't we! Yes Ma'am; it's gone! Ummm, oh my goodness, now that really feels good baby. Oh you like that Chant? Shut up and keep going Mr.! Damn my bad; ok! Ha-ha! I'm sorry D; I didn't mean it like that. Yeah whatever; yes you did. Baby; it feels so good; that's all. Ummmm, good like that! Oh my God Donnie! I want to feel this feeling forever and ever, please don't stop Donnie. The lustful, chemical combustion between the lovers last for hours and hours on end until they both drift away into a deep sleep, both their bodies still connected to each other. As the Egyptian Musk dissipate and the Sun rise above the skyline, its beams cast among sleepy eyes from a night of intimate passion.

Knock-Knock! Knock-Knock! Knock-Knock! Donnie! Donnie! Donnie; get up! What is it baby? Someone is at the door. This time of morning! Knock-Knock! Knock-Knock! Hold on, hold on! Who in the hell can that be! Oh it's must be the movers baby; today is Saturday; our furniture is being delivered. Knock-knock! Dammit; I said I was coming; hold on! Put some clothes on Chantel. I am baby; I aint gone show off your goods. Ha-ha! Woman you're crazy.

Knock-knock! Yeah who is it? We have your furniture sir! D opens the door. Good Morning Sir; where did you want this bedroom set; we have the living room set coming up next. Oh just put it in the backroom bruh; it's empty. Ok no problem. Are you guys going to set it up for us; I don't have my tools with me. Yes; we can do that for you sir; no problem. Thanks man; I really appreciate it. You're welcome; just doing my job sir. Hey D; did you want some pancakes? What kind are you making? You know the kind you put syrup on; I'm not doing anything fancy Mr.!

I don't know Chantel; how do yall make pancakes in Detroit? Don't start with me Donnie or you can have some orange juice and toast! No Chant; I'm just playing; I want pancakes. Alright; don't play like that; you'll be hungry. Chantel! Yes Donnie! I love you baby. Umm-hmm; get away from me; you're getting plain buttermilk pancakes; nothing fancy. Come on baby; can I get some pecans in them. Boy you better stop dreaming; plus we aint got no pecans. Alright; I know, I was just joking. Excuse me sir; where did you want the couch and love seat. You can sit it all down in the living room; we'll decide later. Sure; no problem.

Donnie jumps hops on the kitchen counter and sits there watching Chant as she fixes breakfast. Ring-Ring! Is that my cell? Yeah I think it is D. Ring-Ring! Here you go! Thanks Chantel. Umm-hmm; you're off today so don't even think about it D. I know; I know. Hello! Hey Donnie! Hey; who is this? It's Tameka from HUD! Oh hey; what's up? I was calling to tell you that your company got approved. Oh that's great; thanks Tameka! Chantel stops whipping the pancake mix then looks up at Donnie with a side eye. Hey Tameka, can I call you Monday? Aww; I wanted to go out and celebrate; how about we grab a beer at the Shark bar later. Not today Tameka; I have a lot planned but thanks for the good news; I'll talk with you when I get back to work Monday. Ok Donnie; you're welcome; I'll bring the contracts by Monday. Sounds good; see you then Tameka.

Who was that? Oh that was just Tameka from the HUD office; she was calling to let me know that we got approved to renovate some HUD homes. And she couldn't tell you that Monday? I guess she was excited Chant. Excited my ass; don't have me come up to that office and regulate shit.

Whoa; calm down baby; it's nothing. Umm-hmm; it better not be nothing Donnie. An uncomfortable silence over-came the front room as the sound of the whisk got louder and louder while Chant stir the pancake batter. Donnie removes himself from the kitchen then walks to the bedroom to help the movers set up the bed. Hey fellas; yall need some help in there? Every muscle in his body told him to keep walking and not to turn around. He could feel Chantel's cold stare piercing through his back. Bam! Fix your own damn pancakes!

Batter flies all over the counter and kitchen sink. Chant! Why you do that! Bye Donnie; I'm going to the Waffle House! Baby; are you serious? Bye Donnie! Bam! The door slams as Chant leaves the apartment, dressed in pajamas and house shoes. Man this woman is crazy! Sir which way did you want the head board? Oh I'm coming man; I want it on the left side of the window. Alright fellas, let's turn it around, you heard the man.

Ok class, listen up; your assignments for the rest of the week will be to compare narratives between; Edgar Allen Poe and Ernest Hemingway. Each writer has certain distinctive styles which separates their work from the masses. But my challenge to you will be to find some similarities between the two. The entire classroom sighs with despair. Hold on; don't get discourage; do the research; you may be surprise at what you find. But Professor Q! Yes Cal; what is it?

I am a fan of Hemingway and I really don't see any comparison. Well that's your opinion; isn't it Cal? Yes Professor, it is. Listen guys, I want you to really dig deep into this assignment, your final grades depends on it. Uggghhh! The entire class sighs again. I know; you guys love me right. Well our time together is up for today, see you guys on Wednesday; I'm looking forward to hearing what you have to say. Class is dismissed! Hey Professor Q! Yes Joanne; what is it? Ashley and I were wondering if you could give us some extra help after our classes today. What do you guys need help with Joanne? Well, you know I really don't get all of this comparing writers and stuff. I don't read anything outside of these College text books! Ha-ha! I understand you there Joanne; I was the same way back in college.

So does that mean you will help us Professor Q? It depends, Ashley! Depends on what Professor? If you guys even make an attempt to do the work yourselves! Ring-Ring! Ring-Ring! Hold on girls; I need to take this. Ring-Ring! No wait a minute Professor! Joanne grabs Quentin by the hand, pulling it away from the phone, causing it to hit the floor. Ok girls just take a go at it first and if you still need help afterwards; I will consider it. Please help us Professor Q; we promise you won't regret it. Ashley places her left hand on his chest while Joanne continues holding his right hand. Try it first then I'll think about it. Ring-Ring! Ring-Ring! Ok girls; I have to go. Alright Professor; we'll see you Wednesday! Later girls; see you then!

Ring-Ring! Hey Professor! Yes Darrel; what is it? You got some smoke man? Excuse me! I'm saying; my Uncle said he went to school with you and that you had that Kush. Darrel; get out of my classroom son. Ring-Ring! But Professor Q! Darrel out! Come on Professor; why you holding back! Young man; I'm not telling you again! Alright, alright but you could've let me hold something, dang! Ring-Ring! Hello! Damn; it's about time! Hey Cynthia; how are you baby? I'm ok; what the hell is up with you? I just finished up my last class for this evening; why you say it like that? Because I heard you talking to those fast ass girls the first time I called. What are you talking about Cynt? Don't play stupid Q.

I'm serious baby! I'm referring to the ladies that ask you to help them after class. Oh; they just wanted some help with an assignment. Um-hmm, it sounded like they wanted more than that to me! Cynthia you're being paranoid, stop tripping. Yeah ok; Professor Q! Baby, I'm about to head to the house; did you want me to pick up something for dinner? Don't be changing the subject Mr.; we're going to discuss this at home. Well I'm stopping by Jr. Cricket's to get me a shrimp and Flounder basket; did you want anything? Yeah get me one too and pick up some Root beer. Root Beer! Yes; what's wrong with that Q? Nothing; I'm getting me a six pack; some real beer. That's cool; I'll drink one of those too. Ha-ha. Bye Cynthia; see you at home; what time are you getting off? I have to finish up with this one last case, so maybe an hour and a half. Cool; see you then baby. Alright Q, later!

Traffic is bumper to bumper on Covington Highway over in Decatur. Donnie floors the gas, runs the red light then whips the F-150 on a sharp right turn, causing the empty cups, cans and bottles to roll off the dash. Man yall need to clean out this damn truck! I know Unc; Thomas is responsible for that! What's wrong with your hands Donnie; you can clean it too nephew. Uncle Ted, I have more important things to do. Besides; all this mess is from Thomas and his crew, look at it! Micky D's bags, Sonic cups, Church's chicken boxes, it's all kinds of shit in here. Is all this your trash Thomas?

Well; the fellas left some of it in here too Unc. Just clean it up and where is this house already? It's just up here off of Wesley Chapel, Unc. Where; not that abandon thing with the windows all busted out! No the one next to it. Damn! That one is worse! How much are they asking for it Donnie? The owner want's $24,000 for it. Huh, for this piece of wood and bricks; go ahead and pull in the driveway let's take a look at it.

Donnie backs the F150 into the drive way of the abandon house, parking amidst the 6 foot tall grass and over grown bushes. I can tell yall right now, that this thing is maybe worth, 10,000 if that! Don't talk too soon Unc, let's look inside first. Thomas, trust me, I've been doing this long enough; the inside is going to be a disaster! Well let's go find out! Donnie turns off the engine then they all exit the truck. The tall grass hid the front porch and steps from view. Stray cats ran in and out of the domain amongst the piles of old clothes that lay on the porch. Shattered glass lay on the ground under the windows as the smell of urine reeks from the inside. Boys this place is a nightmare; I don't even want to go in. Come on Unc! Nah, you go first Donnie; lead the way!

Yellow paint; peeled away from the wooden columns and shutters that balanced the front of the house. Solid red bricks stood firm all around, showing some glimmer of hope. Donnie, Thomas then Ted enter through the doorless front door. Black, red and yellow graffiti mask the dirty white inside walls as old urine smelled carpet lay on the floor. God dang; it smells like a rest stop bathroom up in here. You might be right Unc; I'm not sure about this. Hold on Donnie; don't give up just yet; let's see if there is some value in this place first. But you said! I know what I said but everything has a price and the lower we get it, the more we can make. We are, in the real estate investment business; remember? So do you think we can make a profit off of it Unc? If we get it at the right price; we can Thomas.

Now let's do some adding and subtracting nephews; let me show you youngsters how it's done. The first thing that we look at is the location. It's off of a busy highway; Wesley Chapel, you got Krogers, Burger King, A shopping Center across the street. It's a few blocks from I-20 and it's in a section 8 zone too. That's guaranteed dollar signs right there boys. If we can get the owner to sell it to us for 10 maybe $12,000.00 we can sell it for double or three times that once we renovate it. Well how much do you think we can renovate it for Unc? I don't know Donnie, why don't you take a walk around the property, get an estimate then we can call the owner and negotiate. Alright I can do that, let me get my pad and pen out of the truck. Go ahead; Thomas and I will be checking out the plumbing and electrical work. Ok be right back.

So what's going on with Nadia nephew? She's ok Unc. No, I mean are you serious about her, the two of you looked pretty hunky dory on the cruise. Yeah I am; I'm taking it slow right now though. And why is that; you aint getting any younger. I know; but it's so many fine ass women in Atlanta; I don't want to get tied down. So what's going to happen when you start dating the next fine one? Man, I'll cross that bridge when I get to it. Well don't think that you will be able to run the streets forever Thomas, take a cue from your cousin Donnie and find a good girl to settle down with. Time waits for no man son. Alright Uncle Ted; I got it, now chill with the lecture. Beep-Beep! Why is Donnie blowing the horn? I don't know Thomas; let's go see what he wants. Beep-Beep!

Ted and Thomas make their way from the back of the house then up to the front room where they could see Donnie through the broken window panes. Damn; who the hell is that? Oh that's Tameka, Unc; the rep from

HUD. What she doing here; is this one of their properties? No Unc; I don't know why she's here. She sure is smiling hard up in Donnie's face; that's for sure. I see that Unc; maybe he called her. Well let's finish in here nephew, let them do their thing. Alright cool.

Hello Ms. Tameka! Hey Donnie! What brings you over? Oh I was just passing and noticed you standing by the truck. Is this one of your investments? We're looking at it for now, it's in pretty bad shape, so I'm not sure yet. Well; I can see it needs a lot of work. Yep, that's an understatement. Ha-ha! What's so funny Tameka? You standing there with that look on your face; it isn't that bad; I'm sure you can fix it then make a big profit off of it. That remains to be seen. Oh I'm sure you will; so when are we going to get that drink Sir? What drink Tameka? You know; to celebrate your new contracts with HUD. Oh, umm- What's wrong Donnie? Oh nothing, you look good in that red dress. Aww, thank you! You're welcome.

Tameka's flawless red skin, gleamed under the Decatur Sun light as her bright smile showed off her pretty white teeth, complimenting her big hazel eyes. Her toned calves demanded attention as she stood there bow leg in matching red open toe pumps. Passing cars slow and beep as they go by and catch a glimpse of her astounding beauty, all 5'6' and 115 pounds of it.

Well I have to be going Mr.; here's another card; call me when you are ready for that drink. Ok sure; thanks for stopping by. No problem; talk to you later Donnie! Yep! As she pulls away in her white company car; D could only think back on the other day when Chant stormed out of the apartment. He stood there until Tameka's car disappeared from view, shakes his head in shame, grabs the pad then walk back inside. Ok nephew, now that you're done flirting. Can we get back to work? It aint even like that Unc; I'll be back with that estimate. Um-hmm, I hear you playboy. The sound of broken glass, crunch underneath Ted and Thomas feet as they inspect the inside wiring and plumbing while Donnie walks the outside.

"What's up Queen City!" "It's Saturday night and we got the NFL Celebrity party going down at Club Crush!" "Our Panthers play the Cowboys tomorrow, so come out and join the pre-game party." "This is your boy Mr. Elavincent, on Charlotte's Number 1; Hip Hop and R&B station; Power 99."

Ring-Ring! Ring-Ring! Hello! Hey Q; what's up boy? Hey Marc; what's going on bruh? Man I'm in Charlotte, and boy; it's some bad ass women down here playa! Marcus; you just gone be a ho forever; huh? Q I aint married; I'm living the single life my brother; don't hate the player, hate the game. Yeah whatever; where's Harold? Oh they had curfew; he's in the room sleep. That's where your ass needs to be.

Nah I'm sitting in this girls living room that I met at the mall; she's bad as hell too Q! Then why are you calling me? She's in the shower; I had to tell somebody bruh; this girl is fine! Marcus you're pitiful- Yo; I have to go; hear she comes! Click! The fresh smell of dove soap, fill the air as the steam seep through the bathroom door. Beads of water roll down her naked body as she walks towards him. A vision of a smooth, flawless, Hershey's kiss would describe her best. Sweet to taste but yet so deadly if consumed by the unexpected, a diabetic. Marcus a connoisseur of woman couldn't resist. The temptation was too strong, so strong in fact that it blinded his vision to the picture hanging over the fire place, the one on the table by the couch and most of all the size 19 Jordan's sitting by the door. The only thing on his mind was the taste of her sweet black cherry.

Damn baby; you're looking sexy as all out doors; bring that ass to poppa! Thank you

Marc; be gentle with me; I'm fragile. Girl; the last thing I want to do his hurt you. Come here! Marc gets up from the couch, grabs her by the hand then pulls her close. Umm, you're soft girl. The name is Chasity; Marcus; did you forget? Nah baby; you smell so good; let me get comfortable! Here; let me help you. Chasity reaches down to unzip his jeans as he removes his shirt then kicks off his shoes.

Umm; nice six pack there! Thank you; now come here, you sexy chocolate thing. Their bodies embrace from the sure attraction that they both share for that moment. As their tongues dance with one another, the couple surrenders to the couch; Chasity underneath, Marcus on top. Oh my; you're so hard! Yeah you like that, don't you baby. Umm-hmm, do you have a condom? No; for what! I just had my check up last week and all is good; just relax while I put this snake in you. But- Ohhhh, yes! Yes you feel so good right now, oh my God! Cling! Did you here that? Hear what girl? I thought I heard something. Nah, you're hearing things Chasity. Ummm, ok don't stop; it feels so good. Cling! In and out, he went as she moved up and down to his rhythm. Cling! Marc I heard it again! I didn't hear anything, come on, don't stop now girl! The front door swings open, Marcus shouts out while looking surprised. What the fuck; oh shit! Marc jumps up as a tall 6'8" silhouette figure; move hastily towards him. Help! Rape! Rape! What bitch, I aint rape you! Rape! Rape! Baby; get him! He raped me!

Click-Click! Whoa shit; hold on player put down the gun; I aint rape your girl. Look I can prove it; we met at the mall and she asked me to come over- He's a liar; I don't know this man; he rape me! Click-Click! Baby no! Please don't kill him; I don't want you to go to jail. I'll call the police; just hold him there! What; don't kill him! You just said he raped your ass and you don't want me to kill him? No I'm calling the cops now. Hold on Chasity; tell the truth girl; I aint rape you!

Come on bruh; just put down the gun and let me go! Shut up nigga before I put a cap in your ass. Hello 911; what is your emergency? Yes a man just broke into my place and raped me! Ok Ma'am; calm down; is he still there? Yes my fiancé has him at gun point.

Alright just stay calm and don't shoot him; the police are on the way. Thank you; tell them to please hurry! They will be there soon Ma'am! Ok thank you so much! You're welcome! Well what did they say Chasity; are they coming? Yeah they are on the way! Yo this is fucked up man, you can let me go! Shut up nigga; you aint going no damn where! Oh shit; I know you man; don't you play for the Hornets? Shut up before I shoot you fool! Man my bad; look my cousin plays for the Cowboy's; I'm his manager; you know how these groupie girls are bruh. I swear I aint rape your girl; she gave me the ass playa! Clunk! Thump! Baby; why you hit him with the pistol?

That dumb ass wouldn't be quiet; he aint dead; he's just unconscious. Now I better not find out that he was telling the truth; if so I'm putting these 19's up your ass! He rape me; I aint know that fool. Gosh; why would I lie about something like that! Fuck what you talking about; you heard what I said Chasity!

Darkness cast upon his eye lids as the sirens got louder and louder. Marc lay unconscious as the cop's radio for a bus to roll him away. A few bumps, turns and injections later, he awakes to a cold concrete bench, tan cement walls, handcuffed to the handicap rail in front of the desk down at Charlotte Mecklenburg booking. Hello there sir; I see you finally decided to join us! Hey man; why am I cuffed to this damn rail and where am I? You're in jail son; you raped a girl tonight! Officer I aint rape that bitch man; I swear. Yeah, yeah we know! You're innocent! Yeah man; I am. Shut up with that excuse; we've heard it all before. Here; you get one call; make it count! The officer hands Marcus the phone to make a call. Damn, thanks! Yep and hurry up!

Ring-Ring! Hello; Thanks for calling the Carlton at West Lake; how may I help you? Yes can I have room 349 please? Sure hold one moment. Thanks! Ring-Ring! Ring-Ring! Hello! Hey bruh, you up? Yeah Marcus; what's up? Man I'm downtown. So what shawty; I need to rest; I aint coming out. No Harold; in jail man. Marcus what in the Hell are you doing in jail! That ho said I raped her, because her NBA playing boyfriend walked in on us. Marc you can mess up a wet dream; I told you stop whoring around so much. You got a bail yet? Nah bruh, can you call Donnie and have him ask Chantel to get me out; I need a lawyer.

I don't know Marcus, this is Charlotte and I don't think they have a license to practice law here. Damn; that's not good; can you call him anyway? Yeah I got you; when can you call back? I don't know; I'm in holding right now; they're going to process me in a minute. Alright shawty hang tight; we'll get you out. Thanks bruh; I appreciate it. Yep; keep your damn dick in your pants next time nigga. Harold don't rub it in. "Alright times up; hang up that phone!" Later Harold; I have to go! Bye Marc!

Ring-Ring! Hello! Hey Donnie; what's up my brother? Harold what's going on player; you got a game tomorrow shouldn't you be sleep or something? Man I was but oh boy called me from jail. What; from jail! What did Marcus do now? This fool was boning some chick at her place when her man walked in on them. Wow; are you serious? Yeah shawty and that aint the bad part! Damn; what else? She called rape on his ass and now he's locked up here in

Charlotte. See; I told that fool to stop whoring around so much. Well he needs a lawyer; can you ask Chantel to help him? Yeah; I'll call her right now Harold; get some rest player we got this. Thanks D; talk to you later. Yeah Harold, no problem man!

Ring-Ring! Hello thanks for calling The Hudson Law Firm; how can we help you? Yes, I would like to speak with Chantel please; this is Donnie. Sure Donnie; hold on a minute. Thanks! You're welcome; I'm connecting you now. Ring-Ring! Hi; this is Chantel. Hey baby; what you doing? Hello D; I'm working on a case; what's up? Well Marcus whoring ass is stuck in Charlotte. What do you mean by stuck? He got locked up! For what; what was the charge? Apparently this girl said he raped her after her boyfriend walked in on them having sex. Oh my God; that is serious; are you sure they charged him with that D? That's what Harold said. So I'm calling you to see if you guys can help him? Donnie my license is only good for Georgia and so is Cynthia's. Damn, how about your boss? Hold on baby; let me ask her. Ok no problem.

Hey Latrice! Yes Chantel; what is it? Can you practice law in Charlotte? Yes I can; why do you ask? Our friend Marcus has been charged with rape and he needs a lawyer. Wow; did you say rape? Yes Ma'am! Well did he do it Chantel? No, the girl called rape after her boyfriend walked in on them. When did they lock him up; has he seen a judge yet? It just happened a few hours ago and no he hasn't seen a judge yet.

Alright; you guys take over here at the office for me; I'm going to head over to the airport and catch the 7 O'clock flight to Charlotte. Cynthia; call our travel agent and book me a first class seat. Chantel, tell Donnie that I will be there in a few hours and not to worry. Thanks a bunch Latrice; we really appreciate it. Hey that's what we're here for, now get back to work; we have other clients to attend to; I got this one. Cynthia you called yet? Doing it now Ma'am! Ok see you guys sometime tomorrow; I'm headed to the airport. Ok Latrice! Chantel places the phone back to her ear.

Hey baby; Latrice is flying to Charlotte tonight; she's going to handle it. Cool; tell her I said thank you baby! I will; just call Harold back and let him now. Alright I will! Do it now Donnie; I will see you later; I have work to do. Ok; love you; see you when you get home. Yep; love you too D!

Girl it was only a matter of time before something like this was going to happen; Marcus is trifling. I know Cynthia but I don't think he raped her. So what if he didn't this serves him right; he needs to stop being such a man whore. Well look at it this way girl; at least our men have good solid careers going and are not out there with him, whoring around. Amen to that Chant; Amen to that.

That's more reason to keep a close eye on them though Cynthia. Women are no good; if they see you with something special; they will go after it. You're right Chant; I called Q the other day while he was about to get off work and the phone kept ringing and ringing then all of a sudden I heard voices. What kind of voices? Two women talking in the background! What were they saying Cynt? They were asking Q if he could help them with some project after class. I can tell he was uncomfortable from the tone of his voice but these bitches were aggressive. I mean; they kept on and on, until he eventually got them to leave.

I couldn't see what was going on girl but it sure sounded funny. Cynthia aint no telling; these girls nowadays will do anything to get to the top. Yeah I know; that's why I put it on him that night. Girl when Q walked in the door; I was in my Vicky secret's; red outfit and smelling good; shit he's still talking about that night. What; you put it on him Cynt! Umm; better ask somebody. Ha-ha. Cynthia you're a mess!

I would have done the same thing! There's just one girl I have to keep my eye on around Donnie though. I'm not sure if it's something but you can never tell. He got this call Saturday morning while the movers were there. Some chick named Tameka called to congratulate him on some HUD contracts or something like that. I couldn't hear the whole conversation but D cut it short and got back to business. He didn't say anything else about her but bitches are slick; I need to meet this Tameka so I can see what she's working with; you know sluts go crazy when they can smell money. Girl it's probably nothing; Donnie loves your ass; look at that ring in your finger! Yeah I know; aint it pretty! Ha-ha! Chantel; stop it! Don't show off.

8. Drama.

Hey cuz I just got off the phone with our realtor; guess what? What Thomas; don't play; spill the beans cuz. She sold two properties yesterday; at list price! Quit fooling around Thomas; say word! Word up Donnie; she just hung up; we made $185,000.00 yesterday! Yeah baby; now that's how you make money T! We need to go celebrate though Donnie! There will be time for that later; we have to get started on that property on Wesley Chapel. What, that piece of junk we looked at the other day. Yeah man; I bought it for $11,000. Donnie that's a lot of work, do you think we can profit? Hell yeah cuz; just don't get too crazy when you go to Lowes; we got a $13,000 budget on this one. 13; you mean 30! No Thomas; 13 and don't go over. Knock-Knock! Hello anybody here! A soft female voice interjects and interrupts their conversation. Hey fellas; how are you guys doing? Hey Tameka; what's going on Miss? Hi Donnie; I just stopped by to drop off this bottle of champagne. Cool; thanks Tameka, you didn't have to do this. Oh it's nothing; my girlfriend told me that she sold two of your properties yesterday and I just wanted to congratulate you guys on a good job. The homes you remodeled looks really nice; you're going to make a lot of money in the A.

Well thanks for the compliment Tameka; we try to make them as perfect as possible. And they are Thomas. Well I just wanted to drop this off to you guys; my girls and I are having drinks over at Pappadeux's after work; you two should come by. Thanks for the offer Tameka; we'll try to stop by if we have time. Ok that's great Donnie; call me if you can make it. The first drinks are on me; have a good day. You too Tameka; later!

Donnie; she's fine as hell cuz; you better watch out. What you mean; by watch out, Thomas? Man that lady likes you cuz; first; she shows up at the work site, now she's bringing you gifts at the office. Tameka wants to give you that cookie and you're not saying or doing anything to stop it. You know Chantel is crazy; don't let Tameka catch no ass whipping. Thomas you tripping; it aint nothing like that! Alright D; don't say I didn't warn you. I aint worrying about that Thomas; I love Chant; I aint even thinking about cheating! That might be so but I'm just telling you how it looks from the outside. I'm your family and you know I wouldn't tell you anything to hurt you. Well thanks for looking out for me Thomas; I'll try to be more careful around Tameka; so she doesn't get the wrong idea.

Hell; we can nip that in the bud today D! How so? Let's call Nadia and Chant and invite them to go over to Pappadeux's with us tonight. That way Tameka and her girls can meet Nadia and Chant and you won't have to worry about her making any more passes at you. Shit I'm down; we can call them after we finish this paperwork. Alright bet! This better not back fire Thomas! Man it won't!

Luxury cars park along the curb while some cruise up and down Ocean Boulevard as Tamara sit pool side, enjoying her fresh Italian bread, dipping it in her olive oil, oregano season based sauce while she waits for her main course. The warm ocean breeze blowing across her face; held a faint smell of sea water as it continuously blew across the sand, the green grass, busy boulevard then across her table. A mixture of Hip-Hop, R&B and Cuban music electrify the atmosphere from the medley of patrons riding and enjoying the Miami scenery.

Ring-Ring! Hello! Hey baby! Hey Marcus; I'm surprised you called. Yeah I just wanted to hear your voice; I don't have long to talk.

Aww; that's nice of you, why are you in a rush Marc? Aint nothing Tam; I'm here in Charlotte because Harold has a game tonight. Oh ok; how do you like your new job? It's cool; I'm doing a lot of traveling. Umm; how many girlfriends you got now? Baby you know you're the only one I'm in love with. Marcus; don't sell me that BS; I know what time it is. I'm just having fun with those girls Tam; aint nothing for you to worry about. Do you at least use a condom Marcus? "Your call will end in 60 seconds!" What the hell was that! Huh? What was that Marcus? Oh that was nothing; I have to go Tam; I'll call you later! Click! Tam takes her phone away from her ear then looks at it, still confused as to what just happened.

Ma'am; here's your rack of lamb and garlic, mashed potatoes. Ummm. Thank you; it looks so good! You're welcome; can I get you anything else? Yes; bring me a bottle of Merlot, please. Sure; not a problem; I'll be right back! Thanks!

Ring-Ring! Hello! Hey sis; where are you? Hey Nadia; I'm in Miami having lunch at my favorite Italian Restaurant before my ship leaves; what's up? Girl I wish I was there with you, anyway I called to tell you about Marc. What about him; I was just talking to him. What; did he call you? Yeah just a few minutes ago! Oh, I was calling to tell you that he got locked up in Charlotte because a girl called rape on him. That sneaky bastard; he told me he was in Charlotte and couldn't talk long then this operator came on the line; saying the call would end in 60 seconds. Ha-ha! Tamara you're my sister but sometimes you can be so lost. Whatever Nadia; I'll call you tomorrow, I have to finish eating.

Here's your wine Ma'am! Thanks baby! Tam! What girl; I have to eat! You need to let his ass go; he's only going to bring you down with him. It aint that serious Nadia; it's just a sex thing. Well; make sure that dog wears protection! Yeah; I aint no dummy sis! How are things with you and Thomas? Oh I'm so glad he moved to Atlanta; I've never been so happy. Well that's good for you sis; I'm glad that you are happy. Thank you sis; I'm meeting Sylvia in a few hours for drinks she's upset that Marc is locked up. Does she know about you and him yet? No she does not Nadia; and you better not tell her. I'm not going to say anything; it's not my place but you should. For what; it aint her business!

She's our friend Tam, that's why! Nadia I don't have time for this right now; my ship leaves port in a hour and I need to eat. Can we talk about this later? Sure, call me when you get to your next stop. Ok I will; bye Nadia! Bye Tam!

Ring-Ring! Hello! Hey Nadia; I'm pulling up at Slice now; how long before you get here. I'm on the way now Sylvia; I should be there in a few minutes. Ok I'll get us a table and a bottle of wine; we have a lot to talk about. Alright

Sylvia; see you in a bit. Ring-Ring! Damn; why is this girl calling me again! Ring-Ring! Yeah what is it Sylvia! Baby; it's Thomas! Oh hey baby; I'm sorry; how are you? I'm good Nadia; what are you doing after work? I'm going to meet Sylvia at Slice right now; she's upset at the whole Marcus situation and wants to vent.

Ok I understand that; go be there for your friend. Why you ask baby? Oh; me and Donnie wanted to meet you and Chant over at Pappadeux's when we got off. Aww; I'm sorry baby but I already told Sylvia that I was on the way. It's cool Nad; I'll let Donnie know; we'll be ok. Are you sure Thomas? Yeah, we'll be ok. Alright love you baby; see you when I get home. Yep; later Nadia!

Welcome to Slice Ma'am; what can I get you to drink. Hey; can I get a glass of your Riesling? Sure; will you be joining us at the bar? Nah my girlfriend is meeting me here; I'm going to grab a table. Ok no problem; did you want me to bring her a glass also? As a matter of fact; just bring a bottle of Riesling. Got you covered; I'll bring it over to your table and here are two menus for you to look over. Thank you!

Joyous voices occupy the air as several patrons, eat, laugh and drink among each other. The sleek wood finish bar and matching table tops add to the neighborhood ambiance as southern rap tunes play in the background.

Sylvia sit waiting patiently alone, admiring couples and groups of patrons enjoying each-others company. A smile appears upon her face as she see Nadia walking pass the large picture window at the front of Slice. She stands to her feet and happily waves her over as she enters. Hey Nad; over here! With a smile she waves back then makes her way over. Hey girl; how you feeling; did you order yet? Just a bottle of wine; sit down girl; I'm so happy to see you. I'm glad to see you too Sylvia; how's the interior decorating business going. It's going great; I'm about to hire some help; I've been so damn busy.

 Hello ladies; here's your Riesling! Thank you sir! You're welcome; are you ladies ready to order? Not yet honey; I just got here; give us a minute. No problem Ma'am; I'll be back in a few. Honey you can call me Nadia; I feel so old when you say Ma'am! Ha-ha! Ok Nadia; I'll be back in a few ladies. Alright we'll be here! Ha-ha! Sylvia you're crazy; now what's on your mind; why you call me all upset? And don't tell me it's Marcus. Yeah; unfortunately it is; Latrice called me and told me what happened. Did you know she was still in Charlotte; they're holding his bond hearing back for some reason. Oh lord; what else has that boy done? I don't know Nadia; we're only friends but I think I've started catching feelings for him. But why!

I wish I had the answer to that question girl; I'm over here worried about his whore ass and he aint even call me. Umm! It sounds like you're the only one with feelings here Sylvia. Maybe he hasn't had a chance to use the phone yet. Girl stop making excuses; you know that boy can use the phone; at least once a day. If I were you; I'll leave his ass alone. Hell; you're not gone want him no more anyway, once he gets out of jail. Nadia the boy is in jail, not prison and he's only been there a few days; let's not get carried away now. Well; I'm just saying; that's all.

You need to stop being negative; Latrice is a great Attorney; I'm sure she will have him out soon. Speaking of Latrice; what did she say about the case Sylvia? She said that the girl only called rape because she got caught by her man. Marcus claims it was consensual. Umm, umm, umm. And this is the guy that you're sitting here sobbing over; girl you need to go decorate some houses are something; Marc is a whore and will probably be one until the day he die. I love him like a brother but the truth is the truth honey.

Yeah you're probably right; enough of my drama; how are things with you and Thomas? Syl; I've never been happier; he's been treating me like an angel. Aww; that's so sweet; I'm so happy for you. Thank you! Are you guys getting serious? It's still new but things are good; I won't complain. I hear that girl; take your time. Umm-hmm; I aint in no rush; I'm still a mother first. Excuse me ladies; are you ready to order? Oh damn; we're just running our mouths, we didn't even look at the menu! I tell you what; let's just keep it simple; why don't you bring us a medium pizza. Sure Nadia; what kind did you guys want?

Sylvia; I want some pine apples and Canadian bacon on mine; how about you girlfriend? That sounds good; make one side pine apples with Canadian bacon and the other with black olives; Italian sausage and green peppers. Ok ladies, enjoy your wine! I'll go put that order in. Thanks Honey! So how's Tamara doing these days Nadia? Funny you asked; I was just on the phone with her before I got here. She's doing great; she's in Miami now about to leave on another cruise. Gees; I want her life; that girl stays on the go! Yep that's Tam; travel lista! Ha-ha! Is that what you call her Nad? Ha-ha! Yep!

Oh girl; I almost forgot! Forgot what Sylvia? I have tickets to the comedy show tonight; you want to come with me? Sure why not; I have to call Thomas and let him know but I would love to join you girl. Great, then it's all settled; I can't wait to get some of those lemon pepper wings! Sylvia your ass is going to get fat! Keep it up! Nah; I'll go run a few miles in the morning and I'll be fine. Now that's something that I aint about to do child. What? Run, that's what! Ha-ha! Nadia you're crazy! No I got good sense; I just smoke too much. Child I'll be huffing and puffing before I get through the first mile. Ha-ha! Stop it; you're making my stomach hurt! I'm serious Syl!

Ring-Ring! Thanks for calling the Hudson law Firm; please hold! Ring-Ring! Thanks for calling the Hudson Law Firm; please hold! Oh; I'm sorry Ma'am; I didn't see you standing there; welcome to the Hudson Law Firm; how may I help you? Yes I had an appointment to see Ms. Chantel. Sure; have a seat and I'll get her for you. Thank you. Oh you're welcome.

Ring-Ring! Hello this is Chantel! Ms. Chantel; you have a young lady here to see you. Thank you, did you get her name. No but I can! Great can you do that for me? Sure hold a sec; excuse me Ma'am; can I get your name? Yes it's Monica; I spoke with her last week about the D.U.I. Thanks so much! Chantel; it's Monica; she says she spoke with you last week about a D.U.I. Oh ok; I'll be up in a second. Alright; I'll let her know and you also have a call holding on line two. Thanks hun! You're welcome! Ok Ma'am, you can have a seat; she will be with you momentarily. Great thanks! You're welcome; did you want a bottle of water or something? No; I'm fine, thanks. Sure.

Ring-Ring! Hello! Hey Latrice; are you busy; Monica is here. Hey Chantel; I have time; I'm just sitting in this damn hotel room; looking over Marcus's case. Ok great; did you want to listen in? Yeah just put me on speaker. Alright; it will only take a minute; I'm going to get her now. Ok Chantel.

Hi Monica; I'm Chantel; nice to meet you! Hello Ms. Chantel; nice to meet you as well! Monica if you would gather your things and follow me; we can get started. Sure! Monica I have my boss; Ms. Latrice on the phone; she's going to listen in on our consultation. You don't mind; do you? No Ma'am; that's fine. Great; just have a seat right here in front of my desk please. Did you want a drink of water, coffee, Tea? No' I'm good.

Alright; I guess we'll get started then; Latrice are you there? Yes Chantel; I'm here! Hello Monica! Hi; Ms. Latrice. So Monica; start from the beginning and tell us what happened that night and take your time; we don't want to leave anything out. Ok Chantel; it was my graduation night from Spelman. Me and several of my friends we're celebrating over at a bar, not too far from campus. One thing led to another; drink after drink and before you knew it; the night was turning to day. I thought I was feeling pretty well; considering the amount of alcohol I had consumed. I remember getting in my car; leaving the bar then waking up in Grady Memorial Hospital.

That's when I saw the Atlanta police standing over my bed and they gave me the bad news that I was involved in a head on collision with another car and that the driver didn't survive.

Monica's voice starts to tremble as tears roll down her cheeks. It's ok Monica; accidents happen; we'll do what we can to help you.

Her voice now cracking with fear, she attempts to speak once more. I never meant to hurt anyone; it was supposed to be a joyous occasion. I am the first of five sisters to graduate college. Now, now, now, my life is over! You're still young Monica and besides, we don't have all of the facts of the case yet. So don't give up hope just yet baby. But Ms. Latrice; my brother had to put up his house to post my bond; I got my entire family into this mess. I understand why you feel that way Monica but let Ms. Chantel and I do our jobs. That's why your Father hired us, now go home with your family and get some rest; we will start working on your case tonight and stay close to your phone; we will probably be calling you later. Ok, thank you guys so much for taking my case; I am so sorry that this happened; if I could change anything; I would have stayed home that night.

You're welcome Monica; we got it from here. Ok Ms. Chantel; bye Ms. Latrice! Bye baby! Come on Monica; I'll walk you out. Chantel; I'll call you later! Ok Latrice! Alright Monica; get some rest and remember to stay by your phone; we'll probably be in the office late working on your case. I will.

Wow; what was all of that about Chant? That's the young lady that called about the D.U.I.; she hit and killed someone on her graduation night, a few days ago. Aw; that's so sad; are we taking her case? Yeah Cynt; I'm starting on it tonight; are you helping? Girl I still have some depositions to do; so no! Come on Cynthia; don't be like that; I would help you! Only if I finish my work then maybe I'll think about it. Well I'll buy us some Krispy Kreme's if you do! Umm, umm, umm. Look at you bribing me; that's against the law;

Attorney! Ha-ha. Come on Cynt! Only if there hot Chant! Yes! Thank you girl! Umm-hmm. Ring-Ring! Get your phone! Ring-Ring!

Hello! Hey baby; what's up? Hey Donnie; I was just bribing Cynthia with some Krispy Kreme's. Bribing her for what? For help with this D.U.I. case I just took on. Oh, so does that mean that you are working late again? Yeah probably a few hours; why what are you doing? You got a surprise for me or something? Nah; I was calling to tell you that me and the fellas are meeting over at Club Nikki's to watch female boxing tonight. Alright; don't be giving those strippers my money either!

Chant; now you know I'm going to tip something now. Ok $20 that's it! Girl you tripping; I can't have no fun with $20! Alright 40 then! Bye Chantel; gone back to work; I'll see you at home later! Oh don't try and hang up now mister; I'm not done talking. Bye

Chant; I love you! Donnie! Donnie! Click! Uh! I know he didn't just hang up on me! Wait until he gets home; these legs are going to be closed. Oooh Chantel; don't be like that; you know he's gone want some after leaving that club. Umm-hmm; I know Cynt; that's why he aint getting none; gone hang up on me. Girl they just having fun; don't make a big deal out of it. I'm just joking Cynthia! Yeah bitch; whatever, you serious! Oh no, you didn't! Just for that, you're not getting any Krispy Kreme's. Hold on now; don't be playing with the Krispy Kreme's. Ha-ha!

Thomas, Ted and Q sit in the F-150 as Donnie drives down Stewart Ave, passing the Prostitutes, hustlers and drug dealers. He makes a right turn into 1785 Stewart Ave then parks up front by the door. The October weather, on the brink of fall gave way to a comfortable night. Patrons sparingly enter the black and blue building as a few girls here and there walk pass them with small roller suit cases. Loud music sounded off, every time the entrance door opened as the bright neon sign above the entrance that read Club Nikki; illuminate the parking lot.

Alright fellas; we're here; whatever you don't want to spend; leave it in the truck. Donnie; you must be crazy; didn't you see who was walking up and down Stewart avenue; I aint leaving nothing in this truck cuz! Thomas; stop tripping this aint no worse than Dade County! D; forget what you're talking; I know folks in Dade; nobody knows me here and your black ass either; tell em unc! Man no one is coming on this lot to mess with that truck, don't you see all these security guards out here; both of you need to stop that non sense and let's go look at some ass! Ha-ha! Yeah that's right Ted; tell them knuckle heads.

Quentin; stop instigating! Donnie your unc has a point though bruh. Man whatever; let's just go in; they got that female boxing tonight!

Ya'll just miss the whole damn point; don't be asking me to borrow no money tomorrow either! Nephew; I don't need your money. I'm not talking to you unc; I'm talking to Thomas and Q over there. Oh ok!

The fellas finally make their way up to the entrance. "Welcome to Club Nikki gentlemen; it will be $20 each tonight." Here you go baby; I'm paying for four! "Ok; how did you want your change back?" Nah you keep it baby; that 20 is for you! "Aw thanks babe!" You're welcome baby! Thanks Unc! Yep; you got the first round Thomas! Alright no problem; I got that.

"Welcome to Fight Night gentlemen; it's Tuesday night in the A and that means it's time for female boxing!" "It's yo boy Chap on the tables and you know we are about to get it in." "So get your drink on; tip the girls, get some damn dances and get ready for the hottest Tuesday night in the A baby!"

An array of chairs line the walls with several more rows lined evenly in front of them, creating more rows. Blue, yellow, orange and red balloons hang through-out the club. A mixture of men and women patrons, enjoy table dances and drinks of their choice as the club continue to fill. Sounds of Outkast, blast threw the speakers and bounce, off the walls as sexy shake dancers entertain the crowd. An empty boxing ring sit in the center of the club as on lookers await the announcement for the first bout.

"Me and you, your momma and your cousin too" "Rollin down the strip on vogues" "Comin up slammin Cadillac doz."

Man there's some fine ass dancers working tonight! Slow your roll Donnie; you know Chantel's crazy ass is jealous. Thomas don't even go there bruh. You know it's the truth D! Quentin you don't have room to talk, Cynthia's way worse than Chant bruh! Both of you need to stop worrying about your women and enjoy this scenery in Nikki's. That's the problem with you young guns; don't know how to have fun. I agree with you there unc; I'm with you. Ted pauses then looks at Thomas.

Thomas; what are you waiting on to get those drinks, nephew? And make your cousin's a double, this might be one of his last nights with the boys as a single man. Uncle Ted; we aint even set no date yet; don't go there. Well she has a ring on her finger; that's enough right there Donnie. She aint like that unc; I'm still going to be able to hang out. Alright; if you say so Donnie; Thomas, get him a double like I said.

I got it Unc, what you guys want? Let me get a goose and cranberry T! Alright Q! What about you Donnie? Make that double a crown and coke cuz. Cool, and you unc? Bring me some of that bumpy face nephew with some Oj. What's Bumpy face? Gin nephew; gin. Oh, why you call it bumpy face? Because the face of the gin bottle is bumpy! Damn, that is right; it sure is unc! Thomas, just hurry up; we'll be over by the wall getting some dances. Ok Unc; yall get me a girl too!

Donnie; Ted and Quentin turn away from Thomas then walk over to the row of chairs by the wall. How much are dances in here Q? $5 Donnie! Shit that's all; I'm about to get me at least 20! Boy Chantel is gone whip your ass; don't go home smelling like perfume Donnie. Quentin I got a change of clothes in the truck bruh. Ha-ha! Man your ass crazy! Damn D! Look at that fine ass redbone right there. Yeah, she is straight Q!

Hey baby; come over here and give us a dance. Ted reaches in his jeans pocket, pulls out a stack of cash then waves the sexy redbone over. Hey poppa; what's your name? I'm Ted; what's yours baby? I'm Candice hun; can I dance for you? Yep, go ahead and do your thing sexy. Umm, umm, umm. Girl you are fine as all out doors- Ring-Ring! You better get your phone poppa! Ring-Ring! Just keep dancing Candice; I'll get it in a sec! Ring-Ring! Ted leans back in his chair and flips open his cell phone while constantly watching Candice as she continues to dance there in front of him then answers his mobile. Ring-Ring! Hello! Hey babe; what you doing? Hey Latrice; I'm at the bar with Quentin and my two nephews. Oh ok, that music is loud, can you go somewhere quiet so I can talk to you. Nah baby; it's too crowded in here; I might lose my seat.

Well; I was calling to let you know that I'm still in Charlotte; Marcus finally has a bail hearing in the morning; I should be back in ATL tomorrow night. Alright; get some rest and let me know if you need some money for his bail. That's sweet of you babe but Harold says he's going to take care of it. Hell that's even better; well call me when you get in tomorrow; we can go get some dinner. Ok Ted;

have fun with the guys; see you tomorrow. Alright Latrice; later!

As the music plays, at least 30 naked women seem to groove in unison to the beat all at once. Piles of dollar bills fell to the floor while guys and girls alike enjoyed an Atlanta treasure. Smoke; now fill the air along with the hundreds of people that occupy Nikki's as the ring announcer enters the center of the ring, awaiting his first two contestants.

"Ladies and Gentlemen, it's almost that time!" Here you go Donnie; one double crown and coke. Unc this is yours and Q that's you! Thanks Thomas, grab a seat boy and get in on this. Shiiit; I'm about to Quentin. Damn, these women are fine as hell. Alright nephew, don't fall in love with these strippers now. Unc I'm from Miami; this aint nothing. Yeah ok, but this is Atlanta cuz! Donnie shouts; as all four fellas lean back in their seats, drinks in one hand, money in the other while dancers surround them.

9. Close Circle.

"All rise for Charlotte, Mecklenburg court's; Honorable; Judge Hawthorne!" Thank you Bailiff! You're welcome judge! You all may be seated! District Attorney Smalls, what's the first case? Good Morning your honor! Morning! Our first bond hearing is for Ms. Latrice's client, Marcus; she's here from Atlanta, your honor. Good morning Ms. Latrice; it's been a few years since you've been in my court room. Yes it has; Judge Hawthorne. Well good to see you; and what did you have to say about your client?

Your honor; this is his first time ever being in a court room and I want to ask if he could be released on his own recognizance? Ms. Latrice; Marcus is charged with Rape; that's a very serious charge. I agree judge but it's simply a misunderstanding; I can assure you that the sex was consensual. Save that for trial Ms. Latrice; I'm setting bail at $300,000.00. But your honor; my investigators- Ms. Latrice; unless you want to leave your client here until trial; I suggest you take this bond and leave my court room. Excuse me Judge! Marcus; be quiet! No Latrice; I can speak for myself! Yes Marcus; did you have something to say? Yes your honor! What is it son? Don't take it out on my attorney; I'll pay the bond but I'm innocent and we're going to prove it! That's fine son; your bail is set; the officers will take you to out processing. Have a good day Ms. Latrice! Thanks your honor!

Marcus I'll be waiting for you across the street at the Crown Plaza, in the lobby. Ok Latrice; did Harold give you some cash? Yeah I already have a bondsman waiting to post bail; he's waiting on my call. Alright thanks, see you in a few. Ok Marcus time to go; you can speak with your attorney later. The officer walks around the table and grabs Marc by the arm.

Man, don't be pulling on my arm like that; I can walk! You keep running your mouth and we'll make sure these release papers get lost for a few days. Oh my bad officer; I was just joking! Yeah that's what I thought, now keep walking.

Ring-Ring! Hello; thanks for calling the Hudson Firm; this is Chantel speaking! Hey Chant; how are things at the office? Everything is cool Latrice; did Marc get a bail hearing? Yeah, the judge gave him a $300,000.00 bond. Damn! I know right; anyway he'll be out in a few though. Cool; I'll let Donnie know. Well I was just calling to update you; I'm taking Marcus over to the Coffee Cup for some dinner, so we can discuss his case then I'm catching the last flight back to ATL. Alright tell Marc I said hi and we'll see you at the office tomorrow. Ok Chant; good bye!

Latrice places her cell back in her purse; stops at the corner then waits for the crosswalk sign. The cool brisk, North Carolina air had a different feel to it than it did back home in Georgia. Downtown traffic flowed evenly with no congestion while people seem to take their time walking to and from their destinations. As the walk signal illuminates she makes her way across the street and into the Crown Plaza Hotel where she was residing, far from her usual place; The Westin.

Fresh brewing coffee and sliced oranges scent up the hotel entrance as she walk through the sliding doors. Good afternoon Ms. Latrice; did you still want us to bring your bags down? Afternoon and yes I did sir but not right this minute; I'm waiting on a friend but I will call the front desk when it's time. Ok let us know when you're ready. I will!

Latrice walks over to the lobby area and takes a seat by the large window; gazing at traffic as cars roll by. In the distance, she notices Marcus exiting the Jailhouse, just across the street from the justice building. With his confident swagger, he makes his way towards the corner, stands at the light then starts chatting with two women who also were waiting there at the crosswalk. As the light change and he walks toward the Crown Hotel, Latrice pulls out her cell to make a call.

Ring-Ring! Hello, thanks for calling State Taxi; how can I help you? Yes can I have a taxi over at the Crown Plaza Hotel, off McDowell over by the courthouse? Sure Ma'am; what's your destination? I'm going to the Coffee Cup on Clarkson off of West Morehead St. Ok Ma'am we have a unit in the area; they will be there in 2 minutes. That's great; thanks! You're welcome; thanks for calling State Taxi.

Hey Latrice; come meet my new friends- Marcus we don't have time for that; come on let's go! But Trice- She pulls Marc by the arm then leads him back through the sliding doors just as the taxi was pulling up. Come on Marcus; I'm sorry ladies but we have to be going! Damn, can I at least get their numbers before we go? Nope; our rides here and I have a plane to catch in a few hours. Ok; let's go then. I'm glad you came to your senses; now get in the taxi sir. Hello folks, are we going to the Coffee Cup? Yes sir! Alright buckle up; we'll be there shortly. Hey Trice; thanks for coming; I really appreciate it. Don't mention it Marc; just tell me what happened that night?

Man I was on the couch handling business when her dude walked in and pulled a pistol on me! Hold on, let's start over! How did you meet this girl? I met her at South Park Mall then we went to the Cheese Cake Factory. We talked a bit; had some drinks then we went back to her place over on South Boulevard. Damn Marc, you didn't even know the woman and you went back to her place? She was a jump off Trice; she knew what it was. Unbelievable; anyway, just continue.

Well we get to her Condo and she takes a shower while I chilled on the couch. "Ok folks; we're here!" Thank you sir! "You're welcome; that'll be $15.00." Damn $15.00 and we only went a few miles; ya'll worse than Atlanta. "I'm sorry sir but that's what's on the meter." I got it Marcus just go find us a seat. Nah I got it; it's the least I can do. Here you go man. "Thank you sir; you guys enjoy your meal." Yeah umm-hmm; come on Trice.

As they enter the Coffee Cup, years of history is evident from archive photos of Athlete's, Celebrities and locals that hang on the walls. Aroma of grilled biscuits, bacon, fried chicken and pork chops fog the atmosphere. "Welcome to the Coffee Cup folks; can I get you guys something to drink?" Marcus and Latrice take a seat at the historic maple wood top bar as the waiter greets them. Sure, can I have tea and lemonade mix? "Sure; and you Ma'am?" I'll have the same! "Ok coming right up and our special today is the smothered pork chops with mash potatoes." Umm, that sounds good; I'll have that! "Ok Sir; I'll put that in for you." I have to look over the menu; I'll let you know when you bring our drinks. "Ok Ma'am."

Now what happened after she got out of the shower Marc? Oh yeah; so I was just chilling on the couch when she came out. Oh girl came right over to me, took off my clothes and we started getting it on; right there on her living room couch. Did you use a condom Marc? Ummm, I don't think so; we were both kind of bent. Boy why do you live that way; you're gone catch something you can't get rid of. It was just that time Trice; I usually stay strapped up. Anyway, go on. So I'm doing my thing; she's calling my name and screaming and shit but I keep hearing this sound, like keys shaking. I asked her if she heard something but she said no, so we kept doing it. Then I heard it again and that's when the door came open and this tall ass shadow appeared over us. The next thing I knew; she started yelling! Rape-Rape! Rape-Rape!

I was surprised at the whole scenario, I pleaded with the guy but that's when he pulled a pistol on me then bap! What happened after that? I woke up handcuffed to a silver rail at the jail house. The officer let me make a phone call and that's when I called Harold. Well right now; it's her word against yours and the judge as well as the jury; usually goes along with the woman's side when it comes to rape.

But I aint rape her though, Latrice! Can you prove that Marcus? How Trice? I don't know, maybe she will take a deal. A deal? Yes if we can't find a way to get her to change her mind. Well I have her number; do you want me to call her Trice? No I'm your lawyer, let me do that; let's just eat and I'll call her when I get back to Atlanta. Thank you Latrice; I owe you. Nah just make sure you pay me for my services; that's all I ask. Oh baby; don't worry about that; you're getting a big bonus if you get me out of this mess! Ha-ha! Alright Marcus; I hear you! "Ok folks here are your drinks!" Thank you!

Donnie's old Camry looked totally out of place as he and Chantel cruise on to the Atlanta; Mercedes Benz lot. Oh D, look at those on the left; they're so cute. Three, car salesmen watch while the couple pull up to the all glass showroom and parked their Camry right up front. Yeah they're straight Chant but let's check out the entire lot first. Alright baller; I hear you talking. What's our budget? We should be able to afford at least $32,000 Chant; what do you think? It depends, Donnie! On what, Chant? Are we financing or buying out right? We're financing baby; I'm not trying to empty our small savings; we just started putting that away.

Ok Donnie; that's a plan; now open the door so we can finally get rid of this God awful bucket. Hold on Chant; this bucket took us a long way. You're right D but all this must come to an end. How much do you think they will give me for the Camry as a down payment? Ha-ha! Boy, open the door and stop day dreaming!

It aint funny Chantel! Oh yes it is; now can we get out now? Ha-ha! Girl you're lucky I love your ass. Muah! Chant leans over and kisses D on the cheek. I love you too Donnie; now open the door. Finally he opens the door, steps out then holds the it ajar as Chant slides across the seat. Hello folks; how are you guys doing today? We're good bruh; we want to look at some new cars. Great; I'm Rollin; what's your name sir? I'm Donnie and this is my fiancé; Chantel! Hey Chantel; congratulations guys! So did you all have any particular class in mind? Umm; did you hear that Donnie? Do we have any particular class; I like the sound of that! Ha-ha! Yes baby; I heard him.

My man, she was looking at those on the front row over there. Oh ok those are one of our most popular models, the E-class. Why don't you guys walk with me over there so we can take a closer look? Alright Rollin, lead the way brother!

Sure; right this way folks! Miles and miles of Silver, Gold, Black and White colored; 2002, E430 4MATIC'S align the first two rows as they stroll between them. So is there a particular color you want to try? Yeah, can we test drive the black one, Rollin? Of course Chantel; you guys wait here and I'll go get the keys. What do you think Donnie? I like the black too baby, let's see how it drives. I'm sure it drives better than the Camry, Donnie. Hey don't go bagging on the Camry now; it got us this far.

Awww, I'm sorry D; did I hurt your feelings? Chant chill, we can go home and just keep the Camry. Boy whatever; you must be crazy! Ha-ha! Got you! That's not funny Donnie! Alright guys; I need to hold one of your I.D's while you test drive. Sure Rollin; you can hold mine's. Thank you sir; you guys can take it for a spin and just park up front when you come back; I'll be inside. Cool; we'll be back soon Rollin!

Chant grabs the key, opens the front door then slides inside the luxurious E-Class as D enters the passenger's side. Ummm, it smells like new leather in here. Yeah, it does smell good in here Chant; let's see how this baby rides. She pulls off the Buckhead car lot then makes right onto Peachtree. I like this right here Chantel, now all we need is a nice house, some kids- And we need to talk about that some more Donnie. What's there to talk about Chant? Them kids, the house and a wedding date! Ha-ha! So are you ready to set a date then?

You're the one that's doing all the talking, mister! I'm ready girl; aint no doubt over here. Oh really! Yep, you heard me. Well I think we need to take it one step at a time D. We can set a date but I'm not ready for kids and I rather we save up some more money before we go looking for a house. I can agree to that Chantel but the house is going to be easy, we can renovate one or get a good deal on the market. Okay Donnie I'll let you handle that, since you're in the business. But the kids will have to wait sir. Alright and did you want to set a date then?

It depends, Donnie; do you want a big wedding or a small one? We can just go to the court house and get married; we don't need all of the hassle. Boy, don't make me slap you in this car! I was just kidding Chantel, how about November? That's in 6 weeks Donnie! Well when? We can do a December date. Are you sure Chant? Yeah that will give us time to plan and get things in order. Ok baby then it's all set; how does the car drive? It's perfect; I love it! Alright now let's see what they will give me for the Camry! D; don't even bother; you might as well drop it off at the junk yard. Girl you're crazy; you can drive the Camry to work and I can drive this Benz to the office. Humph! You are high; aren't you! Ha-ha! I'm just kidding; I can take the F-150, like always.

Yeah I know! Ok let's take this back so I can write Rollin a check; I have some business at the office. On a Saturday; Donnie! Yeah I need to look over these HUD contracts before Tameka comes by to pick them up next week. I sure am hearing this tricks name a lot lately; I think I need to meet her. I think you should too Chant; she's cool. What do you mean cool; D? You know a good person. Oh really; is she cute? Huh? You heard me D; is she cute? Yeah-she's straight. How come you paused, Donnie;

is there something that you want to tell me? Nah; why you say that baby?

Nothing; just make sure I meet this Tameka; I need to put a face to this name I keep hearing. Alright baby; I will make sure you meet her. Thanks; I sure will appreciate that sir. Umm-hmm, no problem! How are Thomas and Nadia by the way? Oh their good Chant, cuz is in love with that woman. That's good, because she really needed someone in her life. Oh yeah, why you say that Chant? Because all she ever did was work, work, work! Thomas has made her slow down, and start enjoying life again. Yeah I guess you're right Chantel.

How is your new best friend Cynthia; I still can't believe you two are getting along. Yall hated each other at the AU. Actually we were cool until your ass came along with those dreads, causing all kinds of confusion. Damn my bad Chantel; I just had to have your sexy ass. Oh, I know I had your nose open. Ha-ha!

Oh really! Yep, there's only one Chant baby. Look, see, you put a ring on it! Ha-ha! Girl your ass is crazy, park this car.

Beads of water speckle the windshields of several cars as they align Sylvia's drive way from the evening's light drizzle. Luda's; Southern Hospitality, echo through-out the front and backyard while family and friends gather inside to celebrate Marcus coming home from a brief jail stay in Charlotte. As fried fish, chicken and crab legs scent up the kitchen the music jolts the atmosphere. "Cadillac grills, Cadillac mills" "Check out the oil my Cadillac Spills" "Matter of fact, candy paint Cadillac kill" "So check out the hoes my Cadillac fills." .

Damn Sylvia; these crab legs are good girl! What kind of season did you use? Thanks Nadia; it's just some New Orleans season and I poured a few bottles of Corona in the pot with some lime juice. Damn; they taste great! I'm glad you like them girl.

Alright man look; enough of the secrets! Whose girl were you cutting in Charlotte; I heard it was one of those ball players. Thomas you wouldn't believe me if I told you! Marc nothing surprises me bruh; hoes are trifling. Well the only thing I will say is; he played for the Heels in college. Aww!   That   can   be anybody. I'm just fooling with you T; Latrice told me not to talk about it until the case was over. Alright that's what's up; I'm about to grab some of this chicken before it's all gone. Ok Thomas; I need to go holler at one of my shawty's anyway. Did you see Tam around here? Yeah, she was sitting on the stairway eating a minute ago. Cool; let me go find her fine ass. Boy; your ass likes playing with fire; don't you? Aint no ring on this finger T; last I check I was a single man.

Yeah I hear you; go do your thing then Marc; I'll be in the kitchen with my ol lady; eating some of that chicken. Bet it up; I'll see you in a few. Thomas leaves the foyer and heads to the kitchen as Marcus finds his way over to the base of the stairs. So what's up baby; you miss me? Marc; don't start this foolishness; Sylvia's right there in the kitchen. So what; she's busy entertaining anyway. Come with me; I want to talk with you in private. Nope; this is fine right here. Come on Tam; don't start acting all stuck up and shit. Marc you got a girlfriend; and besides you lied to me the last time we spoke. What do you mean Tam; I aint lie to you. Yes you did! When? When you called me from jail and didn't tell me what was going on; I had to find out from my sister.

It wasn't even like that Tamara; I figured your sister Nadia had told you already. Well why did you play stupid when the operator came on the phone saying the call would end in 60 seconds? Because I was embarrassed baby; that's why! Marcus you're full of SUGAR-HONEY-ICE-TEA! What does that mean Tam? You figure it out! Marc reaches down and grabs Tamara by her left hand.

Come talk to me for a minute baby; please; just one minute. Ok Marc; one minute and that's it. Cool; come on! The couple; leaves the stairs, walk up the hallway and into the restroom then close the door behind them, leaving it cracked just a little.

Hey Chant; turn that up; I love me some Alicia Keys! Oh shoot; sing it Nadia! "I keep on fallin' " "In and out of love" "With you" "Sometimes I love ya" "Sometimes u make me blue." Alright ladies; who wants some Pinot; I'm about to pop this bottle! Pour all of us a glass Q. Ok Cynt; set the glasses up for me baby. Ok hun! Man look at you two, love birds. Don't be hating now, Chantel. Child; do your thing; trust me I'm not hating. I'm happy for your mean ass; Q was just what you needed. Yep, she sure was a mean ass when I first met her. Alright Quentin; don't be co-signing. Baby you were an evil little devil when I first met you. No I wasn't! Shit; yes you was woman! When Q?

So you're telling me that you don't remember the first time I met you. Yeah I remember that day; you were passing out some fliers to your party. Umm-hmm and you didn't even show up, even after I gave yall some V.I.P passes. Baby we had to study for our finals, that's really why we didn't come. Yeah tell me anything now; it doesn't matter. Oh really and why not? Because I got you now Cynt! Ha-ha! You aint funny Q!

Nadia walks away from the others as they gather around the island, sipping on pinot and conversing. She reaches in the fridge, pulls out a large glass bowl and slides it on the island in front of the others. Ok dig in guys; this is my famous seafood salad. Here are some plates. Yum, I love your seafood salad girl! Thank you Chantel! You're welcome Nadia.

Hey Trice; hand me that plate of fish baby. Which plate Ted? The whiting, right there beside that loaf of bread. Oh ok, I didn't see it.

Thanks! Are you going to season it? I already seasoned the breading baby, so all I have to do his coat it and fry it. Alright mister; I hope you know what you're doing. You just take a chill and let me know how they taste after I'm done. And you know that I will too, Ted! Umm-hmm; and you can only have one piece. Yeah whatever Ted; don't start no mess. Ha-ha! What you mean baby? If it's good; I'm getting more than one piece that's what I mean. Oh you think so! Ha-ha! That's not funny Ted; don't play with me! I love you Trice! Umm-hmm.

Sylvia, are you going to start the fire place? Yeah Sage; Donnie is bringing in some logs now. Cool; I love fire places! Me too Sage; especially this time of year. I've been meaning to ask you about Harold. What about him Syl? How's he doing; when did you speak with him last? He's ok I guest; I seen him a few weeks ago when they came to play the Falcons. Great; are you two getting serious now? Hell no; that little boy needs to do some growing up before I waste anymore of my time with him.

Hold up Sage; what happened? Did I miss something; I thought you guys were getting along. It was nothing certain Syl; we may have gone on a few dates but the last time did it for me. Oh do tell! Well, Mr. Harold leaves me a voicemail to stop by his hotel room and see him. When I got the message I was close to the hotel; so I stopped by. And? Well, when I got there, I knocked on the door, Harold opens it but he wasn't letting me in. I can tell something wasn't right; I sensed that vibe; you know. Umm-hmm. So I got tired of talking through the door, pushed it open and there was these two naked bitches just lying there on his bed-No Sage! Yes girl! I don't have time for his drama and all the groupies; so I left him right there and told him to lose my number.

Wow that was deep! Did he expect you to join them or something? Child I don't know what that fool was thinking but I am not the one! Alright Sylvia, did you want me to put both logs in? Yeah Donnie; thank you baby! You're welcome sis; I'll get the fire started.

Well did you talk to him since Sage? No and I don't want to either. I feel you though Sage, it's has to be hard dating a guy who has a lot of money and he's a famous athlete too! I'm not trying to be funny when I say this Sylvia but- But what? Marcus aint no better, he's right there with him and all the groupies. That's why he's in this mess now. Yeah I know Sage but we're just friends; we are not committed to each other. Alright Sylvia, remember you said that. Oh I'm good girl, I got it covered. Then I'm happy for you Syl. Thank you girl; I'll be right back; I need to use the bath room!

While the music plays in the background and friends converse among one another; Marcus and Tam are deep in conversation. Marcus I really don't have time for this foolishness, we only had sex once and you think you own me. No I don't babe; and are you sure it was only once. Yes I'm sure; see that's the problem right there. You have so many women that you can't even remember who you slept with. That's not true Tam! The hell! I just hope that you're wearing protection; I'm surprised your ass aint dead from aids or something yet.

Look; I do wear protection and besides none of those women matter. You're my favorite and I don't care about any of them like I do you. Boy you don't care about me; just because we had sex in Sylvia's pool, you think that makes us a couple. If you think that, then you really are thinking with your penis head and not the one between your shoulders. You can't tell me that it wasn't good Tam! It was ok; I've had better; get off of yourself; boy. Bam! The restroom door swings open and hits the wall.

What the fuck! Oh shit; Sylvia! Hey baby! Don't hey me Marcus; get your slut ass out of my house! And Tam! You're supposed to be my girl! You slept with him and didn't tell me! Both of you; get out! Get out now! Hold on Sylvia! I don't want to hear it Marc! Get out! I'm sorry Syl. Tam I can't believe you! The loud shouting attracts the other guest in the house, causing them to gather around the hallway in front of the rest room.

Hey hold up! Everybody calm down; Marc come with me! No Donnie; Sylvia is tripping! No bruh, your ass is tripping, now come on! Donnie jacks Marc up by his shirt collar then walks him into the kitchen. Hey Latrice; get Sylvia baby and take her in the living room. Ok Ted I got her, you guys please hurry and diffuse this mess. Come on Tam, let's talk sis. There's nothing to talk about Nadia; I aint do anything; that's Marc's slack ass. Yeah I know but you should have told her like I said Tam. Now look! Well, I told her that I was sorry sis. Come on Tamara; let's go in the living room, so you guys can talk this thing out. Alright, I guess.

Boy this is too funny Cynthia; I told them to leave Marc alone, didn't I tell them. Yes you did Chantel. Well let's go around here with the rest of them so we can straighten this thing out. Girl; we may be lawyers but I don't think we can ease this one over; let's just let them talk it out Chant. Umm-umm-umm. Let me get another glass of wine first girl. I'm gone need it. Ok Chantel, I'll be up front with the others. Yep; be there in a minute!

Latrice takes a seat in between Sylvia and Tamara. Ok ladies look; this is no way to handle this; we all have been friends for far too long for this little thing to come between us. I know you two feel disrespected by Marcus but it's not either of you guys fault. Sylvia, Tam didn't want to tell you because she didn't want to hurt you. Tam on the other hand you were wrong for not saying anything. But if you ask me; both you guys deserve this because we all know how Marc is; at the end of the day, he's our brother. So let's just agree to leave his ass alone, and make sure that this doesn't happen again. Ok Sylvia! Thank you Tam! Sylvia! Ok, ok!

Hell no girls; I need you ladies to make a truce right now, to never sleep with Marcus or neither one of your friends men ever again. Can we do that ladies? Trice leans back on the couch between the two ladies then looks at them both. Yeah we can do that. Great, now hug each other and make up. Tam and Sylvia leans over Latrice's lap then hugs each other.

Well that's the end of that Marcus; see man; you're always starting something. Leave these girls alone bruh. Man they aint made no truce; watch me cut one of them tonight. Ha-ha! Boy you just don't believe fire is hot, look at you facing a Rape charge and you're still hopeless. I aint Rape that girl Donnie; I swear. I believe you bruh but you need to convince a jury not me.

Hey Donnie! Yeah what's up Chant; I'm about to make the announcement; can I? Sure baby; go ahead and tell them. Chantel walks to the front of the living room then stands by the fire place. Alright everyone; I have an announcement to make! Everyone pauses then gives Chant their undivided attention. Well; Donnie and I have decided to set a date! We're tying the knot on December 15th and we want you all to be in the wedding. Aww! Everyone claps and cheers while congratulating Donnie and Chantel. Thank you guys! Congratulations brother! Thanks Marcus, you need to find a wife. Hah! Imagine that; come on everybody let's have a drink to Donnie and Chantel! Marc pops two more bottles of wine, fills the glasses, passes them out then join the others in celebration.

10. Rose Pedals.

Knock-Knock! Hey Q; get the door baby! I got it Cynthia! Knock-Knock! Hold on; I'm coming! Who is it? Me bruh! Oh hold tight; let me unlock the door Donnie. Hey man come in; hi Chant! Hey Quentin; it smells good in here. Thanks Chantel, Cynthia's in the kitchen finishing up dinner. Well you two guys do what you do; I'm going to see what smells so good. Alright baby! Come on D; I was out on the balcony. Cool, let's go.

The aroma of candy yams, macaroni and cheese and pot roast fill the apartment air. Hey Q! Yeah what's up! Stop right there bruh! What is it D? Man what the hell is that? What man? Q; don't tell me that you and Cynthia sleep on that! Yeah that's our bed; what's the problem?

Quentin for real; a damn king sized, heart shaped bed, bruh? Yeah fool! And yall got red satin sheets and pillows too! Donnie; bring your ass on, stop tripping. Ha-ha! It's Valentine's Day every night in here huh? You damn right; don't hate.

Look, whatever floats your boat brother; that's yall's business. Donnie exits the slide doors then follow Q on the balcony. You want a beer D? Sure man. Q reaches in the cooler that he keeps on the balcony then tosses Donnie a beer. Thanks bruh! Yep! So when are you and Cynthia tying the knot? Hold on D; that's you and Chantel; I aint no-where near getting married brother.

You say that now Quentin, but if she ask then what? We'll just be engaged for a few years. Ha-ha! Your ass would do that, wouldn't you? You damn right! Quentin, tell me that's not what I think it is! What D? Those plants right there! Oh that's just my personal stash. Boy your ass is crazy; does Cynt know about it? Man she waters them for me and everything. Ha-ha! Does she even know that it's marijuana? Nah, not yet! Q your ass is going to hell. Man whatever.

As the October winds blow the brown, orange and yellow leaves across the deck, the delicious smell of dinner creeps through the open doors, enticing them to come back inside. Can I ask you a question Q? Yeah D, what's up? Are you still selling that stuff? No man; but I would if I had to. Good because you can't be a professor and a drug dealer. Hey that was good money in college Donnie. That maybe so but you should be making good money now. You know; it's funny you asked that Donnie.

Just the other day, one of my students asked me for some smoke. Damn, how did you handle that situation? I told him to leave my classroom. What made him ask you that; you keep some joints on your desk or something?

No man; he said that his uncle went to school with us and told him that I was the weed man back in the day. Ha-ha! Now that's funny right there. No it's not D! Quentin; don't be getting all serious and shit; you were the weed man! Kiss my ass Donnie. Hey guys! Come eat; the food is ready! Alright Cynthia; we're coming baby.

Come on Donnie let's go eat; I'm starving. Alright let's go; I sure hope your girl can cook. Well; I'm still living and I've been eating her cooking for the past three months. Ok, let's go then.

Cynthia and Chantel both stood over the table waiting for the fellows to come in. The mac and cheese, pot roast and yams sit in the center of the table in white serving dishes as the guys approached. Four empty plates along with silverware and four glasses of tea sit around the table awaiting the main course.

Alright guys; sit down and let's eat. Ummm, this looks good baby! Thank you Q! Here, I'll fix the plates, you guys just relax. Aww thanks Chantel! You're welcome Cynthia, thanks for inviting us; it's the least that I can do. Donnie; Cynthia and Quentin all take their seats while Chantel fills everyone plates. Ok there we go; now we can eat. Hold on Chant; there's something I want to say before we eat. Sure what is it Cynt? Well; we invited you guys over for a reason. Oh shit; don't tell me! You're pregnant! No girl; do I look pregnant to you Chant? No but you could be in your second week. Ha-ha! Baby you're crazy; chill out and let Cynthia tell us why they invited us over.

Donnie, Chant we consider you guys to be our closest friends, so we wanted to tell you first. Tell us what Cynt; hurry, you're killing me! Ok Chantel; here it is; Q and I eloped yesterday! What the hell! Wait a minute; come again! You heard her right D; we're married bruh. Oh my gosh; congratulations girl! Thank you Chantel. Man I just asked your ass about this out on the balcony and you- I know man; I didn't want to ruin the surprise. Well I'll be damn; we need some champagne with this fine dinner; so we can celebrate! That's not necessary Donnie; we can do that later when we tell everybody else. Ok suit yourself man, I'm happy for you guys bruh. Thanks D!

Cynthia did you guys plan this or what girl? No it just happened; Q asked me to marry him and said he didn't want to wait. He just had to have me as his wife. Damn; I would have never thought that you guys would have made it this far. Do you remember when you two first met? Oh I remember Chant; she was playing hard to get! No I wasn't Q! Yes you were baby. No I just didn't come to your party because we already had plans. Well it doesn't matter now; you're all mines!

Aww, aint that sweet! Look at them Donnie; two love birds. Umm-hmm. Now can we eat;

I'm hungry as hell. Donnie! What Chant! Be nice! I am; this is family; they know I love them, now can somebody bless this fine meal so we can dig in! Sure I'll do it; let's bow our heads. Ok Quentin, go ahead my brother.

As the clock strikes 9; another work day begins for Nadia. So how was your day off Nadia? It was good Cap; I needed the rest. I hear that Nad; all this overtime has gotten me worn out. Yeah but that check sure looks good; don't it? Oh yeah and my wife loves cashing it too. Ha-ha! I bet she does Cap! Buzz-Buzz! Look at monitor 7 Nad and see who that is buzzing the side door. Oh it's a delivery guy. Thanks; let me go see what he wants. Cap pushes the intercom button by the front desk PC. Yes how can I help you? "Yes I'm with FTD; I have a delivery." Ok step back from the door so I can buzz you in. "Ok!" Buzz!

Nadia; make sure he signs the guest book; he has a delivery. Ok Cap; I got it. The delivery guy enters the side door, dressed in a three piece blue suit, red tie and white shirt with one dozen roses in his right hand and a card in the other. Damn Cap; he's sharp for a delivery guy huh? Sure is Nad! How are you doing sir; who is the delivery for? It's for Nadia; are you Nadia? Her eyes now stretch wide as golf balls, heart pounding, she reluctantly answers. Yes- that's me.

He hands her the Roses then the card. Curiously she opens it to see who sent her flowers and it read. "Dear Nadia, from the moment that I first laid eyes on you; I knew I had to have you." "So to show you how much I care, these flowers are just a little something to let you know that I love you." "Love Thomas."

Aww this is so sweet! Thank you sir! You're welcome Ma'am, there's one more thing. Really and what is that? He reaches over the counter, gently grabs her right hand then serenade's her with a Heatwave; love ballad.

"Always and Forever, each moment with you"
"Is just like a dream to me that some-how came true" "And I know tomorrow will still be the same" "Cause we got a life of love that won't ever change and.."

Oh my God; that is so beautiful. Thank you so much. Now that's what I call class right there Nadia; tell Thomas he took care of business on this one. Damn, now I feel like I have to do something for my wife. Ha-ha! Stop it Cap; you're too funny. But I'm so serious. Oh this is too much; I'm about to cry; can I take a quick break Cap? Sure go ahead and call him; I know that's what you want to do. Thank you Cap! Yep, no problem! Hey do you have a card young man; I may need your services. Yes sir; here's two! Thanks and you did a god job with that song. Thanks a lot sir. You're welcome; have a good day young man. You as well!

Ring! Ring! Hello! Hey Thomas! Thank you so much! You're welcome Nadia; so I take it you liked the flowers. Hell yeah, and especially the song! That's what's up, I'm glad you do baby. What are you doing right now? About to use the bathroom then headed back to work. Ok, well I'll see you when I get off; thanks again Thomas. I love you. Love you too Nadia, bye, see you later.

Hello sir; welcome to Atlanta; Bank and Trust are you being helped? No I just got here. Ok what can I do for you? I just came to drop something off for my friend Sage. Sure; if you'll have a seat, I can go get her for you. No you don't have to get her; can you just give her this box? Yes I can do that for you. Harold stretches out his right hand, revealing a small black velvet box, wrapped in a yellow bow. And may I ask your name sir? Yes it's Harold. Did you want to wait? Yeah, I'll just have a seat here on the couch. Ok' I'll be right back. Thank you!

The assistant hastily walk down the cream carpet hallway and into Sage's corner office. Excuse me Boss! Yes what is it? A gentleman named Harold just asked me to give this to you. Where is he? Is he still here? Yes but he said he would wait out front. He just told me to make sure you got this box. Well don't just stand there; let me have it. Oh I'm sorry; here you go Ma'am. Thank you; you can go now! Yes Ma'am.

As her assistant walks back up front; Sage sits the box in the center of her desk, gaze at it for a moment then proceeds to untie the yellow bow. She places the yellow bow off to the side then slowly removes the small velvet box lid. Wow! Did he really! Ha-ha! All Sage could do was talk and laugh to herself as she look down at the black key with the gold Lexus symbol in the middle. Calmly she rolls away from her large desk, stands up, fixes her skirt, slips on her jacket, grabs the box and heads up front.

Hello mister! Hi Sage! What is this? It's just a little something to say I'm sorry. So you just go around buying luxury cars for people when you want them to forgive you? No, that's not it. Really, it sure looks that way to me. Isn't this a car key? Yes! Is it for me? Yes! Then there you have it; it is what it is. But- Here; keep your keys; I don't need your car. I have my own and by the way; I'm a Mercedes woman. Well that's fine; I can get you a Benz. No thank you; bye Harold! But Sage! She turns away and heads back to her office while talking to him. Bye Harold; next time call before you try and drop in on me; I have work to do!

I was only trying to apologize, Sage. Harold I'm not one of your groupies; I don't need your handouts and that school kid stuff doesn't work on me player. You don't need me anyway; I'm only one woman. Last time I checked you needed two girls to make you happy or is it three now? Come on Sage- Bye Harold, see yourself out; have a great day!

Damn; is she always this stuck up! Excuse me sir? Never mind; did you want a car? Who me? Yeah; aint you the only one sitting here shawty! Oh yes sir. Well here; it's all yours, the title is in the glove box, consider it an early Christmas gift. Oh my God; are you for real! Calm down shawty and don't tell your boss; I'm sure she'll make you give it back. Ok I won't! Oh shit- I mean thank you so much! May God Bless you! He's already blessed me shawty; now I'm blessing you; have a good day! Thank you, thank you; thank you! Yep, bye shawty!

Ring-Ring! Ring-Ring! Hello; thanks for calling the Hudson Law Firm; this is Chantel how can I help you? Hi Chantel is Ms. Latrice in? She should be here in a moment; can I take a message? Yes can you have her call Chasity please! Sure; did you want to leave a number or does she has already? No thank you; she already has it. Ok I'll give her the message. Thank you! You're welcome Chasity.

It's going to be a long day Cynt! Why you say that Chantel? I have two new clients coming in, plus two hearings today. Oh that's nothing; at least you haven't started trial yet. Latrice asked me to take lead on this 5 year old case she had. Hmmm, what case is that? I don't know child; I'm about to fix my morning coffee; sit at my desk with some Maxwell on and review the case files.

Good Morning ladies! Hey Latrice; we were just talking about you! I sure hope it was about something good Chantel. Of course; you know we love you; Boss lady. Hmm, wait until I give one of you a bad case then we'll see how long that last. Ha-ha! Any case that's paying the bills; isn't a bad case. Latrice pauses, looks at Cynthia then taps her on the shoulder. Oh snap; say that again Cynthia! I'm just saying; it's true isn't it. Yes Ma'am it is and by the way I heard that you are newly-wed now. I sure am; I'm sorry we didn't have a wedding; we just wanted it to be something personal and sacred.

Hey girl; I understand! Congratulations! Thank you Latrice! You're welcome honey! Did I get any calls this morning? Oh yes; now that you mention it! A young lady named Chasity called. Chasity? Yes, she says that you already have her number. Yeah I have it; I'm just surprised she called. Oh ok. Thanks Chantel; umm it's going to be a long winter.

Latrice places her Gucci bag and hand full of mail on the receptionist counter in front of Chantel and Cynthia. Two white envelopes and a small 2 inch by 4 inch black and white piece of paper fell off the counter down in front of Chantel. Oops; here you go Trice this fell off the counter. Wait a minute! Chant pauses, glances at the paper then looks back at Trice then down at the paper again. Is this what I think it is! Yes it is Chantel! Whoa and is this yours? Yes Ma'am; I just got it about an hour ago. What is it Chantel? I'll let Trice tell you Cynt! Well what is it guys, don't keep me waiting! Alright; calm down girls; I just left the doctor because I was feeling sick the past few days.

He did some test and that is what I walked out of the Doctors office with today. Let me see that Chantel. Here you go Cynt! Oh my God; is this a BABY! Yes Cynthia; please lower your voice. I don't want the whole world to know. Wow! Latrice you're going to be a Mom? It looks that way Cynthia. So is it Ted's? Yes Chant it is. Did you tell him yet? I will tonight before he heads back to Texas.

Wow; I bet he's going to be so happy. I sure hope so girls, because I worked really hard to keep this body in shape, now it's about to be put to the test. Don't worry about that Latrice; you'll bounce back after the baby as long you keep working out and eating good; you'll be fine girl. Thanks Chant; I needed that. You're welcome boss. Sniff-Sniff. Cynthia I know that you're not over there crying. Sniff-Sniff. It's just good to see all of us happy; I'm in love and married; Chantel is getting married and you're having a baby. Sniff-Sniff. Cupid really does exist. Girl if you don't stop that crying with your crazy butt.

Aww leave her alone Chant; she's just emotional. No she's not Boss, she's crazy. Ha-ha! You know she got a check while we were in school, that's how we bought groceries every month, off her crazy check. Ha-ha! Chantel cut it out, that's not funny and I'm not crazy Latrice. You two are a mess; alright come on, let's get to work and where's our secretary? Chant sent her to Krispy Kreme's! Ooooh Cynthia stop lying; you know you sent her! Well it better be enough for me or both of you madams are going to be sorry. You know we got your raspberry filling and lemon creams Trice.

Great, let me know when they get here Cynthia, now hand me my ultra sound picture and let's get to work! Yes Ma'am! Latrice picks up her bag, and mail then grabs the photo from Cynthia and heads to her office. Wow that baby had a big head Cynt, did you see it! I heard that Chantel! Oh I'm sorry Latrice! Umm-hmm; just wait until you get pregnant; Donnie has the same big ass head as his father and Uncle! Ha-ha! Ha-ha! Ha-ha! Ha-ha! Shut up Cynt it's not that funny! Ha-ha! Ha-ha! Oh my stomach hurts! Cynthia whatever! Go to your office!

Don't get mad Chantel. Just wait, I'm eating all the Krispy Kreme's. Aww; we still love you Chant; don't be mad; you started it. Chantel picks up her coffee then heads to her office, upset and smirking all at the same time. See I knew you thought it was funny. Ring-Ring! Shut up Cynthia and answer the phone. Ring-Ring! You're supposed to be answering- Ring-Ring! Bye Cynthia; see you later; get the phone please. Ring-Ring! Ooooh Chantel; just wait! Ring-Ring! Hello; thanks for calling the Hudson Law Firm!

11. Nine to Five.

Hey bro; go by Lowes and pick up 40 of those 4x4 studs; I'm leaving the office in a few minutes. I'll meet you guys over at the house when I leave here. Alright and I think we need some more nails too Thomas. Ok get a few boxes and bring me my damn receipts; I don't need Donnie on my ass about not having a receipt. Alright boss; I got you; see you later. Ok bro; see you in a few. As Thomas places the phone on the receiver the office door opens and there she was. Her CK1 perfume preceded her entrance, Tameka's fit body seem to be even more noticeable through her fitted black dress. Now standing right in front of him across the desk, eye level because of her Choo pumps, Thomas taken aback by her beauty finally managed to get out a few words.

Hey- Hey- um Tameka. Hi Thomas; how are you doing today? I'm fine; what brings you by; my cousin isn't here, he's out looking at some new properties. What makes you think I came to see Donnie? Because you're always flirting with cuz; you know he has an ol lady right. Ha-ha! Is that what you guys are calling us these days? Old ladies?

It's just a saying Tameka; that's all. Well thank you for the update Thomas but you're wrong about me. How so; every time you come around, you're always in cuz face. I'm not interested in Donnie, Thomas. Shit, I can't tell; you might as well be sleeping with him, much as you come around. Ha-ha! You silly boy! Nah I have good sense woman. You're not as smart as you think Thomas. Tameka walks to the left side of the desk, takes a seat on the edge then with her left hand grabs Thomas by his shirt and pulls him around the desk slowly. Oh whoa; what are you doing Tameka! It's you that I have eyes for Thomas; not your cousin.

So what do you think of me now? Am I still coming around too much? Tameka; this aint what you want; I'll do you. Oh really now?

Damn right; I'll bend your fine ass over this desk. Hmm, I think you're all talk Thomas. She releases his shirt then walks towards the entrance. Hey don't leave now girl; what are you; scared? Click-Click! With two swift turns Tameka locks the office doors. Oh ok; you want to take it there huh? Are you sure about this Tameka? She remains standing in front of the door, grabs the bottom of her dress, lifts it up over her head then drops it at her feet. Do you think I'm ready now Thomas? Zip! He drops his pants, walks towards her, pulls off his shirt then there bodies collide.

As both their hearts beat at an alarming rate; Thomas and Tameka indulge in each-others forbidden ecstasy. With one swift move, he removes her black thongs, lifts her up then carries her over to the desk. Papers, pens, books and envelops, fall onto the floor as the thrust from their bodies upon the oak desk pushed them away. Oh I've wanted you for so long, please put your black love inside me. Oh, I'm about to- Damn Thomas!

 This how you want it! Yes like that! Um-hmm, you like this black love; don't you Meka! Oh God yes! I love it Thomas! Click-Click! They both look up as the door swings open. What the fuck Thomas! Tameka! Get yall's nasty asses off of my desk! Damn cuz, what you doing here! Oh Donnie; I'm so sorry! Really Tameka! In my office though, Jesus! Thomas put some damn clothes on. Donnie; she came on to me cuz; look at that body; I couldn't say no! Man I don't want to hear it; I'll be back in 15 minutes. Clean my office up!

 What you doing Meka! Putting my clothes back on! Chill, we got 15 minutes, come on don't stop now. Nah I'm embarrassed, maybe another time. Damn, aint this a bitch! Tameka puts her clothes back on then hurries out the office as Thomas stands there in aw, naked, clothes in hand. So when are we going to finish! Bye Thomas!

"Hello folks, this is your Pilot speaking." "I would like to thank you for flying with us this morning." "We are now approaching Charlotte Douglas International Airport." "I ask that you please return your seats to the upright position and buckle up." "We should be touching down in 15 minutes." "It's a warm 65 degrees in Charlotte and the time is 11:00 am." "Thanks again for flying with us."

Ring-Ring! Hello! Hi, is this Chasity? Yes it is! Hi this is Latrice; Marcus's attorney. Oh hey; good morning. I just landed and I should be at the Westin downtown within an hour. Oh ok. I'll call you after I check in so we can meet up and discuss what we've spoken about over the phone. Ok Ms. Latrice; I'll go ahead and get dressed so that I can be ready when you call. Alright Chasity; see you then. Ok thanks!

As the black limo roll over and around the cobble stone driveway; two Westin Valet stood adjacent the hotel entrance awaiting Latirce's arrival. Hello Ms. Latrice; welcome back to Charlotte. How are you doing today Ma'am? I'm fine young man; thanks for asking. You're welcome; do you have any bags. Just this one here baby; I can take it myself. Are you sure? Yes it's no problem, I'm sure I can handle it. Ok Ms. Latrice; enjoy your stay and it's good to see you again. The Valet runs pass her, pauses then opens the door. Thank you; have a good day young man. It's my pleasure Ma'am.

A sea of huge; gray marble tiles cover the hotel lobby while white satin drapes stream down from the ceiling at every column. Hello Ms. Latrice; welcome back, we have your usual suite all ready for you. Thank you hun! How long will you be staying this time? Ah two days at the most hun. Ok great; do you have your Starwood Preferred Guest card with you? No but I do know my SPG account number. Super and what is that number? Oh it's 7-9-8-4-5-3-2. Ok, thank you for that information; I've applied these dates to your account. Did you need a bell hop to assist you this morning? No, I'm fine; I'm going over to the restaurant to grab some coffee and a bagel. Well, enjoy your coffee Ms. Latrice and remember we're here if you need us. Thanks hun, did you want anything? No Ma'am but thanks for asking. Ok see you later.

Ring-Ring! Ring-Ring! Hello! Hi Chasity this is Latrice; what time are you available, so we can talk. I'm free now Ms. Latirce; where are you staying? I'm uptown at the Westin. Oh cool; I'm on South Boulevard not too far from you. Really, are you at home? Oh no; I'm about to go inside the House of Pancakes, for some breakfast. Hmm, how about I catch a taxi over there, we can speak over breakfast. Sure I'll get a table for two. Thanks Chasity, see you a few.

Latrice stops just in front of the hotel restaurant then walks back over to check in. Excuse me hun, can you take my bag up to my room? Sure, no problem, I'll have someone get it now. Thanks, I'll be back shortly. Alright, Ms. Latrice! Casually she turns around then heads out of the side doors and walks to the corner, to catch a cab. In a few seconds two white taxi's slow right at the corner to assist her. "Where you headed Ma'am?" Right around the corner, House of Pancakes on South Boulevard! Alright jump in; it will only take a few minutes. Thank you hun!

You're welcome, so where about are you from? Me; I'm from Atlanta just in town on business. Ok, is this your first visit to Charlotte? God no; I'm here at least three times a year. Cool; what's your profession, if you don't mind me asking? No I don't and I'm a

Defense Attorney. Really; you look young to be an Attorney. Ha-ha. I don't know if I should take that as a compliment or an insult. Oh I'm sorry Ma'am it wasn't an insult! I know; I was joking with you and my name is Latrice; you don't have to call me Ma'am.

Well it's nice to meet you Ms. Latirce; I'm Harvey. Nice to meet you Harvey! After one right turn and one mile later down South Boulevard; they arrive at the House of Pancakes. Ok Latrice; this is your stop; enjoy your breakfast; the food is great. Oh really; what do you recommend? For me; the grits and liver pudding is the best. Um-um, no I think I'll pass on that one Harvey; how much do I owe you? Just $6 Ms. Latrice! Great, here's a ten; keep the change. Thanks! You're welcome Harvey!

The aroma of fresh biscuits, coffee, bacon and syrup meet her as she enters the restaurant. Welcome to the House of Pancakes Ma'am;

how many people are in your party? Oh no thanks, I'm meeting someone here. Ok Ma'am you can take a look around to see if they're here yet. Latrice, places her red coach bag over her right shoulder, takes out her cell then calls Chasity. Ring-Ring! Hello! Hey Chasity; I'm at the restaurant. Alright I'm standing up waving, is that you in the grey suit with the red bag? Yes that's me! Cool, I see you, turn around and look to your right.

Ok I'm looking! Oh there you are; in the panthers hat, right? Yes! Trice makes her way over to Chasity. Hi Ms. Latrice, nice to meet you! Nice to meet you as well Chasity! I ordered us both a cup of coffee; I hope that was ok. Thanks; that's fine, now as I recall, you want to speak with me about your side of the story. Yes Ma'am. Now as a law of the court, I recommend that this is a bad idea. Did you discuss this with your lawyer first? No Ma'am; I feel bad because of the way things turned out. How do you mean Chasity? Well Marcus didn't rape me. Oh really; then what happened? Chasity leans back in her chair, takes a deep breath then fiddles with her fingers. Hello ladies, here's your coffee and some milk, the sugar is right there beside the napkins. Thank you! You're welcome ladies; are you guys ready to order? Oh can you give us a minute? Sure ladies, take your time.

Why don't we just start at the top Chasity. Tell me when and where you two met and how you guys ended up at your place? Her hands now shaking nervously, she attempts to pour some milk in her coffee. Well, I was at the mall shopping when I first met him. You said first met him, did you guys have another encounter before you went to your place. Yes Ma'am. Ok continue. I was at the mall buying my boyfriend a birthday gift and Marcus was in the jewelry store as well. He noticed me looking at some men watches; I needed some advice about a Cartier watch and a Movado I was trying to decide on. So I asked him and that's how it started.

Ok then what? He took my cell phone off the Jewelry case and called his phone, he did it so fast I didn't realize it. We laughed about it, after I realized what he done. I told him that I was faithful to my man and that I couldn't call him and that he should erase my number. He said; ok no problem I understand. After that I went my way then he went his. And Ms. Latrice; I'm going to be honest I was attractive to him but I had no intentions on sleeping with Marcus or ever seeing him again. He was just so charming when he called me!

I hear what you're saying Chasity but the fact still remains that I am his attorney and we are here right now, discussing those ill intentions. So what is it that you want? You've already admitted to me that he didn't rape you, so what's next? Well I'm engaged and I really don't want to drag this thing out in the courts and the media; my fiancé is a famous athlete and this is the last thing that we need. But you lied; Chasity! I know but can you please help make it go away; I don't want to take this thing any further. So are you saying you want to drop the charges?

No I can't do that! My fiancé will be furious; I was thinking about settling out of court and that way I can always tell him that I settled to keep our business out of the media. How much are you asking for Chasity? I will take no less than $500,000.00. I'll have to make a few phone calls first but I can't promise you anything; that depends on what my client wants to do. Ok Ms. Latrice; when can you let me know something? I'll go call him now, give me a few minutes; I'll be back. Alright; Ms. Latrice!

Ring-Ring! Ring-Ring! Hello! Hey Marc; this is Trice! Hey Trice; what's up? She closes the restaurant door behind her then paces slowly up and down the side walk while talking with

Marcus. I'm in Charlotte, meeting with Chasity; she just admitted to me that you didn't rape her- Hell yeah; so it's over? Hold on; don't go celebrating just yet! She's worried that her business will get out in the media if we go to court. Did you know that she's engaged to some NBA player or something? I wasn't interested in all of that Trice; I only had one thing on my mind that night. Umm, why am I not surprised! Well anyway; she wants to settle out of court. Will that keep me out of jail? Yes it will! How much does she want? No less than $500,000.00. Damn; that's some expensive pussy! $500,000 dollars! Yes Marcus; so how do you want to proceed? Hold on a sec Latrice.

Marc places his phone on the hotel room bed. Hey Harold! Yeah shawty, what's up? Man can I get a loan? What kind of loan? 500 stacks! What the hell for? Man this damn Charlotte chic wants a payoff or my ass is going to jail for rape because it's obviously my word against hers. Damn nigga; that's two game checks!

Come on man, please! Marcus you're working for free for the next year fool; I mean that shit! Bruh I don't care; I need this! Ok shawty; I got you! Whew! Thanks Harold! Yeah shawty; maybe now you'll keep yo dick in your pants!

I don't know about that but I can promise you I won't get caught up like this again. Yeah I hear you shawty! Marc picks his phone up to give Trice the news. Hey Latrice; tell her I can have $400,000.00 in her hands by tomorrow but $500,000 is a reach. Alright I'll go talk to her; if I call you back, that means she's not in. If you don't hear from me in 5 minutes it's a go. Alright Trice; thank you sis! Yeah, you owe me big Marcus! I know and I got you! Don't worry; I'll get mines, talk to you later and tell Harold I said Hi! Alright will do; bye Trice.

Latrice gathers herself, places her cell in her purse then enters the restaurant. Ok Chasity, I just spoke with Marcus, he says all he has at the moment is $350,000.00. But if you are willing to settle for that; I can have it deposited into your bank account, first thing tomorrow. Chasity takes a deep breath, holds it, releases then answers softly. Ok sure, by what time tomorrow? By noon; I will deposit it myself. I can do that Ms. Latrice, thank you so much! You're welcome; now before we can do that I need a written confession and agreement to the terms and the charges will be dropped, you can write it, right here on this legal pad. I'll deliver it to your attorney and the judge myself.

That's no problem; Ms. Latrice! Great let me get you a pen and here's the pad; just flip those first two pages back use the first blank sheet you see. Chasity slides her coffee to the side, flips to a blank page then starts writing her statement while Latrice crosses her legs, sips from her cup and looks on.

Downtown traffic, crawls on Luckie and Baker Street as Donnie, Poppa Rich and Ted stand on an empty lot between the cross streets, shadowed by the Coco Cola center. Well Pops, Unc this is it! What's it son, this is a big ugly empty lot. Yeah nephew; we're in the Real Estate investment business, not construction. We are not building anything on this land. See, you two old timers got it all wrong. This very property that we're standing on is going to bring the company so much passive income; you want believe it!

Donnie the only passive thing on this property will be the homeless who is passing by now but will be sleep right here tonight! So Pops you're telling me that you don't see my vision. I'm sorry son but I agree with Ted; let's not get into the construction side of things. Listen to your daddy nephew; he's making sense. Alright look you two; this is going to be a paved parking lot; where patrons can park while their downtown. Oh really?

Yes Unc! Now can you see it Pops? Oh yes; I see it now son. Great idea; how much will you be charging to park? Anything I want Pops; it's my property. That sounds good and all Donnie but what about when there's not a big event downtown? Uncle Ted someone will always need to park, I can charge $5 one day, $7, $10, hell even $20 if it's the right night! I'm happy for you son; this was a great decision; you have my blessings. Thanks Pop, and what about you Unc? As long as it make dollars; it makes sense to me Donnie; do your thing nephew! Thanks Unc; now that we have that out of the way; celebrations are in order.

Hold on son; it's too early to celebrate! Wait a minute Pops; I'm not talking about this. You mean to tell me, that your brother didn't tell you that he was having a new baby! Baby! What's Donnie talking about Ted? Oh Latrice is pregnant. Well I'll be damn, congrats brother! Thanks Rich! You're welcome; now you have to start all over again though. Man I know but it is what it is bro. Plus Trice is a good girl; it'll be ok. See; that's why I stay away from those young chickens; Donnie is twenty something and I'm done raising kids. Now it would be nice to have a few grand kids to spoil. Pops don't start with that; Chantel and I still have to get our careers straight before talking about rug rats. I hear you son; just putting a bug in your ear.

Well you'll just have to settle for a niece or nephew for now, via Uncle Ted! Ha-ha! You two jokers aint funny; let's go over to Magic City and get some wings and a cold beer. Damn Unc; you love those strippers don't you? Donnie how can you live in Atl and not son? That's the question! Ha-ha! Come on old men; let me take yall buts to the shake club. Then let's go son; it's your treat too. Yeah pops; I got it.

Say nephew; are you ready to tie the knot. The big day is a few weeks away! I'm good

Unc; it's not like anything will change much; we're already living together. Ha-ha! Ha-ha! Ha-ha! What's so funny Pops? You! What! Did you say that things weren't going to change! Son change is the one thing you can count on happening in a marriage; especially in the beginning. I don't think so Pops; Chantel is pretty straight forward. Ha-ha! Ok nephew; let's talk about it, when we get to the club. Ha-ha! Unc your ass is crazy! Pops get your brother! He's right though son. Aw man whatever, you two are tripping; come on let's just go have some fun.

As dusk began to set over the Atlanta Skyline, the three gentlemen make their way back into the F-150. Peels off the vacant lot and into oncoming traffic, in route to 241; Forsyth Street, the bright red, break lights, disappearing in the distance.

Hello; welcome to the Hudson Law Firm, how can I help you? Hi young lady; I'm

District Attorney James and this is; Attorney Byrd. We're here to speak with Ms. Chantel. Ok sure; you guys can have a seat and I'll let her know that you are here. Thanks! You're welcome! Ring-Ring! Ring-Ring! Hello, this is Chantel. Hi Ms. Chantel, there's an Attorney Byrd and a District Attorney James here to see you. Ok thank you; can you show them to the conference room and offer them some coffee; I'll be there in a few. Ok Ms. Chantel; no problem!

Excuse me, Mr. James! Yes Ma'am! Ms. Chantel will be with you guys shortly; she asked if you could wait in the conference room. Sure young lady; and where is that? Oh you can follow me, I'll show you! Did you guys want some coffee? No I'm fine, thanks for asking. You're welcome Mr. Byrd! I'll have a cup; black no sugar, no cream! Alright here's the conference room, make yourselves comfortable and I'll be right back with that coffee Mr. James. Great, thanks!

As the phones continue to ring and clients walk in and out of the busy Atlanta Law firm, James and Byrd sit patiently, while Chantel makes her way down the hall. She clears her throat, straightens her dress, stops, places her case folders firmly in her right hand then enters the conference room. Gentlemen! Hello Ms. Chantel! Hello, you guys don't have to stand up, how are you? We're fine and yourself? Well that depends on what kind of news you have for me James. I think it's pretty good, considering it's a DUI case. This was clearly an aberration you guys. That may be true Ms. Chantel but someone has lost their life.

And I understand that Byrd, let me assure you that Monica is very remorseful for this incident. She has a squeaky clean record and has just graduated from Spelman. No matter how remorseful Ms. Chantel, she has to do some jail time! How much time are we talking James? Well; we think 24 months jail time and

3 years suspended is fair. Come on James, two years! She just graduated; I say a year jail time and we can do a DUI program along with a monitored suspended 4 year sentence. What level monitoring are we talking Ms. Chantel?

Let's do two DUI classes a month, ankle bracelet and random urine test to monitor the drinking. If you throw in the no-drinking pills I think we can work that out. I'm sure I can do that! Did you want to check with your client first, Ms. Chantel? She's calling me on her lunch break; I'll speak with you after that. Well, we'll be headed back to the court house, I'll be waiting on that call and thanks for the coffee. You're welcome James; I will call you guys as soon as possible. Alright; if she doesn't agree to that, we may have to go to trial; I don't think we can offer a better deal. Oh, she'll agree! Ok, we'll speak later then! Later; have a great day Mr. Byrd and you too James! Thanks!

Byrd and James make their way out of the firm as Chantel stands by the receptionist desk waiting for them to exit. Ok baby, get my client Monica on the phone ASAP! I'll be in my office! Yes Ma'am, I'm on it.

Chant stops by the break area, grabs a bagel and makes a cup of coffee then walks in her office just as the phone rings. Ring-Ring! Ring-Ring! Hello, this is Chantel! Hi Ms. Chantel, I have Monica on the phone! Ok put her through.

Hey Monica! Hi Ms. Chantel! Hi; I just spoke with the DA. Ok what did he say? Well of course you know that you will have to do some jail time. Oh my God, how much? All together 5 years- Oh no, no, no, I can't do it! Monica calm down, 4 years of that is suspended. What does that mean? It means that you will have to do a year in jail and participate in a DUI program while incarcerated then once that year is over. You will be on an ankle monitor along with taking the no-drinking pills. Oh my God, what are no-drinking pills? There pills that keeps you from drinking alcohol, and even if you try to, you will be so sick that you can't stand it!

Lord, help me! Monica it's this or a trial, and as your Attorney I must warn you that if you lose at trial you could get life in prison. God my life is over! Monica I would recommend the one year and four years suspended. Unless you want to take your chances at trial, it's your life and I can do whatever you want me to; just let me know. Ms. Chantel, thanks for everything, I'll take the deal but can I have some time to spend with my family before I go. Sure I'll speak with the D.A and see if we can get a few more weeks. Thank you so much, I really do appreciate all that you have done. You're welcome Monica; I'll call you as soon as I get a court date. Alright thank you; bye-bye!

12. Forever.

Lithonia, Georgia; Brownsmill Rd. a block from Panola Road; Harold's huge tan and stone Mansion over shadows all others on the block. Amidst the trees and atop of the hill, it's hard to miss it and all its beauty. In the middle of November with green grass of summer; he, Donnie and Thomas gather on the lawn along the crescent driveway.

Damn Harold; this is nice brother! Thanks Thomas; I got it for 1.5! 1.5 Million! Yep! Must be nice bro! It's a cool starter home; my team mate knows the realtor; he gave me a deal. Harold it's only you; what are you going to do with all of this house? Hell, your butt is hardly in town. Calm down Donnie; it's a Christmas gift for my Mom. Oh ok, that's what's up!

Speaking of her, that's why I called you two over. And why is that? My mom's likes to grow flowers and all that but I don't want her messing up my lawn. Man you just said this was for her. It is D but if I let her plant flowers in the front yard, it's going to cost more money to landscape this thing all over again.

Man stop being cheap, you can afford it. That doesn't mean I have to do it though Thomas! So what did you want us to do? Donnie I was thinking about a green house in the back then she can grow whatever she wants! Are you sure? Yeah D, can you guys do it? Yeah that's easy, where did you want it and how big? Cool, come on let's go around back, so I can show you.

Hey you guys go ahead; I need to take quick smoke! Thomas we're outside, you can smoke where ever! I know Harold but I don't want you to catch a contact and shit. Oh you're about to light up a blunt? Yeah man; did you want to hit it? Nah shawty; we'll be in the back. Alright! Come on D; let's go; how long does a job like this takes? Maybe a week at the most, if we work on it every day! That's what's up! Harold and Donnie make their way around to the side of the Mansion, through the back gate and into the back yard. Ruff! Ruff! Ruff!

Oh! What the Fu- Down boy! Down boy! Harold when did you get a big ass Rottweiler! My bad D; he's not gone bite. Man, get that fool! Ruff! Ruff! Ruff! Ruff! Hell I think he wants to bite me though! Down boy! Stay here Donnie; let me chain him up. Man aint no chain can hold that big ass monster. Come on boy! Harold grabs the beast by the collar then walks him over to a tree in the corner of the yard and chains him up. My bad D; that's my girls dog; she keeps him over here to watch the house while I'm not around.

I sure hope he's not here when my crew starts working on this green house. Nah shawty; I'll make sure he's at my girls. Cool and who is this girl that I never met. Oh she's a cheer leader for the Falcons. Um, that figures. What's that supposed to mean D? Man what's up with Sage? I don't know D; I can't get her to bite bruh. That's the problem right there Harold; she aint no fish, she's a woman. You know what I mean man; everyone can't be like you and Chantel.

Harold, Chant wasn't easy, it took a lot of work. Any woman worth having is going to take some work. That's how you know that you can trust her. What do you mean by that D? Think about it, like this bro. If it's easy for you to get her then it's easy for the next man as well. The harder it is to get her, means she won't just leave you for the next man that comes along. Damn, I never thought about it that way man. Yeah you think she's a fish! That woman is a successful banker and she's doesn't want for anything. Get it through your skull that she's a woman and just be patient with her. If she's interested; you'll know. How will I know that?

It's a vibe Harold, a connection that you will feel. The fact that she even gave you a chance, should tell you that she's interested. Yeah but the last time I went to see her, she gave me the cold shoulder, even walked off from me. Why did she do that? What did you do? I went to her job to give her a present. That's cool, what did she say? She said she didn't want it! What did you get her? A new Lexus!

Boy you're stupid! That woman has BMW and a Benz; she's doesn't need your money or a car. Man what was I supposed to give her then? Definitely not that; you disrespected her! How so Donnie? By treating her like one of those groupie chicks! I'm confused shawty; I don't know what to do? It's easy Harold; give her time and respect, that's more valuable than any gift.

I'll see Donnie; right now I'm done. Alright that's your choice, now where is this Greenhouse going? Right here, in the center of the yard. Cool, how big do you want it? I don't care D; just make it big enough to keep her busy. Ruff! Ruff! Damn look at that's monster, that's a big ass dog back there Harold! Where did you get that thing?

That's my girls dog Thomas. Oh ok, that's a beast right there bruh! Yeah he protects the house pretty well. Shit I bet; so what's up with this project? I was just telling D that to put it right here Thomas, in the center of the yard. Cool, when do we start? You guys can start tomorrow Thomas!

That's straight; I'll call the crew when we leave here. Sooo Donnie; are you ready shawty? Ready for what; Harold? Your wedding man! Oh; I'm ready as I will ever be! So you're not nervous? Why would I be Harold? That boy aint nervous Harold; he's just crazy that's all. Man whatever; you two fools crazy. All I'm saying Donnie is; you're about to be with one woman for the rest of your life. There's nothing wrong with that Harold; I'm not a player like you and Thomas. One good woman is all I need.

Well you have my blessings shawty and Thomas, you aint no player! Donnie; you better school your boy. Oh he got some game Harold; a little bit, he's just slack with it. Damn cuz, why I got to be slack! Harold I walked in on this fool banging a chick on my office desk. I'm talking, butt ass naked, her bootie juice all over my damn papers and shit. Ha-ha! Thomas, you might be a player shawty! Good move! Man both of yall nuts, come on Harold show us the inside of this 1.5 Million dollar house! Ha-ha! Right this way boys; let me show yall this here castle! Man where's your pool at?

Thomas you can't swim, why are you worry about a pool. Because we need to be having some pool parties while your ass is at camp. Man this is my mom's spot, that aint gone happen. Ha-ha! Boy your mom's is bout it! Thomas shut up cuz, you aint got good sense. Don't tell him nothing D; I'm gone body slam his ass. Ha-ha! Come on Harold, I'm just joking bruh. Thomas just come in and close the door behind you.

Hey Latrice! Come out here quick! What is it Cynthia? Latrice jumps up from her desk then makes her way to the front of the office. What Cynthia? Look outside, in front of the building, it's Ted! Ted? Yep! She hesitantly walks over to the door to see what all the fuss was about. Oh my God! Ted what is this! She yelled out of the front office door. Come see it baby; it's my gift to you. Wow Ted; a freaking new Navigator! Yes and I had the 20 inch rims custom made just for you. But I already have a Benz, Ted and I like it. I know but you're about to have my baby and that Benz is too small for car seats, strollers and all that kid stuff.

Well thank you; I love you so much! Yeah I know! Aww, you're a mess. So take it for a spin and stop by the mall while you're at it. For what? I left some cash in the glove box, so you can go baby shopping. Really; that's so sweet; aren't you coming with me? No I have to meet Donnie and the grooms at the church for rehearsal. We're planning something special for Chantel. Ok then tell everyone I said hello. Alright baby, call me when you get done; so I can see what you got. Sure thing; give me a kiss Mr.! Muah! See you!

Cynthia do you have your cell on you? Yes I do! Good; call Chantel and tell her to hold down the fort while we test drive this baby. Ok calling now! Ring-Ring! Ring-Ring! Thanks for calling the Hudson Law Firm; how may I help you? Hey it's me; Cynthia. Can you put Chantel on the phone please! Sure Cynthia, hold one moment! Um-hm. Ring-Ring! This is Chantel. Hi Ms. Chantel; you have a call, line 2! Thanks!

Hello; Chantel speaking. Hey girl; it's me! Where are you and why are you calling me at the office; aren't you down the hall? Nope, Latrice and I are about to go for a ride in her new Navigator! What; and leave me with all this blame work! We'll be right back Chant; we promise! Yall better not take all day Cynt! Hey don't yell at me; our boss told me to call. Whatever Cynthia; just don't be gone too long. We won't! Bye Cynt!

What did she say? She wasn't too happy but she's cool. Ring-Ring! Ring-Ring! Oh this is Quentin; hold on a sec Latrice. Sure answer your phone, girl. Hey baby! What's up wifey; what you up to? Oh; I'm wifey now? You've always been wifey baby. Well, how come this is the first time that I heard you say it. Cynthia I call you that all the time around the fellas. I don't know why; besides you haven't placed a ring on my finger yet! Oh, here you go! I'm just joking Q; what are you doing?

Over at this church with the guys, we're practicing this thing Donnie wants to do for Chantel, at the wedding. What kind of thing? It's a surprise, and if I tell you; you're going to open your big mouth. No I won't Quentin; I promise. Nope forget about it; I just called to speak any way; I'll see you later tonight! Ok hun, love you! Love you too Cynthia!

Man, put that phone down and stop caking! Donnie; can I talk to my woman bruh! Chill Q; I'm just foolin with you. Now let's get this thing right; where's Marc? Out front; talking to some girl! Can you go get him please while I start this music! Yeah, I'll get him! Q runs through the church entrance, retrieves Marcus then returns just as the music starts. Purple cushions line the seats for the congregation while stain glass windows compliment the ambiance of light wood finished furniture and wine colored carpet.

Ok Marcus; you have to hit this note good man! Donnie; I'm lip sinking fool; I can't sing like no damn Ohio players! Marc just try it; we all know you singed in the school choir before. Even though, you did it to get women. Alright play the track Donnie.

"You know what I think heaven is, I think heaven is you." "You know that place where I can find Happiness" "A close place to your loviness" Damn Marc, you sound good boy! Yeah he's alright! Don't hate Quentin! He's straight Q; that was cool. Ok so when am I supposed to sing this? Right after me and Chantel kiss! Ok got it! I'm talking about right after the preacher say; "You may kiss the bride." Don't worry Donnie; I got you covered bruh. Thanks Marc, I really appreciate it.

Ring-Ring! Yo are we finished D; I need to take this call. Yeah we're done. Cool; this honey right here is fine as Beyonce'! I can't miss this call bro! Ring-Ring! Hello! Is this

Marcus? Yes it is! Hey what's up? You baby; with your fine self. So when am I going to see you? I'm over at this church right now but we can link up in an hour or so. That's cool; I need to drop my daughter off anyway. Well you go ahead and take care of that then meet me at the Shark bar after. Ok Marc; I'll call you when I'm on the way. Alright sexy; see you later! Ok; later Marc!

Yo D, Quentin; see you knuckle heads later! Alright Marc; don't do anything that we wouldn't do. Donnie, you already know what it is man. Yeah that's why I said that! Whatever, I'll call yall tomorrow when I get to Tennessee. For sure; holler at you later Marc! Yeah later; Mr. Marcus! Ha-ha! Marc stops, turns around then looks at Quentin with a smirk on his grill. You got jokes Q! Just saying; that's all.

Hello! Hey where are you? I'm in the parking lot Nadia, waiting on you. Oh ok, I'll be on break in five minutes. Ok baby; I got some smoke too. Ha-ha! Not that stuff you had last time! No, I got you some Reggie. Who is Reggie? Ha-ha. Nah baby; it means regular. Oh ok, be out in a few minutes. Alright; I'm parked on the end by the fence. K!

Sade's Love Deluxe; serenade through the speakers of the SUV as Thomas relaxes comfortably in its plush butter soft leather seats. Kush smoke; fill the air as he recline back in the driver's seat, waiting for Nadia to come outside. "There must have been an Angel by my side" "Something Heavenly led me to you" "Look at the sky" "It's the color of Love."

Ok I see you, jamming to Sade! Yeah this is my joint baby; how's work? It's ok; what you bring me for lunch? This smoke! Ha-ha! I am hungry Thomas. Ha-ha! I got you some tacos. Tacos! Yep; there shrimp tacos from that place you like. Oh let me have them then. Wait a minute; here take this blunt, it's just for you rookie. Hey, I'm still getting used to this baby. Um-hm. Thomas reaches in the back seat then hands Nadia her bag of Tacos.

Thanks baby! You're welcome and go slow with that blunt; you still have to go back to work. I thought you said this was some regular or something. I said Reggie but you still need to take it slow though, ok. Alright Thomas; light it for me. Nadia places the blunt up to her lips, he lights it then she takes a long pull. Sloooowww down, Nadia! I got it Thomas. Ok, I warned you woman. This is not so bad; I'm not seeing things like before. Whew; we sure don't need that again! Ha-ha. That's not funny Thomas. I know baby, I'm just kidding.

You better eat those tacos; you're going to be hungry as hell when you go back to work. Um-hmm- She takes another long drag off the Reggie while answering him, opens the bag then starts to eat. Damn these are good! I don't remember them being so good! Your ass just has the munchies, give me that blunt! Hold on baby, just one more pull. Alright, one more Nad, hurry up. She takes one last drag. That's enough, woman! Aww Thomas; you aint right, why you take it? Because you're about to clock back in and you don't need be too high at work, remember what happened last time, now.

Ring-Ring! Ring-Ring! Get your phone baby! Aww, it's just Donnie; I'll call him back when your breaks over. Well I only have 6 minutes left anyway. How did the rehearsal go the other day? What rehearsal? The wedding Thomas! Oh, it was straight we just went over a few things; we have one last rehearsal before the wedding with everybody so we can do an actual walk through of the real thing. When are you picking up your tux? Tomorrow! Oh cool, can you get my dress while you at it. Sure baby, I can swing by there for you. Thanks Thomas; it's time for me to go back. I'll see you when I get off. Muah! Ok; later Nadia!

As he watches Nadia walk back inside the building; he glances down at his phone to check the missed call. The caller I'd read- Ring-Ring! Ring-Ring! Hello! Hey big daddy! Hey Tameka! What are you doing Thomas? I'm about to leave my girls job; what's poppin? You mister; I thought about you all last night. Is that right? Yes sir it is. Well was it something good? Oh yeah that's why I called, I need some more of that black love.

You can get it girl, just say when! Now! Now; are you serious? Yep, can you meet me in College park? Sure where about? At the Westin; off Riverdale; I'm sitting here, all alone, chilling at the bar. Well hold tight; I'll be there in twenty minutes, order me a Henn and coke. Ok poppa; call me when you're 5 minutes away; I'll order it then. Say no more; in route now. Great; see you soon mister!

As he pulls on to the 285 bypass, anxiety over comes him, sharply reminising the last time he and Tameka's bodies intertwined. The way her legs gripped tight around his waist, how warm she was inside just that forbidden scene that replayed constantly in his mind every day since. Ring-Ring! Ring-Ring!

Yeah hello! Hey baby; can you come back, I left my badge in the truck, I need it to clock out tonight. Damn Nadia; I'm like 30 miles away! Well turn around; and where are you going anyway? I need to check out this new property, that's why Donnie called earlier. I thought that you were going to pick up your tux and my dress? I am but I need to handle this first. Alright, can you come by before I get off work then? Sure baby; what time do you get off tonight? At 9 Thomas! Ok I'll call when I'm on the way. Thanks baby; love you. Love you too Nadia; bye-bye. Thomas comes to a complete stop, just in front of the Westin entrance.

Hello sir; welcome to the Westin; will you be checking in or just visiting. Just visiting! Great thanks for visiting us; I can park your car if you like. Sure man; I appreciate it! You're welcome sir and here's your ticket. Thanks bro! Ring-Ring! Hey mister; where are you? I just pulled up; walking in now. Awesome; I'll order that drink then; I'm at the bar. Um-hmm, I see you; damn you're looking sexy over there. Thank you!

Her natural hair; fell flawlessly upon her shoulders, resting on her cobalt blue blazer which complimented her black skirt and cobalt blue stilettos. Her beauty demanded attention at all times and this evening wasn't an exception. Cautiously he approached, his stomach in a not from that feeling of betrayal. He knew this was wrong but some-how, Tameka just felt so right.

There you are; thanks for coming mister; how was your day? You're welcome and my day is going good so far. So far, huh? Yep! Well, have a seat; I promise I won't bite; at least not yet.

See; you're just a handful aren't you Tameka? More than that Thomas, maybe two hands; what's wrong, can't you handle it? Didn't I already? That was just an appetizer; today is the main course. Ha-ha! In that case make that drink a double, bartender. Sure; no problem sir!

A subtle chatter from spirited patrons and the several TV's that sit behind the bar fill the atmosphere of the huge hotel lobby, bar and restaurant. Tameka and Thomas drink happily among the other patrons as the fresh aroma of grilled onions, peppers and lamb seep from the kitchen. Patrons constantly check in and out of the Five Star Hotel while riding up and down the escalators and glass elevators while some gather in the huge banquet rooms for their scheduled trade shows, meetings and presentations. Smoke gray ceramic tiles, cover the lobby and walk ways, a huge glass front leaves you in awe at the vision of cars passing by on the interstate, planes taking off and

landing at nearby Atlanta Hartsfield Airport
and the constant flow of cars pulling up to the
Valet.

Um-hmm that was good, are you ready to
leave this bar? Yes Ma'am, I only have an hour
or two anyway. Tameka reaches in her purse,
takes out a bill then leaves it on the bar. Hey I
could have paid for the drinks. Nah, I invited
you over, this one is on me sir. Alright; I'll
leave the tip then. Thomas I left him a $50 bill;
he already has a nice tip. Cool, let's go, I'm
ready. Meka picks up her white and cobalt
blue Prada bag then walks away, Thomas
closely behind. Her soft perfume; linger in his
path, drawing him closer to her forbidden
fruit. In seconds they find themselves looking
at patrons below from the rising glass elevator.

Reluctantly; both of them fought off tensions
to jump each-others bones while in the
elevator. Ding! Silently they hastily rushed off,
walk down the hall then into suite 599. Oh my

God, I want you so bad Thomas! I've been thinking about that day at your office, every-day since! Shit, me too Tameka, come here and take those clothes off! No, we don't have time Thomas! Just drop your pants and come here! I don't have on any panties anyway!

Say no more! Oh yes, take me Thomas; take me! Thomas picks her up; she wraps her legs around his waist as he thrust her up against the cold window pane. Um-hmmmm, yes give it to me baby, damn your wood is good boy! Yeah you like it! You like it? Yes Thomas, yes! Ring-Ring! Ring-Ring! Um- your phone is ringing Thomas. Forget that phone! O-o-ok! Ring-Ring! Ring-Ring! Damn Meka; you gone make me leave my girl! Ring-Ring! Is it good to you Thomas? Hell yes! Ring-Ring! "Hi you reached Thomas from the 305; leave a message!"

"Thomas this is me; I get off in an hour and I need my badge!" "Where are you?" "Call me back!" Oh my God Thomas; I'm coming, I'm coming! Then bring it on girl, bring it on! Ohhhhh, yes! Yes! Yes! Ummmmm, thank you! That was wonderful, you better check your phone; I wouldn't want you to get in trouble with your girl. Ha-ha! Too late for that Tameka! Ha-ha! Nah-uh, she won't know if we don't tell! Girl you're a trip. Shaking his head, he feels the guilt while he puts back on his clothes then heads back downstairs to head over to Men's Wear House. Bye Thomas! Talk to you later Meka.

"Good Morning Atlanta; this is your boy; DJ Boogie!" "It's a nice 70 degrees out and two weeks from Christmas." "Now here's something for all you lovers!" "One of my favorites; Promise by ATL's own Jagged Edge!" "Nothing is promised to me and you." "So why will we let this thing go" "Baby I promise that I'll stay true." Alright son this is it; in a few more hours and you'll be a married man. Are you ready for this? Yeah pop; I'm ready! Ok driver, take us to the church! Hold on pop; we can't leave until Quentin and Thomas get in the limo. They're in the limo ahead of us Donnie. Ok where's mom? She's in the limo with Chantel. Is Uncle Ted riding with us? Nope; he and Latrice are already at the church. Can we leave now son? Yeah let's do it! Driver let's go! Yes sir!

Three; stretched white, Navigator limos, cruise one behind the other in route to Atlanta Baptist Church. A few miles later, upon their arrival, Chants limo cruise around back while the others stop in front of the church steps. Several guest; gather out front while others walk in to be seated. The grooms step out of the limo, dressed in chocolate pin striped tuxedos with yellow vest and bow ties then headed to the side entrance as Donnie joined them dressed in his Chocolate brown tuxedo with the penguin tale jacket, yellow vest and bow tie.

What's up cuz, are you ready? I'm ready Thomas; do you have the ring? Yeah man, I got it. Where's Harold and Marcus, Q? In the room, waiting on us! What room? The one the grooms are using man. Oh ok; do we have some sandwiches or something in there; I'm hungry. No but we have some chips and water. That will work! Are the bridesmaids all-ready, Thomas? I don't know Donnie; I just got here, same as you bruh.

Call Nadia and make sure cuz, can you do that? You're tripping cuz, they're in the same building. We can check on them when we get in. Donnie; calm your nerves brother, I'm sure everything is under control. Alright Q; I'm good. Damn Thomas, it's about time yall get here; where you fools been? What's up Harold, we just got here man. Hey Marc what's up; Donnie you good? What up; I'm good. You better be; your Uncle just came in and said we got 45 minutes.

Damn, that's it! Where's my pops? He's coming; he was right behind me Donnie. Gentlemen what's happening! Here he is now! What up poppa Rich! Hey Harold, you're looking good out on that field young man; when am I going to get some 50 yard line tickets? Pops, I got you man, just call me. Alright; I'm going to hold you to that!

Hey! Hey! I see the gang is all here; are you ready nephew? What's up Unc, I'm ready man. Good because your Bride is looking beautiful over there young man. Marcus; are you staying out of trouble? Yes sir! Man, stop lying! Chill Q, aint nobody ask you! Well, Latrice told me about your situation with that girl in Charlotte. Man; that's all over. Yeah but you need to be careful Marcus, next time your friends may not be there to bail you out. Yeah, I know Ted; I'm working on that. Knock-Knock! Who is it?

It's Cynthia, Q! Yeah baby; come in! Hey baby, what's up? It's time for us to go out now, all the bridesmaids are meeting up front. Ok Cynt; we're coming. Great, you guys all look so nice! See yall up front!

Fellas, I appreciate all of you guys for this. Pops, Uncle Ted, thank you too! Son, I wouldn't miss this for the world. Where's Chantel's dad anyway? Oh, he's going to be sitting on the front row of her Families side. Cool, he's giving her away, right. Yeah pops, he is. Marcus, did you remember that song? Yep; I got you covered brother. Thomas, you got the ring. Yep; now stop procrastinating and let's get to that alter; Donnie.

Donnie pauses, takes a deep breath, looks at his Father, uncle, Cousin and friends then opens the door. Let's do it! Right behind you, D! They shouted then follow behind as he exits the side door and heads to the front to pair up with the bridesmaids.

Pure joy and love fill the air as the grooms paired with their bridesmaids. Quentin and Cynthia stood in front while Nadia and Thomas, Ted and Latrice along with Sylvia and Marcus stood behind. All stood waiting patiently for their queue to enter the church and walk the isle. Alright Thomas; are you guys ready? Yep let's get it started bro! Cool; hold tight; the music should start in a minute guys. Everyone; remember to pace yourselves and don't walk too fast! As soon as you here the Debarge song and the doors open, it's on. You guys got that? Yeah Q; we got it man.

Thomas, I'm serious! Yeah bruh, now chill before you mess us up. Ha-ha! The ladies laugh as the fellas go back and forth.

"You knew you had me" "With your sensuous charm" "Yet your love so alarmed as I walked on by" "In awesome wonder you had to know why."

One after the other, they enter the church amidst flashing cameras and smiling faces. At the end of the isle as the song play they all took their selected positions. Donnie and his Mother make their way down the aisle slowly, until he reached his position, she let go of his arm then took her seat on the front row as Donnie stood their nervously waiting for his bride. A brief silence came over the church as the music continues to play while all eyes were on the door.

"Love me in a special way" "What more can I say" "Love me now" "Love me now, 'cause I'm special." Cameras flash as gasp of joy fill the room upon the site of her entrance. Chantel's long white, beautiful gown drape her body as it glide effortless behind her over a bed of roses that seem to sparkle as she walk down the aisle. Her Father, all smiles, held his daughter tight while on that walk he hoped would one day come. The preacher stood patiently waiting as she surely approached.

"We are gathered here today to celebrate one of life's greatest moments, to give recognition to the worth and beauty of committed marital love, and to add our best wishes to the words that shall unite Donnie and Chantel in marriage."

"Who gives this woman to be married to this man?" Chantels Father let's go of his daughters hand then answers as the groom accepted her. *I do!*

"The commitment that the two of you are about to make is the most important commitment that two people can make, you are about to create something new, the marriage relationship, an entity that never ends. As you stand here today, are you now prepared to begin this commitment to one another?" *I am!*

"Have you come here freely and without reservation to give yourselves to each other in marriage?" *I have!*

"Donnie and Chantel, I would ask that you both remember to treat yourself and each other with dignity and respect; to remind yourself often of what brought you together today. Give the highest priority to the tenderness, gentleness and kindness that your marriage deserves. When frustration and difficulty assail your marriage – as these do to every relationship one time or another – focus on what still seems right between you, not only the part that seems wrong. This way, when clouds of trouble hide the sun in your lives and you lose sight of it for a moment; you can remember that the sun is still here. And if each of you will take responsibility for the quality of your life together, it will be marked by abundance and delight."

"Donald James Robinson; will you have this woman to be your wedded wife?" *I will!* "Will you love and comfort her, honor and keep her, in sickness and in health, and forsaking all others, keep yourself only unto her as long as you both shall live?" *I will!*

"Chantel Brittany Holloway; will you have this man to be your wedded husband?" *I will!* "Will you love and comfort him, honor and keep him, in sickness and in health, and forsaking all others, keep yourself only unto him as long as you both shall live?" *I will!*

"Since it is your intention to enter into marriage, join your right hands, and declare your consent (before these witnesses) by repeating after me:"

"I, Donnie, take you Chantel to be my wife, to have and to hold from this day forward, for better or for worse, for richer or for poorer, in sickness and in health, to love and to cherish, as long as we both shall live."

With a twinkle in his eye, he happily repeats the lines to his bride. A tear fell from her eye as she inhales the moment her heart desire.

Psst! Thomas! Oh, my bad; here you go D! Donnie reaches over and takes the ring from Thomas, picks up Chantel's hand then slides it on. Chantel, take this ring as a sign of my commitment and fidelity to you. Tears fill the wells of her eyes as reality began to sink in. Just then she reaches over to the Reverend and retrieves Donnie's ring as she spoke.

I, Chantel take you Donnie to be my husband, to have to hold from this day forward, for better or for worse, for richer or for poorer, in sickness and in health, to love and to cherish, as long as we both shall live.

Donnie, take this ring as a sign of my commitment and fidelity to you.

"Donnie and Chantel, in so much as the two of you have agreed to live together in Matrimony, have promised your commitment to each other by these vows, (and) the joining of your hands (and the giving of these rings), by the authority invested in me by the State of Georgia, I now pronounce you Man and Wife."

"Congratulations, you may kiss your bride."

Pure energy from filled hearts explode in the atmosphere as friends and family, clap, cry and aw as Donnie and Chantel lips interlock in front of them.

"May I present to you Mr. and Mrs. Robinson!"

As the crowd cheer; Marcus leaves his groom's post then head over to the microphone as the piano man began to play the Ohio Players rhythm to Heaven Must be Like this while Marc serenade the Newlyweds as they slowly began to walk down the aisle of the church towards the exit as everyone watch with tears of joy and hearts of love.

"You know what I think Heaven is, Heaven is you" "You know that place where I can find

happiness" "A Place close to your loveliness"
"Somewhere to rest my aching mind, aw, aw"
"Where there's no time, your love's- just so
divine"

 "Heaven must be like this" "It must be like
this….."

THE END.

MELISHA ROSS

ANTWAN 'ANT' BANK$

Thank you for reading; Everlasting Romance; by ANTWAN 'ANT' BANK$ and MELISH ROSS. Please be sure to leave a review. We would love to know what you think. You can read more from these Authors as well as other PRINTHOUSE Books Authors. Titles are available everywhere that books are sold.

www.PrintHouseBooks.com

PRINTHOUSE BOOKS

Read it, Enjoy it, Tell A Friend!

Atlanta, GA.

It is a theory that women's minds are very complex. This author believes differently. Like their counter the male; women love, they suffer loss, have self-esteem issues, and are always on the path to find what truly makes them happy. My belief is; the only thing that separates the two, are the way they process the same thoughts.

The creator of this book wants to take you on a journey. This journey is filled with love, heartache, finding peace, suffering, loss, acknowledging their beauty, realizing the strength within, and finding true self.

MADE; Crime Thriller Trilogy.

Three years ago, I lost my wife and family to this messed up economy. After that nothing was there to hold me back, with no more support from Uncle Sam; I decided to pave my own way. Never one to break the law, I traveled down the straight and narrow but to no avail, thanks to this Bitch ass Cop; name Espinoza. So again I found myself in a corner. But as I gathered my thoughts and tried to come up with a plan; it was by fate that I met who would later become the love of my life.

Sabrina in her own fortuitous way introduced me to the life I have today. Still no wife nor kids in the picture, even though they constantly held a place next to my soon to be cold heart. I witnessed my life change in a split second. Now that I think back on it; mine did that very day I dropped Pharoah's punk ass in that back parking lot. I should have known things would never be the same after that day. I still get a thrill when I think about the look he had in his eyes when I took his life away and the smile that remained on Sabrina's all that day.

As I sit here smoking on this Cohiba, in this Mansion, with all this power, all this money and all the blood on my hands from those fools that stood in my way. My heart still beats fast at the sight of the cars, money, houses, women and the sound of hot bullets piercing warm flesh. See I live for this shit because there's nothing else out there for me; but this. Don't blame my mother, don't blame my pops. Blame Uncle Sam for placing that M16 in my hands and brain washing me to kill without feeling a damn thing. Blame this messed up economy; that has so many people struggling. Yeah I made a choice and I am happy with it. Because of that; me and my crew will protect what's ours until the day we die. See we don't plan on going to no prison, jail or nothing like that. Yes we plan to go out with a fight, last man standing! Death before Dishonor; that's how we roll! Gangsters make the world go round and Sin City is its axes. It's time for me to stop talking now; you have a story to read; see you on the inside.

The word Adoration can be defined as fervent and devoted love or simply put; to worship. During our time on Earth we will all experience this powerful thing called Love. This novel will take you on a journey seen through the eyes of four couples and their relationships. For Love we endure amazing things and some of us will go to the limit to keep it.

Love can fill your heart with joy or leave it filled with hate. Adoration explores love at several levels; some of them good; some bad. In Book One of this Series; hearts *will break, tears will fall, blood will shed and bells will chime; all in the name of love.*

Millions travel to the City of Angel's every year in search of that one shot at stardom. But most fail and find themselves caught in the underbelly with the homeless, the drug attics, prostitutes, thieves and murders. Candy and Joe unfortunately are no different than most and end up living in a different hotel every other night; doing whatever needs to be done just to survive.

The Cover Girl series is about, an Atlanta; Eye Candy photographer; name Malakhi Jones. Pronounced (Mal uh Ky). This short story and many others to come; will take you inside a day in the life of a hot photographer and his daily encounters with several of the industries sexiest Magazine Models and Video Vixens.

While these events are Fiction; anyone in the industry knows; what goes on at the shoot; stays at the shoot! Malakhi is at the top of his game and is connected with every Men's Magazine Publisher,

Casting Directors, Hip Hop Artist and Talent Managers in the industry. Getting a session with him is like winning the lottery; when it comes to being an eye candy Model, in the ATL. Any Model knows; that once the session starts and that camera flashes; all rules will be broken to obtain that success; if not! Then keep dreaming.

Cover girl Series is only available in eBook.

In book 2 of *The Cover Girl Series; Malakhi ventures on an on location shoot, with the Sexy Chocolate, Video Vixen; Lola Love. Her enticing aura almost proves to be too much for the A List Photographer but in true Malakhi fashion; he prevails. The two meet up, downtown on Peachtree street Atlanta; at one of the Cities five star hotels.*

Together, they will create magic for the camera and hot lustful memories in their Jacuzzi Suite. They say a picture is worth a thousand words but only the photographer and the model knows; what exactly goes on, between those poses.

The following collection of spirits; were some of my favorites to mix for the thousands of customers that I served as a bartender back in my 20's. During 1995 - 1996, I worked as a bartender in several Las Vegas Clubs and had a damn good time doing it! I've included a few recipes I picked up from fellow bartenders, some from customers and most I've learned from bartending school.

Mixology is an art and if mastered one can make a really good living serving spirits and conversing with the people you serve at your bar. If you're a bartender looking for some new drinks or you're just someone interested in mixing up some new drinks in your kitchen. This book of spirits is for you. Welcome to the Party Life and remember to drink responsibly.

PRINTHOUSE BOOKS
PRESENTS

F.I.T.H.

What happens:
when bullying goes too far!

A must read for any Parent, Teacher or Kid

ANTWAN 'ANT BANKS
A COMING OF AGE, PSYCHOTIC DRAMA

Earlier in the mid 80's and early 90's; I had the unfortunate opportunity of being friends or acquaintances with two special individuals. Now that I am thinking about it, maybe it wasn't unfortunate but faith that we crossed paths. Their stories we're similar, even though they happened at different times and in two separate parts of the world.

It is through my God given gift that I will deliver their message; through Eric; F.I.T.H's main character. I find it my destiny to help others see life *as they did; at tragic moments in both their lives. The time and location of events and names have been changed to protect them and their victim's families. Hopefully this story will show why it's not cool to be a bully but deadly, when you factor in all the consequences.*

PRINTHOUSE BOOKS

Read it, Enjoy it, Tell A Friend!

Atlanta, GA.

PrintHouseBooks.com

www.ingramcontent.com/pod-product-compliance
Lightning Source LLC
Chambersburg PA
CBHW030912050726
47498CB00003BA/705